# NAPOLEON'S ROSEBUD

# NAPOLEON'S ROSEBUD

## A novel

Humphry Knipe

ISBN-13: 978-1541220393

Baby, baby, naughty baby,
Hush! You squalling thing, I say;
Peace this instant! Peace! Or maybe
Bonaparte will pass this way.

—Old nursery rhyme

*"The daughter of the house introduced us to one of her friends, Miss Kneips, the prettiest person we could see: tall, blonde, handsome waist, fair complexion. Her freshness, her beauty, made us call her Rosebud, and we never called her anything else. Her mother was the widow of an officer of the company and lived there from some modest pension."*
—Comtesse Albine de Montholon, *Souvenirs de Sainte-Helene*

# Contents

A Personal Note

Acknowledgements

# A Personal Note

The print hung on the wall in my grandfather's gloomy little living room in his gloomy granite block cottage in Cathcart, a tiny fort town in what was once British Kaffraria, Eastern Cape, South Africa. It was a large black-and-white print of a short man in a long coat and black hat set sideways on his head, hands clasped behind his back, standing alone on the deck of a sailing ship, gazing out to sea with an expression of infinite sadness. Gathered in a knot a respectful distance behind him were seven officers, hats off, watching the solitary figure with curiosity and awe. It was a picture I stared at often, a cheap print of Orchardson's iconic painting of Napoleon sailing into exile on the *Bellerophon.*

"Who is that lonely man?" I asked Grandfather, already in his late seventies, although not too old to wear his kilt to church on Sundays, a ritual he picked up from his grandfather Henry Porteous Knipe, who plays a small part in the story.

Grandfather didn't expect me to know the name of the lonely man because I was only five or six. "A great general called Napoleon," he said. "We beat him at Waterloo and exiled him to Saint Helena. That's where I come from."

"Did you know him?"

"Oh, Lord, no! That all happened in *my* grandfather's time."

Grandfather, who had been stationmaster of an insignificant South African Railways whistle-stop in the Great Karoo desert, died a few years later when I was nearly twelve. I remember very clearly my dad, the only one in his family who went to college, telling me with more than a touch of pride how Grandfather, near death, had summoned him, and him alone, to his bedside to tell him to remember that a long time ago on Saint Helena the Knipes had been touched by greatness.

We Saint Helena Knipes are an old family but not yet a distinguished one. John Knipe, the original Knipe to settle on the tiny island, was an illiterate tanner who arrived there in about 1676, courtesy of the English East India Company, which needed "small whites" to farm their refreshment station. John was given ten acres of land to grow yams, potatoes, fruit, and vegetables. He was also given two cows. The Company provided him with freshly butchered hides to scrape clean and tan for a fee. It was dirty work. John's sons and his grandsons plowed the same humble furrow. They were planters and jacks-of-all-trades. Some signed on with the Honorable East India Company's regiment. John's great-grandson Samuel was to rise to the modest distinction of being the most extensive cultivator on the island. But it was his relatively penniless brother Richard's daughter, a beautiful girl of nineteen, who was touched by greatness. Napoleon was probably introduced to her the evening he landed on the island, October 17, 1815.

He called her *Bouton de Rose*, Rosebud.

# Chapter 1: Astonishing News

**Saint Helena Island, South Atlantic**
**October 12, 1815**

Charlotte was in the kitchen bottling peaches with her mother and her aunt Emelia when she heard the news. The messenger was her eldest brother, John, a strapping loudmouthed Yamstock, as the islanders were called, who arrived with a great clatter in the farm's courtyard, froth on his horse's mouth.

"Boney!" he yelled, wheeling the animal around. "Boney's coming! He's coming to get you! Reelly, reelly, reelly!"

Brother John had the brains of a sparrow, and when he got excited he spoke with an accent as thick as his skull. He often said silly things that didn't make sense. "Hush or Boney will get you!" was a dire warning that mothers everywhere in the Empire used to frighten their children to sleep. Had John been drinking prickly pear *tungi*, and it not yet noon?

Charlotte's mother, long-faced and short-tempered, launched herself into a question with a busy pump of her elbows. "What you mean, John?" Her nerves were acting up because John was shouting and waving his hat and spurring his horse to rear, although the poor animal was clearly near dropping after the steep uphill ride from Jamestown, which wasn't a town at all, hardly even a village, and the only one for a thousand watery miles in any direction.

"Just what I said!" shouted John, hitching his horse. "Wellington done beat Boney at someplace called Waterloo, and they're done gorn sent him 'ere! Him and his whole fancy court! Hundreds of Frenchies! Counts and

11

countesses in them white wigs, I bet! Enough generals to make up an army! All coming here day after tomorrow or the next day, depending on the wind. Five ships full of rich aristos loaded with livres. The whole island will be swarming with hungry redcoats to guard 'em. Can you believe our luck?"

Charlotte couldn't. Tiny Saint Helena was a speck in the vast South Atlantic, barely five miles wide, the loneliest island in the world. How could it suddenly become the center of the universe?

"Where's he going to stay?" asked Aunt Emelia, a pleasantly plump, kind-faced woman who sat on a stool, quite happy to watch her restless, rawboned sister-in-law do all the work.

"Them say at Longwood, you know, on Deadwood Plain," said John.

This convinced Charlotte that John's news was nothing more than a preposterous rumor that John didn't have the wit to distinguish from the truth. "There's no house there, idiot!" she called out to him through the window. "Only a few drafty sheds!"

John threw open the back door, plucked off his hat, and burned his mouth on half a peach, still hot from the syrup. "Shows how much you know," he said through the peach. "It's been fixed up as a summer cottage for years. Now they're in a tearing hurry to fix it up some more."

"Who told you all this?" Charlotte shot back, making no effort to hide her skepticism, because she didn't have much time for fools and her brother John was definitely one of those.

"The whole town is shouting about it. I got it from your very own best friend, Mary Porteous, who is shouting louder than anyone else because they're putting him up at Porteous House until Longwood's ready. I bet old man

Porteous will wear his kilt every day instead of just Sundays. Not often you have an emperor as a lodger!"

John's mother and aunt stared at him in disbelief. Charlotte flushed with wild excitement. Napoleon, suddenly thrust into her life! What would Daniel say when he heard the news? But of course Daniel would know already. How infuriated he must be, stuck in the outskirts of London, while everything was happening in his backwater home! It was all so impossible. A fairy story.

"Napoleon!" Charlotte said just to taste the flavor of the word. It conjured up images of cannons and cavalry charges and a picture she'd seen of him being crowned emperor by the pope.

"At last someone good enough for you!" said her mother sarcastically. "Your poor father used to go on about him so much it made me quite sick!"

"Rubbish! Daniel is more than good enough for me!"

"Because he writes you all them letters stuffed with nonsense about how Napoleon's bringing the world liberty and equality and revolution," crowed John. "Don't think I haven't read them. You leave them all over the house like your smelly underclothes!"

"That's disgusting! I leave them in a box under my bed, where you have no business sticking your nose!"

John attacked another hot peach. "None of the local lads want to walk out with you because all you want to talk about is Napoleon!" he said. "Hurray! Now's your chance to get your claws into the man hisself!"

"What's all the excitement about?" It was her uncle Samuel, closest Charlotte had for a father since hers passed away ten years ago leaving her mother to live on a small army pension. Instead of squandering his inheritance by playing the gentleman soldier, as her father Richard had done, Samuel had worked his share so that he had risen to

13

the rank of the richest planter on the poverty-stricken little island. But money couldn't ward off old age. He had begun to suffer from gout and shortness of breath. He didn't look like a man who would see many more summers, not that there was much difference between summer and winter on this, the sheltered leeward side.

John, relishing his opportunity to shine, did a silly bow so deep that his hat swept the floorboards and then tried his best to speak proper. "Uncle Samuel, I am pleased to announce that Wellington beat Napoleon at a great battle and that we are about to be honored by the presence of no less a personage than the deposed emperor himself. He is to take up indefinite residence right here, on this very island, courtesy of His Majesty's government!"

Samuel searched John's excited face for the lie but didn't find it. "Bravo for my friend Wellington!" he said on the basis of bumping into the general a few times during Wellington's short visit to the island ten years ago on his way back from India. "So he's caught the cockerel at last! I wager they'll not let him flee the coop a second time. That's why they're sending him here, of course!" Samuel sighed. He was a sharp trader, but he was also a kind man. "Poor devil. I think in many ways he means well. Just imagine being cast down all the way from the golden throne of Europe to this pimple on the backside of nowhere!"

"Does seem sad!" echoed Samuel's obedient wife. "Poor thing."

"But I can see Lady Liberty 'ere thinks it's the most wonderful event since the nativity!" Charlotte's mother said who had a tongue as sharp as a shard of glass.

"It is!" said Charlotte. "That's why we need to go back to town, immediately."

"Well, we can't," said her mother, her thin face hardened by widowhood and the grind of making ends meet. "We've got to help your aunt finish with the peaches."

"Oh, don't worry about the peaches," said Emelia. "I'll get one of the kitchen girls to help."

"No!" said the mother. "Charlotte gets her own way more than enough!"

Charlotte headed for the door. "How can you expect me to bottle peaches at a time like this!" she said. "I need fresh air!"

"Charlotte Knipe, you aren't going anywhere! Oh, how I wish your father was still alive. You never listen to a thing I say. Samuel, you tell her!"

Samuel was smiling. Charlotte was a lovely girl. She was tall, perfectly formed, with a long cascade of blonde hair falling from her animated face. But it was her complexion that was the finest of her natural accomplishments: the fair, luminous skin, the blush more subtle than anything a brush could apply.

"Let the girl go," Samuel said. "This is tumultuous news. A whiff of wind will clear her head better than smelling salts."

"At least take Molly with you, child." Molly was Charlotte's slave, willed to her by her father, Richard, and who was nearly as close to her as Mary Porteous, although of course in a different way. But Charlotte didn't want to take Molly. She wanted to be alone with the Friar. To speak to Daniel through him, as the Catholics spoke to God through a priest at confession. What she'd been doing since the boy—a man by now—left for London five years ago.

"I don't need Molly," shouted Charlotte, already outside. "I'm taking John's horse!"

"No, you're damn well not!" shouted John, sprinting for the door.

But Charlotte had already untied the chestnut, hitched up her thin cotton dress so she could ride astride,

15

and was heading out of the courtyard so fast that John's curses barely caught up with her.

She slowed the tired horse to a walk as the trail wound down into Lemon Valley, the switchbacks ever sharper, the trees thicker. She heard the whispering voices, the dying gasps of the wind barely stirring their leaves. The sighs, the Negroes believed, of slaves freed from ships where the living were left chained to the rotting dead until they were cut loose by the British and dumped in camps downstream from here.

Charlotte crossed the ankle-deep brook, urged the horse up the other side. There, huge against the blue sky, wrapped in a worn, weather-beaten lichen robe, was the rock outcropping called the Friar, which looked east to watch the sun rise over Africa and west to watch it set in South America while thousands of miles of restless ocean sang orisons at his feet.

The tireless trade wind blew from the southeast, so it was tamer on this, the west side of the island, where the Knipe family farmed, just blowing swiftly enough to keep the tropical heat at bay. Except for wisps of dying fog, the sky was clear. The only storm brewing was the one in Charlotte's heart as she slipped off the horse and sat at the feet of the Friar.

Napoleon! How cruel that her father hadn't lived to see his hero, even meet him, perhaps! Although he had inherited good farming land, his passion was for war, not weeds, as he put it. He had served in India for just long enough to catch malaria in Madras. He returned home to take on the less onerous duty of a clerk in the Saint Helena Regiment but his condition worsened so he was invalided out two years later in 1794, the year Napoleon took his first giant stride to greatness by winning the battle of Toulon for the Revolution for which he was promoted to the rank of general at the tender age of twenty-four. Suddenly Richard found a new outlet for his military obsession: following the career of the brilliant young Corsican. As the years passed he refought every Napoleonic battle on paper with tiny wooden soldiers directed by a man on a white horse who wore his hat sideways. When she was old enough he demonstrated Napoleon's elaborate feints and forays to Charlotte who watched, fascinated, following as best she could. Then, in 1805, when Charlotte was nine, malaria made its final charge and Richard Knipe's toy soldiers fought no more.

"If only I were thirty years younger … Oh what an honor to serve such a man!" Charlotte had heard her father say more than once before his death. "What an honor it would be if one of my sons would do it for me!" But his only son old enough was loudmouth John who had no fight in him unless he was full of fiery *tungi*.

Sitting at the feet of the Friar Charlotte's thoughts flitted by like wisps of Saint Helena fog being chased by the perpetual southeaster. Daniel was old enough to fight, but he wasn't a soldier either. She and Daniel had been separated for five years now, linked only by the monthly letters that crossed one another in ships battling the vast Atlantic. When he left the island for Kew Gardens, London, Daniel was a moody boy of fourteen. When he came back, a botanist and a gentleman, he would be twenty-one. What would he look like? He sent her sketches of himself, well-done because he was being taught to do botanical drawings, but not very good likenesses, she could tell, because the faces were all different. She'd sent him sketches of herself she'd done from the looking glass. But none of them caught the vivacity in her green eyes, the perfection of her features, she was vain enough to admit to herself. They were certainly nothing like the drawings that their schoolmaster, William Burchell, had done of her. Kind Mr. Burchell—he was the one who had obtained Daniel his

Kew apprenticeship and the chance to make something of himself. Who had taken something of the local Yamstock accent out of their pronunciation, taught them a smattering of French and the elements of Liberal politics. Often he talked about his personal hero, Napoleon.

The day before a ship swept Daniel off to London, she and Daniel had sat here at the Friar's feet, just as she was doing now. This was his special place, where he went when his black moods took him. When Charlotte's was the only company he wanted.

"I need something to remember you by while you're sniffing flowers like a gentleman in the Royal Botanic Gardens," she had told him.

"Flowers? No chance!" said Daniel. "I'll be sniffing manure!"

"No, you won't! You'll be learning botany. Soon you'll know as much as Mr. Burchell."

"No one could ever know as much as Mr. Burchell," said Daniel.

"Please! A little memento!"

"Such as? You know I have next to nothing."

"A story is all I want. I want you to tell me a story to remember you by. The Friar's story. I want to remember you telling it to me."

He took her hand, brushed it with his lips. "You do have such beautiful hands," he said. "Mr. Burchell captured them perfectly in his drawings."

"Please!"

"You will look after my father for me while I'm gone?"

"Of course I will," she said.

"He's got hardly anyone else who'll…see him."

"I know. Please…the story."

So he told her the story in his freshly broken voice, almost the voice of a man, not quite. It was the sad little tale of a saintly Franciscan friar, hope of the hopeless, who fell madly in love with a mountain nymph and begged her to marry him. The fairy agreed on the condition the friar give up his religion and worship wild nature as she did.

"The day of their wedding finally arrived," Daniel said, squeezing Charlotte's hand. "They were to be married in a chapel that once stood on this very spot. Then at the exact moment they were to be joined together forever, the rock opened with a mighty roar and swallowed the chapel and everyone in it. All that was left was the friar, turned to stone as you see him now, forever searching the horizon for his lost love."

"Daniel," she said, "that was beautiful."

"It's a warning for boys like me to beware of lovely witches like you!"

She'd laughed at that. "You've heeded the warning," she said. "Because you're fleeing to England tomorrow."

"I'm going because I want to be better than just another Saint Helena Yamstock who's born, bred, and dead on the island. Besides, while I'm gone you'll just keep on growing more beautiful." He squeezed her hand. "Promise me you'll wait. At least give me a chance."

Charlotte had gazed into his quick brown eyes with their turbulent black depths. She made her promise. "Yes, I shall."

Dear Daniel! Two years more before he served out his apprenticeship at Kew Gardens and came back a gentleman who would publish scholarly books on the plants of Saint Helena found nowhere else in the world. She took his latest letter out of her pocket—she always kept at least one with her. As usual the lines crossed and re-crossed one another to squeeze as many words as possible onto the single sheet of paper, all that was allowed to qualify for the cheap letter rate.

19

This one was special because it brought the grand news that Lord Byron had just visited Kew and that Daniel had actually spoken with him!

*I am suddenly in a rage about his poems. And of course his pursuit of freedom. I've read his 'Childe Harold' three times and 'Corsair' four. Here's how his latest poem begins. The lady reminds me so much of you!*

> *She walks in beauty, like the night*
> *Of cloudless climes and starry skies;*
> *And all that's best of dark and bright*
> *Meets in her aspect and her eyes…*

*You are the best of dark and bright!* he wrote very small so he could squeeze it onto the crowded page and so save a penny. *How I long to hold you! Two more years, but what's two years in a lifetime? Wait for me!*

"I'll wait for you, I promise!" she told Daniel at the feet of the Friar but she was thinking of the living apparition that was about to appear. The mischievous wind snatched away her words and carried them gleefully out to sea.

"Napoleon! Oh, what will I wear?"

# Chapter 2: The Eagle Lands

Would he find her pretty?

That was the question she asked her full-length looking glass. Molly, her slave, had done her long wavy blonde hair in ringlets. She'd borrowed a green dress from her cousin Elizabeth, rich Uncle Samuel's daughter, because she'd heard that it was the emperor's favorite color and because it emphasized the emerald green of her eyes. It was just a tiny bit short on her, but that had the advantage of showing off her ankles.

On Saturday evening five shots from the alarm cannons on Signal Hill announced that five ships had been sighted. At noon on Sunday another cannon roared, this time from the three-masted man-of-war *Northumberland* to signal it had dropped anchor. Swelled by the congregation that had just spilled out of Saint James's Church, a crowd of island faces, black, white, and yellow, watched from the wharf.

A longboat pulled away from the ship, a hundred spyglasses glued to every oar stroke.

"There's someone in uniform up front!"

"Napoleon!"

"Does he look like his pictures?"

"Is he a monster as they say?"

"It's not him! It's someone tall and thin!"

The thin man in a splendid blue uniform with gold epaulets who was standing stiff as a pikestaff at the prow of the longboat was indeed not Napoleon. He was Admiral Sir George Cockburn, a hard man, fresh from burning down the White House in Washington and now charged with keeping the most dangerous man on earth safe until his permanent jailer arrived.

The outgoing governor, Mark Wilks, replaced because he was thought to be too soft, waited for the boat at the slippery, sea-slapped tier of stone steps, the only dry way onto the island. Next to him stood his daughter, Laura, shielding herself from the vulgar sun with an embroidered umbrella that must have cost as much as Charlotte's slave, Molly. Charlotte, perspiring in her borrowed green dress, narrowed her eyes. She hated Laura, the spoiled little prig who was always oh so languid about her good breeding! Laura who had never bottled a peach in her life. But highest on Laura's list of crimes was that she allowed herself to be complimented as the most beautiful woman on the island. Did she have no shame?

Governor Wilks beamed at Charlotte. "Ah, Miss Knipe! Quite the event, what? Not every day we have an emperor stopping with us!"

Charlotte liked the governor. He was intelligent and educated, prepped by his parents for the ministry although he had chosen government service instead. His wit was sly and his nose never up in the air. He invited her to functions at Plantation House quite frequently, in spite of his daughter's disapproval. More than once Charlotte had caught him looking at her with a lingering gaze that made her blush.

Laura Wilks, impeccably tailored, favored Charlotte with a condescending smile. "Oh, I see you dressed for the occasion," she drawled. "How thoughtful. Perhaps I should have."

Happily all eyes turned from Laura to the longboat, which was now within hailing distance. "Make way!" bellowed a sailor with a barrel chest. "Make way for Admiral Sir George Cockburn on His Majesty's business!"

The longboat hove to, and the admiral stepped out. Distracted, perhaps by the mean prospect of the little one-street town, he stepped into six inches of the South

Atlantic. He ignored the mishap. Although his right foot sloshed loudly in his shoe, he strode forward boldly and introduced himself to the governor, fixing him with his eye as he took his hand, and walked with him and Laura the short distance to the rambling collection of offices and reception rooms laughably called the Castle.

With no introduction and no umbrella (she didn't have anything as grand as Laura Wilks's and wouldn't be seen with less) Charlotte fled to the shade of the Castle gardens. That was where the dreadful Balcombe brats found her.

"Papa's just gone into the Castle!" crowed Betsy, nearly thirteen.

"He's in with the governor and the admiral!" crowed Jane, almost fifteen. "He's going to be Boney's provisioner!" she whispered, as if that were a cabinet-level position. "It's all settled."

"Means Papa could starve him if he wanted to!" Betsy added spitefully.

*Probably will*, Charlotte wanted to say but couldn't. She'd heard all about William Balcombe's light fingers from Mr. Burchell, who'd been unlucky enough to go into the trading business with him back in 1805, the year Charlotte's father died and left his large family with nothing much more than a shack in town, a run-down yam farm, a few lazy slaves, and a meager widow's pension from the company, in whose regiment he had risen to the modest rank of first lieutenant.

Mary Porteous, Charlotte's best friend, plump and plain, pushed her way through the wild-eyed throng. Her face was pink with excitement. "My father's just come out!" she squealed. "Napoleon's to stay with us! Can you believe it! Oh, my mercy, Emperor Napoleon Bonaparte in Porteous House! Of course we're busy kicking out all our lodgers. You can't imagine the bedlam!"

23

Charlotte felt a chill that defied the dusty Jamestown heat. "That means you'll meet him?"

Mary laughed, the high sound of tinkling wineglasses. "But of course! You'll meet him, too. We're family, aren't we? They say there's a handsome young general with him. He's Napoleon's right hand man, apparently." She winked as she whispered the next word. "*Unmarried!* Apparently he's quite the firebrand, if you get my meaning."

"What's his name?" asked Betsy Balcombe sullenly, her bubble popped by this extraordinary news, as if an eligible young general's name should be any business of hers.

But Mary was generous and affable even though she'd drawn a short straw in the competition for good looks. "Gaspard something. French names are so hard to pronounce! But I suppose we'll soon get used to that."

"Is Napoleon coming ashore today?" asked Charlotte, feeling a chill when she said the name.

"Oh, dear no. We aren't half-ready for them," said Mary Porteous. "Tomorrow maybe. Almost certainly tomorrow. What a day it's going to be for Porteous House!"

"*Merde!*" cursed Napoleon.

He was on the afterdeck of the *Northumberland*, examining Jamestown through a telescope. He didn't like what he saw. The village was a fungus of white hovels that had infested the crack between two rearing granite thighs. He'd heard it called the brothel of the South Atlantic. It certainly looked it. He was back in this cabin when he was told that the governor—soon to be ex-governor—of this cow pad, someone called Wilks was calling on him with the imperial party's provisioner, a merchant of some sort called Balcombe who fancied himself one of the local gentry. Napoleon examined them through the well used peephole in his cabin door. Governor Wilks looked like a calm, bookish man with intelligent eyes. But the provisioner was sweating with apprehension, licking nervously at his lips as if he were parched for a drink. Excellent! He would make this shopkeeper his creature.

Napoleon began by refusing to admit the provisioner. Instead, he interrogated the ex-governor about his accommodation, his menu, his laundry, and even handed him two gold watches that had stopped during the voyage (one of them because he had hurled it to the deck in a fit of temper) with instructions to repair them.

An hour later, governor and provisioner dismissed, Napoleon was back on deck gazing at the sheer, thousand foot walls of his prison when Admiral Cockburn approached. The emperor pretended not to see him. Pretended not to hear him when he cleared his throat and asked if the general was ready to go ashore. The *general*! The *emperor* took a last loathing look at the canaille waiting for him at the landing like hungry dogs so they could tell their grandchildren that they'd seen Napoleon Bonaparte with their own eyes.

He would not give them the pleasure. When he eventually responded to the admiral's question, he told the preening rooster that he was not ready and that he would not be ready to set foot on this miserable rock except at night. He would not be gawked at.

The swift tropical sun had fled the scene, and the moon, almost perfectly full, was slicing its way skyward through the tall date palms when Napoleon stepped ashore. The landing, the walk of shame to the lodging house where he was to stay until his residence was ready, all were lit as bright as day by the thousand flaming torches waved aloft by the leering islanders, most of them drunk, every one of them hungry for their bite of history. All they needed,

Napoleon thought, were pitchforks to complete the horror. He had been steeling himself to endure jeers and catcalls, but though the rabble pushed and shoved at the shabby redcoats who lined the road from the landing to the village, the night was eerily silent. The rabble was listening for him to say something, anything to pass down to their descendants.

The only sound Napoleon could hear above the soft hiss of the surf was faint music, if you could call it that, coming from somewhere in the town. It was so badly played that it took him a moment to recognize the piece. It was the butchered first movement of a symphony being tortured by a rump of an orchestra. *His* symphony, the third, the *Eroica*, the one Beethoven composed for him. Oh, the monstrous irony! Only the presence of the leering mob prevented him from weeping.

The Balcombe girls had run off to hold hands with their freshly famous father. Charlotte, with Mary Porteous at her side, had established a spot on the pavement that gave her a gull's-eye view of the procession.

It was the hat that gave him away. The two men walking on either side of him were Cockburn, the ramrod straight English admiral, and an equally vertical French general of some sort. Both wore tall hats with plumes that danced like flames with every step. But the shorter, broader figure between them, who was dressed in a green jacket decorated with a huge star-shaped medal, wore his plain black hat crosswise. The model for a myriad paintings and drawings.

Napoleon!

The miserable band fell silent, for which Napoleon thanked the nonexistent gods. At the top of the seven steps that led up to the front door of the warren where they were going to make him spend the night stood the governor, the bookish Wilks man. Next to him was an absurd figure in a kilt with a dirk stuffed into the top of his left sock and a timid grin perched nervously on his lips, as if it was ready to fly away at the first sign of danger. Perhaps, Napoleon thought, the faux Scotsman would draw his weapon and put him out of his misery. Too much to hope for.

Governor Wilks waved a hand in the kilted man's general direction. "General Bonaparte, may I present your host Henry Porteous, landlord of this establishment."

*General* Bonaparte. Again the insult to the man the world styled emperor, this time right in front of the rabble!

The landlord didn't make the same mistake. "Your *Majesty*," Porteous said with an awkward attempt at a courtly bow. "Welcome to my humble abode."

Napoleon ignored the man. The door was open, so he brushed past him and walked inside. Anything, even the shoddy interior, was preferable to the leering eyes of the mob. The reception room lived up to his worst expectations. It was barely big enough for twenty people if they didn't mind rubbing shoulders. And twenty people it soon contained, men and women, dressed in what he supposed was their Sunday best. He closed his nose to the sour smell of unwashed bodies, ignored the pathetically eager eyes, especially those of Balcombe the provisioner and the two brats who clung to him like clams, closed his ears as the landlord stuttered his way through introductions. Only when he said, "And this is the governor's daughter Miss Laura Wilks," in a tone of voice that indicated someone special, did he focus on anyone at all. Laura Wilks was pretty, but it was in a vapid way, which aroused no interest in him, although he had been at sea without intimate female companionship for over three months. *Merde!*

On droned Porteous the landlord, spewing out names that would be remembered only by their gravestones. Napoleon should have noticed the engraving earlier, no doubt hastily borrowed for the occasion, because it had been given pride of place on the wall facing the front door. It was a cheap reproduction of him in his imperial robes, a golden laurel wreath perched on his head, a parody of the original. To deepen the cut, outside the apology for an orchestra went back to gnawing at the *Eroica*. He was looking for an escape, even more fervently than he had been at Waterloo, when she came in. A tall blonde vision wrapped in green, eyes to match, faultless complexion, no doubt with long legs underneath that peasant's dress, just the way he liked them.

Porteous the landlord was smarter than his kilt and knobby knees made him look. He noticed Napoleon's sudden interest. "Your Highness, may I introduce Miss Charlotte Knipe," he said.

The conqueror of Europe looked her full in the face with that penetrating gaze that turned brave men to stone and beautiful women to water. A delicious tingle ran up the back of Charlotte's neck, a sensation she had never felt before, but her green eyes kept coming back to his as she ran through her repertoire of delightful expressions.

He had found what he was looking for, he was sure of that. For the first time on Saint Helena, Napoleon spoke. "A rosebud among the thorns," he said so softly that it might have been no more than a wistful sigh, heard only because the room was quiet as a wink. The girl was moving something that had not moved since Waterloo. Napoleon made a quick dismissive motion with his fingers that was noticed only by Marchand, his valet, who was an expert at reading his master's gestures.

"Enough!" Marchand boomed at Porteous the landlord. "The emperor wishes to retire."

Porteous showed off the backs of his hairy thighs as he hopped like a goblin up the narrow stairs leading to the second floor. "Of course!" he said. "This way, Your Highness, this way!"

Countess Albine de Montholon, spirited wife of the emperor's chief adviser, was as usual the first in Napoleon's entourage to find her voice. "*Bouton de rose.* Rosebud!" she gushed. "From now on no one must call you anything else! What do you think, Gaspard?" she said in French.

"Very appropriate," said a gorgeously attired young French officer, magnetic even though he was only of medium height, who was examining Charlotte with his large gray eyes. "Rosebud it is if that is acceptable to mademoiselle."

Charlotte's French was barely up to the task. "Yes, yes, of course," she said, hoping her Yamstock accent didn't carry over into the language of love.

Countess Albine clapped her hands. "So that's settled then!" She added a sting in the tail. "We shall call you Rosebud, or Miss Kneips, whichever comes easiest to the tongue."

"Knipe, pronounced like knife," Charlotte corrected, a defiant glint in her eyes.

Albine de Montholon had played word games in the most fashionable salons of Europe, only to find herself in this armpit sparring with one of the local peasant girls. "Exactly. Kneips," she purred.

Napoleon followed the kilted landlord down a narrow passage. Henri Bertrand, grand marshal of the palace, walked one step behind, and Marchand the valet made up the rear guard. Porteous threw open the door to a dusty closet that would no doubt forever after be known as the emperor's suite.

Napoleon didn't hear the man's apologies for the smallness of the room and the narrowness of the bed. "Rosebud," he said. "Is she married?"

29

Porteous's face was alive with smiles, because here was an irresistible tidbit of gossip. The emperor had his eye on Charlotte, his daughter's best friend! "No, sire," he said, "although she pretends to be the fiancée of a boy in England—Kew Gardens, to be exact. He's doing his apprenticeship there." He resisted the impulse to wink. "He won't be back for more than a year."

"They correspond?"

"Regularly, Your Majesty," said the landlord, puzzled by the question.

Napoleon waved at Marchand, who nudged Porteous the few steps to the door. The man at least had the manners to walk backward, bowing all the way.

Napoleon stood at the window looking down at the street, where the drunken crowd had put down roots and the band had gone back to murdering Beethoven's greatest symphony.

"Tell them to stop that caterwauling," Napoleon barked at Marchand.

"At once, sire," said the valet.

"But first tell me about our provisioner, that Balcombe person."

The valet frowned. "He drinks too much."

"All the English do," Napoleon snapped. "Anything else?"

"Admiral Cockburn is going to stay in his guest cottage. Wellington stayed there for five days when he visited ten years ago on his way back from India."

"Ah!" said Napoleon. "Cockburn's going to stay there, is he?"

"That's the plan, sire," said Marchand who immediately caught his master's drift. "It's apparently a little pavilion, nice little place set in the garden, away from the main house, quite private. We'll be passing nearby it tomorrow, on the way to view your residence."

30

"Can't be too bad if Wellington stayed there," Grand Marshal Bertrand said.

Napoleon's bitter bark of a laugh. "How unlucky he ever left! What else do we know about our man Balcombe?"

"Describes himself as an auctioneer's appraiser. But he's a jack-of-all-trades, like most of the locals," said Marchand. "Has crooked fingers in several pies."

"Excellent!" said Napoleon. "Best news we've had since Austerlitz!"

General Gaspard Gourgaud, personal aide-de-camp to the emperor, was indeed a handsome young man of considerable swagger who had the intriguing habit of examining others down his rather long nose. While showing him to his room Mary Porteous had invited him to cool off in the night air with her and a friend, the girl the emperor had just christened Rosebud. She mentioned Charlotte not because she wanted her there but because Mary knew, by the firebrand's air of indifference to her, that she needed to bait her hook with a more dazzling fly. It worked. His gray eyes widened with sudden interest when she mentioned Charlotte's name. He said with a quick smile that he would be honored.

Charlotte was downstairs talking with the kilted landlord. "Papa," interrupted Mary, "General Gourgaud is dying to take some fresh air. I thought Charlotte and I could walk with him to the Almond Tree, since it's just across the street. You want to come along, don't you Charlotte?" she asked, hoping Charlotte would say no.

"Of course I do!"

Mary's father frowned. "I don't know if it's such a good idea," he said, "going out tonight. The town is crawling with drunken soldiers."

The general slapped his sword and shot the landlord an intimidating glare. "Are you suggesting that I am unable to defend the ladies?"

"Oh no, of course not," the landlord Henry Porteous said hastily.

In the bright moonlight the street, lined with its neat white houses, looked like a scene in the theater, Gaspard Gourgaud thought. The tavern, which spilled out onto the pavement, was a sorry imitation of a Parisian street café. He ignored the vulgar stares coming at him from every direction and in turn did his best not to stare at Rosebud, of course a tactical move.

He hardly had time to become acquainted with his vile glass of Cape wine when Rosebud asked the inevitable question: "What is Napoleon like in person?"

"Oh, I expect you will find out very soon for yourself," he said dryly. "I'm much more interested in hearing all about Saint Helena."

"All right then, we have two kinds of mosquitoes," said Charlotte. "One bites you in the night and the other in the day."

"She's being silly," Mary cut in, "they're not that bad. To answer your question, the Portuguese discovered the island in 1502. Nobody here, never has been. Not until Dom Fernando."

"Who is he?"

"Our own Robinson Crusoe," Mary gushed. "He was a Portuguese gentleman, a soldier, who turned traitor in Goa and converted to Islam. The Portuguese were furious. They captured him and – you're going to hate this. The first day they pulled out his hair and beard and eyebrows and dragged him through a pigsty – you know how Muslims hate pigs. On the second day they cut off his nose and ears. On the third day they cut off his right hand and left thumb."

"Mary!" said Charlotte. "You'll give the general nightmares!"

"Then what?" he said, curiously excited, Charlotte noticed.

Mary rushed on. "Then they put him on a boat heading for Portugal. But he jumped ship here in Saint Helena because he didn't want his family to see he looked like a fish."

"Crippled Dom Fernando inspired Shakespeare's Caliban," Charlotte said. "So hooray, you're on Prospero's magic island!"

"I've heard the rumor," said the general. "Your admiral had the crew perform the play when we were crossing the equator. They even had Caliban wear his hat crossways as the emperor does. His Majesty laughed the whole thing off as a silly joke. Said the only line he liked was 'Hell is empty and all the devils are here'. All the devils, he said, except for one. The real Caliban."

"Who on earth did he mean?" asked Charlotte.

"Sir Hudson Lowe. The ogre they're sending out to be our jailer." The young general stifled a yawn. "Now I really must go to bed. It's been a trying day. Do you both live in the boardinghouse?"

"No," said Mary. "Charlotte is with her mother, up the street. There's only one of them. Street, I mean."

Gaspard examined the young woman thoughtfully. She was plain and gauche, but she had an ample bosom that she was pathetically eager to share, he was sure. But the other one was a true beauty. No wonder she had caught Napoleon's eye. He turned to her. "Then I insist on walking you home, Miss Kneips."

Charlotte knew he was teasing her by intentionally mispronouncing her name, so she didn't correct him. "Thank you general."

"Gaspard."

"Thank you Gaspard," she said with her prettiest smile.

"I'll walk with you," said Mary hopefully.

"Best not," said Gaspard. "I might go for a stroll afterwards. I need to be on my own for a change, after being cooped up on a crowded ship for months. I'm sure you understand."

Mary did her best to keep the disappointment out of her voice when she said she did.

At the gate to the modest bungalow, Gaspard looked up at the midnight moon burning down as bright as the sun. "Rosebud, may I kiss you good-night?"

"Certainly not!" she said with a laugh. "We hardly know each other, and anyway I am promised to another."

"Who?"

His name's Daniel. Daniel Hamilton. He's apprenticed in Kew Gardens, London. He's studying to be a botanist."

"Excellent! London is a long way away. Shall we save the kiss until tomorrow?"

Charlotte laughed. "Not even tomorrow!"

When the young general laughed, too, Charlotte found she liked him.


At dawn the next morning, the little cavalcade set out for a preview of Napoleon's residence, still under construction. The emperor, dressed now in the bright green satin uniform of a colonel in the imperial guard, his chest glittering with medals, was seated on a half-decent little black stallion auspiciously called Hope. It was almost like old times. Gaspard rode with him, and so did Admiral Cockburn, who pretended to be in charge. Marchand the valet was there as well, ready to fling himself between his master and the assassins he was convinced infested this foul island like the fleas that had kept him awake all night.

Up the steep, narrow, switchback road, their horses sweated. An hour and a half later, they emerged. Below them was Jamestown. The island lay before them. Westward were trees and houses with the governor's residence, a decent-sized country house painted dove gray, nestling in the distance. But eastward, the windward side of the island, was a scene of desolation. Black volcanic mountains patchily covered by a thin layer of soil. It was arid and virtually treeless.

"Which way do we go?" asked Gaspard.

"East," said Admiral Cockburn.

"Of course," said Napoleon without a trace of sarcasm. He had his spyglass trained on a beautifully manicured little estate below a high heart-shaped waterfall that had just come into view. "Who lives down there?"

"William Balcombe, your provisioner. I am going to stay in his little pavilion, as a matter of fact."

"Oh, you are, are you?" said Napoleon, a faintly ominous ring to his words.

They rode on through a narrow gorge called Hutt's Gate. It should have been called Hell's Gate, thought Napoleon, because it led to Deadwood Plain, a plateau that was dotted with gnarled and crooked gumwoods, native to the island, all leaning their umbrella tops in the same direction, permanently deformed by the relentless southeaster. The party was welcomed by the lieutenant governor who had recently made a halfhearted attempt to convert a clutch of cowsheds into a summer house he called Longwood, an effort that was being redoubled by a swarm of navy carpenters already hard at work.

"Well, General Bonaparte," said Admiral Cockburn afterward, "it obviously needs work, but what do you think?"

Napoleon was thinking of something else altogether, namely how to get his hands on a replacement

35

for the vial of poison that had failed to kill him after Waterloo. He thrust the negative thought behind him and charged back through Hutt's Gate on his way down to the residence below the heart-shaped waterfall. Balcombe's. He had a conquest to make.

Late that afternoon Charlotte, bonnet on and parasol up, was promenading on Sister's Walk, the seaside path cut into the cliffside that towered over the wharf. Because of the tropical heat she was naked under her sleeveless dress, her tall, willowy silhouette with its nipped waist needing no corset to set it off.

She tried unsuccessfully to calm herself by gazing down at the ships, small as matchsticks, swaying their masts in the bay below. She greeted people she knew and ignored the cheeky compliments of redcoats and sailors. Her mind was elsewhere, reliving the previous evening, examining it from every point of view like facets of a diamond.

*Who does that woman think she is to tease me about my name?* she was thinking. *She's nothing more than a prisoner of war. One word to Governor Wilks…oh, no!*

The unspeakable Balcombe girls appeared around a bend of the cliffside path, shrieking with delight at having run Charlotte to ground.

"Rosebud! Rosebud!" they chanted. "Boney wants to sniff Rosebud!"

Charlotte's frown was as disapproving as she could make it. "I beg your pardon?"

"It's true!" said Jane.

Betsy beat her sister to the really extraordinary nugget of news. "He galloped down to the Briars on his way back from Longwood. Ruined our lawn by charging across it on his horse. Insisted on seeing Papa immediately."

Jane would be interrupted no longer. "They talked together all alone for at least an hour while Admiral Cockburn walked up and down, absolutely fuming. And—"

"And then Papa made this big announcement. He said that Emperor Napoleon had accepted his invitation to stay in our pavilion until Longwood is ready for him!" said Betsy.

"You should have seen the admiral's face. He was absolutely livid!" said Jane.

"Because he was planning on staying there himself, as Wellington did," said Betsy.

"Anyway," said Jane, "Boney moved in right away without even going back to town."

"Said he didn't want to be gawked at," said Betsy.

"Turns out he's ever so nice and friendly. Not at all the man-eating monster you'd expect," said Jane. "He and Papa talked politics. I think Papa has quite fallen under his spell." She dropped her voice to an urgent whisper. "I'm sure they're plotting something."

"He likes me specially," said Betsy brightly. "Lets me call him Boney and calls me Miss Beetsy. We played blind man's buff and suchlike. He even asked after you, if we knew you and whatnot. So of course I told him you're one of our best friends and visit all the time."

"She's telling the truth for once," said Jane. "He did ask after you."

"Of course I am! I'll ask Papa when you can come up."

Napoleon, used to being on campaign, settled into his new accommodations quickly. The next morning he asked Balcombe to walk with him in the garden.

He got straight to the point because he owned this creature already. "Tell me about Rosebud's correspondence."

"I believe Henry Porteous told Your Majesty that she writes regularly to her fiancé, who is serving an apprenticeship at Kew Gardens in London. She's been sending him packets of plant specimens for five years."

"Can she be recruited?"

"She will have to be persuaded."

"By you?"

"Not by me, sire. We aren't that close."

"Who, then?"

"She worships you, of course. All Your Majesty has to do is ask her."

Napoleon was impatient to get back to dictating his memoirs, because he was in the middle of his victory at Austerlitz, the most exhilarating day of his life, when his spirit soared into the empyrean and even the tongues of the trees were singing his praises to the highest heaven.

"Settled!" he said. "Now listen carefully. I say things only once, as I remind my secretaries even when they ride into battle with me, writing down my dictation as they go. I will instruct Rosebud from now on to enclose a sealed scroll in her packet of weeds. When the packet arrives in England, Rosebud's inamorato will extract the scroll and hand it over to one of our agents. Do you understand?"

Balcombe said he did.

"You will launch this venture by going to the admiral and betraying the scheme to him."

Napoleon looked Balcombe full in the face, enjoying the man's befuddlement.

"Your Majesty, may I know why?"

"It's a well-worn military maneuver called a misinformation campaign. You will offer the admiral a letter from me, which he believes to be secret. You will make sure he thinks you are a blackguard who has betrayed me for money. That won't be so difficult, will it?"

A smile, slow as a slug, crept over Balcombe's lips. "No, Your Majesty."

After a largely liquid lunch William Balcombe rode into Jamestown, thinking through Napoleon's scheme all the way. The diabolical cunning of the man! The freshly minted double agent was certain he was being followed, but the winding road the locals called the High Road— although it was only six feet wide in places—made it easy to see that he was not. He took a glass of wine at the Almond Tree tavern, where officers and gentlemen met to swap the latest news. A second glass steadied his nerves enough for him to tether his horse purposefully and stride into the Castle's reception room with the assured gait of one who had an appointment. He managed to persuade the orderly that he needed to speak with Admiral Cockburn on an urgent matter.

Admiral Cockburn, already officiating as acting governor, ignored Balcombe when he was shown in. He hadn't recovered his good humor since this man had handed over his very pleasant accommodations to Bonaparte. The cowardice of the man, treating the prisoner as if he were still in command! That puffed up criminal Bonaparte was sorely in need of deflating, and he, George Cockburn, the man who had eaten President Madison's lunch, was just the man to do it.

As if to make this point, Cockburn was sitting in front of a large painting that had kept him company in his cabin all the way from England. It was a portrait of himself wearing a self-satisfied smile as Washington burned behind him. "Mr. Balcombe!" he said eventually. "To what do I owe the pleasure?"

After Balcombe told him, the admiral snorted as if he were trying to evacuate a particularly obnoxious smell from his nostrils. "Let me see if I have understood you correctly. Just by chance, you say, you have overheard that Bonaparte has a scheme in which he will use that Rosebud girl to smuggle secret correspondence to England. She will do this by delivering a packet hiding a secret scroll to the postmaster. The postmaster hands the packet to you, who brings it to me. When I have read its contents, we reseal the scroll with a copy of the imperial seal, which you will supply to us. You return the reconstituted packet to the postmaster, who sends it on its merry way so the girl will remain unaware that we have penetrated her secret. The young man at Kew extracts the scroll from its hiding place in the packet of dried weeds and hands it over to Napoleon's London courier, whoever that may be. The point of this rather circuitous exercise is that we get to read Napoleon's private correspondence without his being aware of it. Is that a fair summary?"

"Yes, Sir George."

"The girl, this Rosebud, will play her part?"

"Yes, Your Excellency. I know her well. She's in awe of Bonaparte. She'll do anything he asks her to do."

"How do we know her young man at Kew will cooperate?"

"He will be told that it is both his patriotic duty and the only way to keep his sweetheart safe from her own folly."

Cockburn interlaced his fingers as if they were pieces of a puzzle. "How well do you know this postmaster?"

"Joseph Cole has been one of my partners for ten years."

"And he will cooperate?"

"Yes, Sir George. I'm sure he can be...persuaded."

"You are, of course, talking about persuasion of the pecuniary kind?"

"I know he isn't well-off. If I may be candid, all we traders on the island have suffered huge losses since the embargo on European goods was lifted after Bonaparte's defeat."

Cockburn fixed Balcombe with a stare that made him squirm. "And passengers no longer have to pay your black-market prices."

Balcombe cleared his throat twice but could think of nothing to add.

"How much do you want?" asked Admiral Cockburn. "Of course we will need to read copies of the boy's responses to the packet or packets if things go smoothly."

Bargaining put Balcombe on familiar ground. "That adds levels of complexity but we'll throw them in for a total fee of a hundred guineas per packet. Half of that will go to the postmaster for the risks…French assassins…the girl's family…our reputations."

"Reputations!"

"Yes, Sir George. This is a small island. It's difficult, often expensive, to keep a reputation."

"Keeping your reputation is your affair. Keeping your mouth shut about this matter is mine. You and this postmaster better keep that in mind."

The admiral fanned his face with the back of his hand, turned his back on Balcombe and gazed with satisfaction at Washington in flames. "All right, agreed. One hundred guineas per packet. Now do get out of here, my good man. The air is oppressive enough."

Although the post office was just a few paces down Jamestown's only road, Balcombe had walked off the insult by the time he got there. The postmaster listened with his mouth open as Balcombe explained in a priestly whisper that he had discovered a devilish Napoleonic plot to smuggle letters out to England in Charlotte's packets to

Daniel, which, out of patriotic duty, he had reported to Admiral Cockburn. He told Cole what he had to do. There was no need to mention the hundred guineas.

Napoleon was sitting in the thick shade of a pomegranate tree. He pretended not to notice he was no longer alone, his eyes staying glued to his book. Balcombe, hat off, stood stiffly to attention, waiting to be spoken to, not even daring to clear his throat. Charlotte, in her best white dress, was motionless at his side, bare hands in full display.

Balcombe had told her she'd caught the emperor's eye that first night at Porteous House and that his instructions were to bring her to him. What he didn't tell her was that Napoleon intended to recruit her as an accomplice in a scheme to feed false information to His Majesty's government. What would happen if Cockburn discovered that the king's men were being sold a pack of lies in repeated doses? What would they do to Charlotte? What would they do to him? The thought had robbed him of sleep until, with the help of his bedside bottle, he found Morpheus in the arms of Bacchus.

Charlotte stared at the man concealing his face behind the book. She could see from the gold embossed spine that it was a collection of Greek tragedies. The first of his features that caught her eye was how small his feet were. It was hard to imagine such a tiny foot on the neck of Europe! His calf in its white stocking was well shaped, although his little paunch wasn't elegant. But his shoulders were broad and his hands beautiful, white and dimpled with fingers that tapered off delicately to perfectly manicured nails.

The slavish minutes crawled by on hands and knees. Eventually the emperor tired of the game. It was time to put the last piece of the puzzle in place. He set down the book, looked the girl full in the face with his bold gray eyes. "Ah!" he said, with relish. "Rosebud."

"Charlotte Knipe, Your Majesty," said Balcombe, unsure what else to say.

"Leave us."

Balcombe did a smart about-turn, which he'd learned during his short service in the navy, put his hat back on, and left her alone with Napoleon.

"How old are you?"

"Nineteen Your—"

"Who was your father?"

"Richard. He died ten years ago this—"

"Where did he come from?"

"He was born here."

"Who was his father?"

"Isaac Kni—"

"Where was he born?"

"Here."

"Name of his father?"

"John."

"*His* father?"

"Also John."

"Where was he born?"

"England."

"When?"

"About 1660."

"What was his first occupation?"

"Apprentice tanner."

"What's a tanner?"

"Someone who tans hides."

"How does he tan hides?"

"You begin with the raw skin of—"

"And then?"

"You flesh it."

"What's that?"

"You scrape off all—"

"Does it stink?"

Charlotte gave a quick smile. "Yes, and attracts flies and—"

"And then?"

"You salt it."

"And then?"

"You lay it out on a table and cure it—"

"And then?"

"Wash it until—"

"And then?"

"Soak it for two weeks in the tanning—"

"What's that?"

"In my great-great-grandfather's time they boiled the bark of the redwood and ebony trees from the forest, but—"

"But what?"

"Eventually they killed all the big trees and the wild goats ate the seedlings. Now instead of Great Wood it's called Deadwood." For the first time he let her finish a sentence.

"Ha! That's where they want to put me. This Deadwood. Yes?"

"I don't—"

He jumped to his feet, seemingly animated by the interrogation. "Come, walk with me." He led her down a path that was shaded with pomegranate trees, their flowers matching the jackets of the soldiers watching him from a distance.

"What do you know about politics?"

"Not very m—"

"You must believe something."

By this time she knew to keep her answers short. "Everyone should be given an equal chance."

"You are American?"

44

"No, of course not! But I do believe in democracy. Most ordinary English people do."

"Yes! In 1804 we tried to give it to them. I planned to empty the Channel of your fleet with the false intelligence that my ships were in the West Indies, busy linking up with the Americans. Then there would be nothing to stop me from landing two hundred thousand men at Chatham and sweeping up to London in four days. I would immediately have declared a republic, abolished the aristocracy, and redistributed its property among the ordinary citizens. Voilà! England would be a democracy!"

In a quick movement, he reached out and pinched her cheek, which Charlotte would normally have taken to be a gross presumption. "What do you think of that idea?"

"I think…" For once she struggled to find her voice. She was thinking of all the upper-class snobs who had looked down their noses at her. She was thinking of Laura Wilks. There was fire in her words. "I think that would be wonderful!"

"I believe you have a fiancé," he said. "A gardener at Kew in London."

"Not a gardener, Your Majesty," she said. "A student. He's studying botany."

"You write to him?"

"Yes. I send him packets of dried plants and flowers. To classify."

"Of course you know that all my letters are read. The English oligarchy fears my pen as much as my sword."

Charlotte's heart beat faster, because she had a sense of where this might be going. "Yes, I can see that."

His eyes caught hers and cradled them. "Do they ever open yours?"

"Certainly not! I've been sending out the Kew packets for years. And the new postmaster, Mr. Cole, is an old family friend."

An unexpectedly sweet smile toyed with the corners of his lips. "Excellent! You shall send a new packet tomorrow." He reached into his pocket and took out a slender sealed scroll. "You will hide this among your herbs."

The next morning Charlotte delivered a packet to Mr. Cole the postmaster. Within minutes Balcombe delivered to it Admiral Cockburn. Kay, the senior government secretary, an aging fixture who had served three administrations already, undid the simple clasp and extracted the cover letter as well as the sealed scroll hiding in the little burlap pouch of herbs.

Kay broke the seal carefully because he was going to have to replace it. Cockburn read the scroll. All it said was: "Important messages to follow if this arrives intact." It was signed *N*.

Then the admiral started Charlotte's cover letter and was swept away by a wave of excitement.

# Chapter 3: Cinderella

*October 20, 1815*
*Dearest Daniel:*

*As I write this, I know that you must already have heard the extraordinary news. An emperor has moved in with us Yamstocks here in little Saint Helena. And not just any emperor, but the emperor Napoleon! I could write this whole letter with nothing but exclamation points, but that would still not do justice to my extraordinary excitement. Not only have I seen Napoleon, but I have seen him all on my own! Just the two of us, tête-à-tête in the Balcombes' garden! At first he fired a fusillade of questions at me, so quickly that I had hardly any time to answer them. For some reason he wanted to know all about my family, where they came from, what they did. When I told him that they started out as tanners, he insisted on hearing all about tanning, down to every last smelly detail!*

*He's younger than I expected. He turned forty-six on board ship in August on his way down here. Not tall, as everyone knows, but not short, either—I think I might be an inch or two taller. But he is very broad in the shoulders and radiates the most extraordinary energy that overwhelms everyone he meets. His ambition is not to rule the world, he told me, but to bring it the gift of freedom. He said he was the bridge between the feudal world of serfs and a modern world that enslaves only machines. He very nearly helped the English declare the Republic of Britain ten years ago but was prevented by the Channel. He still hasn't given up. He knows, as you do, how the ordinary English people are suffering, especially with all the war veterans returning to a country where they can't find work. A spark, he says, will set England on fire.*

*Now I come to the heart of this letter. Napoleon needs our help! Our help, can you believe it? His jailers read every letter that he sends to Europe. They destroy every word that does not suit them. Napoleon could write a thousand letters a day, there are so many who are dying to hear from him. But because all his letters will be read, he will not write any.*

*So what he asked me to do is hide a little sealed scroll right at the heart of each shipment of dried specimens I send you. Since I have been sending you identical packets for five years now, no one will ever suspect. Take a quick look, there is one inside your specimen packet right now! Napoleon's courier has been informed of its arrival. If you are reading this in the Black Dog as usual, he is already there. As soon as you finish my letter he will approach you and give you the password, "Rosebud" which is what Napoleon calls me. Isn't all this so exciting!*

*Please say you will help. I know that there is a small degree of danger, but it is a risk I take for freedom's sake, which I embrace all the more fervently because I can't embrace you for fifteen long months!*

*Be brave, my husband-to-be, just as I am trying to be brave all alone on this lonely island!*

*All my love,*
*Charlotte*

Daniel choked on his urgent gulp of bitter. He had watched men hanged for less than this. Listened to the crowd laughing as the wretches not lucky enough to have their necks snapped by the drop dancing their last dance at the end of the rope, their feet comically searching for stairs that weren't there. As with many others he sympathized with the radical causes that swirled in the sewers of English society and kept Charlotte as informed as the slow post would allow. But treason! The packet of herbs in his pocket, as usual sown in burlap, transmuted to lead.

He could drink no more beer. He also wanted nothing to do with this mad scheme. He would write to Charlotte in the severest terms with instructions to put this nonsense out of her head. He was about to return the letter to the packet, hurry over to the grate that was trying unsuccessfully to keep the room warm, and burn it to ashes, herbs, scroll, and all, when a tiny bird of a man with an angelic smile on his face detached himself from the bar and approached with light steps as if he was trying not to wake a sleeping child.

"Rosebud sent me," he whispered. "You are Mr. Daniel Hamilton, are you not?"

Daniel examined the stranger. He was rail thin and couldn't have been much more than five feet in height. His slightly humped back and beak of a nose gave him the air of a hungry but amiable vulture. He put down his glass on the table and pulled out a chair. "May I sit with you?" he asked, after the fact, because Daniel, overwhelmed by the swift passage of events, couldn't find his voice.

"Who are you?" he asked when the little man had settled himself on the chair with the proprietary air of a hen settling on her eggs.

"Edwards. George Edwards, at your service," he said in a surprisingly mellifluous voice, which he dropped in volume when he added, "I am honored to be to be a friend of Mr. Arthur Thistlewood. Surely you've heard of him?"

Daniel had not and said so.

The man calling himself Edwards whistled, again like a bird. "I'm surprised, I really am," he said, glancing over his shoulder as if to make sure no one was listening. "Mr. Thistlewood is a rising star in the radical movement. He served with the redcoats in America, where he was set on fire by the flame of liberty. He cashiered himself in '93 and fled to France, where he was made captain in the French grenadiers during the Terror." Edwards leaned across the table, his head so low that it looked as if he was going to peck at bread crumbs with his nose. "That's when he met Napoleon, at the siege of Toulon." He crossed two skeletal fingers of his right hand. "They've been like this ever since."

Daniel said nothing, because his mind was a battleground of conflicting emotions with terror leading the charge.

Edwards looked over his shoulder again, as if he was trying to relieve a crick in his neck, and lowered his voice. "Now if you would pass me the enclosure, I'll be on my way."

Terror won the day. "I'll have nothing to do with treason!" Daniel hissed. "Nothing!"

Edwards's chuckle sounded like a contented cluck. "That's because you're afraid. The problem for you is that the girl isn't. Tell me"—there was steel in his gentle voice now—"what would you prefer? Her dangling on your arm at the altar or her dangling at the end of a rope?"

Now Daniel was angry. "She's full of fantasies! What letter? You have no proof! Nothing!"

Edwards laughed out loud. He gestured at a man who sat at the bar. He had a squint that allowed him to watch the door with one eye and them with the other. "Come, sir, my friend over there is a hard man. And there is the little matter of that letter in your hand. It would be an easy matter for the police to be provided with all the evidence they need for Charlotte's conviction on a capital charge. All we are asking you to do is take an insignificant risk to promote the cause of liberty and save the life of the lady you love. Is that too much to ask?"

"Blackmail!"

"No, sir, war. Us against them. The common man against the strutting parasites who feed like vampires on our blood. Bonaparte is freedom's shining star, a freedom that gives every man an equal chance to make his way in the world. You have the power to help us destroy the oligarchy and make England a shining democracy like America. You also have the power to save Charlotte. What say you?"

Daniel forced himself to take a long, calming swallow. He'd been to enough hangings. He didn't want to go to his own. And he could not bear the thought of Charlotte…

Without a word he took the burlap bag out of his pocket, undid the stitching, and found the scroll basking in fragrant Saint Helena herbs. He noticed the seal was stamped with the French imperial eagle. "Here," he said handing it to Edwards.

"Capital!" said Edwards. "You have just struck a blow for democracy!" He beckoned to Daniel to lean closer, dropped his voice. They were conspirators already. "When the next packet arrives, you are to deliver the scroll on the Saturday night following to the Cock in Mayfair, where I will introduce you to Mr. Thistlewood himself. He will be expecting you—we are in close contact with the island, you see. He is most interested to hear everything that Charlotte tells you about Napoleon, and I do mean everything, down to the smallest scrap of gossip! Will you make sure she includes all that in her letters?"

Saint Helena, November 20, 1815.

On the night of the grand ball, thrown in the Castle ballroom by Admiral Cockburn to welcome Napoleon and his court to Saint Helena, the guest of honor wasn't there. The victor of the Pyramids, Marengo, and Austerlitz had no wish to celebrate Waterloo. Even the invitation was an insult. Oh, it was grand enough, embossed with bold gold letters, but it was addressed to *General* Bonaparte! *Quelle horreur!* This Cockburn creature had no delicacy, none at all. Napoleon would not attend his ball.

But Napoleon did give Gaspard permission to throw a warm-up reception in a tent that had been pitched on Balcombe's lawn, the lawn he had torn up with his horse's hooves when he had robbed the puffed-up English admiral of his residence—if you could call the little shack preposterously misnamed the Pavilion a residence! Although he refused to show himself, Napoleon examined the guests through a chink in the Pavilion's curtains. Rosebud, the magnificent creature, glowed in her humble gown. She pretended to listen to Gaspard's war stories but kept glancing furtively in his direction.

Charlotte's sharp eyes caught just a glimpse of Napoleon before he snapped the curtain shut. Here was a man who had been the center of the world's attention, reduced to a Peeping Tom! But perhaps she could change that, if Daniel far away in starving Britain would help her.

At nine the dance party, in high spirits, left Napoleon sulking with his servants and was transported in a cavalcade of little buggies down the winding precipitous road to the Castle that wasn't a castle. Gaspard invited Charlotte to ride with him and then annoyed her by going on about Laura's charms.

The Admiral's Ball, as by now everyone on the island was calling it, was the social event of the new century. Almost two hundred guests, every person of any respectability, were invited. The men were mostly in uniform, the women in their finest. Charlotte wore a pink ball gown, the best Jamestown could provide at short notice. It was paid for by rich Uncle Samuel, because the Knipe name, he told her with a tear or two in his eyes, was now in her hands. Those who weren't invited, which included all of Charlotte's Yamstock relatives, gawked between the redcoats lined up to keep rabble like them at bay. When she was helped out of the buggy by Gaspard, epaulets and medals glittering, Uncle Samuel waved his stick at her approvingly, and a loud lout in the crowd yelled, "Rosebud! Rosebud! Hello, Rosebud! Lovely dress! Bet that one going to come off soon!"

The lout was her brother John, drunk, of course, the one who had announced Napoleon's arrival when she'd been bottling peaches.

Their mother, dressed in her best widow's weeds, elbowed him in the ribs. "Shh!" she hissed. "Don't spoil it for her! She's with gentry!"

"No need to hit so 'ard! You tink I be one dawg?"

Charlotte pretended she hadn't heard this vulgar interaction, and fortunately General Gaspard Gourgaud had trouble understanding John's thick Yamstock accent. A few springy steps across the courtyard on Gaspard's arm and they were inside. The high table was already seated, Admiral Cockburn of course at the center. Mrs. Wilks, the governor's wife, sat on his right, Madame Bertrand on his left, and so on all the way to lovely Laura Wilks, who sat with an officer as decorated as a Christmas tree.

Charlotte felt Gaspard stiffen. "*Mon Dieu!*"

"What's the matter, Gaspard?" she said, because she was calling him that by now.

"Look what the canaille have done! They've placed the governor's wife on the admiral's right! A barefaced insult! That's where Madame Bertrand, as wife of the grand marshal of the palace, should be!"

Charlotte felt like reminding him that there was no palace anymore. "Why?" she asked instead.

He stared at her with genuine astonishment. "You don't know? Because Madame Bertrand outranks her, of course! Wait until the emperor hears about this. He will be furious!"

Gaspard was equally unhappy about the table he and Charlotte were shown to, because they were to share it with the Balcombes, already seated, with Betsy an eyesore in an absurd gown plastered with faux roses.

Admiral Cockburn, flush with brandy, made Gaspard dance with both of the Balcombe girls, although the dashing young general's attention was elsewhere—on Laura Wilks, as she went through her paces with partners from the endless supply of lovelorn young officers prepared to throw themselves on their swords for the privilege of being seen with the ex-governor's lovely daughter. Charlotte did her best to ignore her rival. She had several dances. She pretended to listen intently to kilted Henry Porteous going into too much detail about the correspondence he was having with Mr. Burchell about the proper classification of Saint Helena cabbage trees. She danced with Gaspard.

"Rosebud, I am suffocating in this stuffy tropical heat of yours," he said. "Please do me the honor of taking the air in the garden with me."

Charlotte, who saw that Laura Wilks was watching out of the corner of her eye, was delighted to say yes.

It was a moonless night. The stars in the pristine Saint Helena sky twinkled like Gaspard's medals.

"May I kiss you now?" asked Gaspard.

Charlotte smiled, because the garden was full of social spies and this would certainly get back to Laura. "You may kiss my hand," she said.

Sunday dinner at her mother's.

"That fancy Frenchie done gone and kissed her in the Castle garden! Everyone seed it!" Charlotte's loutish brother, John, blurted through a mouthful of boiled yams.

"The same prince charming that done gone and helped Charlotte out of the carriage just like a regular princess!" cried her youngest brother, Bill, seventeen and just signed up with the Saint Helena Regiment.

Everyone was laughing, and everyone was there. All Charlotte's siblings, as always on a Sunday after church. When her father, Richard Knipe, died ten years ago, her mother and the younger children had moved from desolate Half Moon Farm into this little bungalow in Jamestown. Here her mother struggled to make ends meet on a widow's pension and the meager earnings from Half Moon's vegetables, mostly potatoes and yams and citrus, intermittently provided by John and sold off the front porch.

Today, the Sunday after the ball, the gathering was larger than usual. Twenty people nearly, including Porteous House landlord and company gardener Henry Porteous in his kilt; Joseph Cole, the rotund postmaster recently recruited into the shadowy world of espionage; and rich Uncle Samuel Knipe, who had supplied the fresh leg of lamb—a luxury on a tiny, poverty-stricken blob of rock where you needed permission from the Company to kill an ox, and even the slaughter of a sheep was cause for universal comment.

But this *was* a celebration. A celebration of the honor that Charlotte had brought to the Knipe family name. She'd been a guest of the great man who brooded in the mountains. She'd danced with a general. What a sight she had been, their own Charlotte, dressed in a ball gown, helped out of a carriage by a French general spangled with medals!

"He started with your hand, but I wonder what else you let him kiss!" howled John, washing down his words with so much beer that it ran down his tangled beard and dripped onto the table.

"Don't be so crude, you've just been in church!" snapped their mother.

"All that was missing was the glass slipper," John blundered on.

"General Gourgaud was just being polite," Charlotte said, patience already worn thin but making a point of watching her language. "Thanking me for a pleasant evening."

"Exactly, but how pleasant?" Henry, a year older than Charlotte, chimed in and then bit his tongue, because he was the studious one, Mr. Porteous's apprentice at the Botanical Gardens, who should have known better.

"Your idea of pleasant is wearing nothing under your kilt!" Charlotte shot back, her fair cheeks flushed, because young Henry wore a kilt on Sundays like his master Mr. Porteous, who had adopted him, in an informal way, after his father died. "I wonder why!"

"Mine your moufs, there be little ones 'ere!" screeched Florella, another of Charlotte's siblings, whose brats were slyly throwing food at one another under the table.

"Look who be talking!" belched John, who had sparked the ruckus. "You got a mouth sumpin' like a latrine when you ain't pretending to be a lady!"

Charlotte let her thoughts wander. She was thinking of Cinderella.

The roar of an Alarm Hill cannon told Saint Helena that a ship had been sighted. Hours later the flutter of signal flags announced it was a packet ship. It was February 10, 1816, high time for a response from Daniel. High time to read whether he had the courage to serve liberty. Not that Napoleon would care if he was too afraid to help. The emperor had other conduits, she was sure. But she would care. If Daniel refused to be part of the chain, she was very afraid that it would be the end of their relationship.

When the ship came in that afternoon, Charlotte was at the wharf, watching the mailbags being loaded onto a barrow bound for the post office. She fumed with impatience as she waited at the Almond Tree, chatting with friends and warding off officers for what seemed like hours as she gave Mr. Cole the postmaster time to sort through the mail.

When she couldn't stand the suspense any longer, she walked in on him and sang out, "Anything for me?" as if she didn't have a care in the world. But she did. She cared about what was going on in Mr. Cole's head. She cared that since she sent the first secret scroll to Daniel there had been a tightness in the rotund little man's smile, a sly glint in his eyes. Or was it her imagination? It had to be there somewhere in her mind, impossible to root out, a vestigial sense of guilt, a weed of doubt, that whispered she was betraying her government and could be hanged for it.

"I saw you hovering, so I looked for it," he called out, a little too cheerfully. "Voilà, as they say up the hill. I have it right here safe and sound on my desk. A love letter!"

That afternoon she took Daniel's letter up the mountain to Longwood, the ex-cowshed where Napoleon had been transplanted exactly a month ago. In spite of the ghostly curtains of fog chased in from the sea by the relentless southeaster, it was hot and humid. Napoleon sat her down in the shade of his favorite tree, a banyan with wide-spreading branches close to the house, the only tree that gave it any shade. A redcoat leaning on his musket peered at them. If he bothered to look farther, Napoleon knew, he could pick out more soldiers, circling the house night and day, the noose around his neck.

Instead he listened to the girl read Daniel's letter to him in her cool, clear voice, translating it for him as she went along.

*December 5, 1815*
*Dearest Charlotte,*

*I have received your latest packet with its most interesting enclosure. Many of your samples are plants I have never seen before and may be new to science. Mr. Burchell will know. I miss you more than I can find words to tell. Just imagining you alone among those misty crags, drinking up the sounds and sweet airs of our enchanted little island without me, makes my heart ache!*

*But no one except for me and Mr. Burchell is interested in the plants. Napoleon, that's all everybody asks me about. Does he have eyes like saucers? Does he really have teeth like daggers? You can't believe the number of silly questions I've been asked! My problem is I have so few answers. In your next letter, please tell me everything you've heard about him. What does he wear? What does he eat? How does he pass the day? Even more important, how does he pass the night! I hope he doesn't keep a rosebud in a vase next to his bed!*

"Ha!" barked Napoleon. "I think I am beginning to like this Daniel of yours. He has seductive ideas!"

Charlotte ignored the coarse quip and read on:

*Has Byron's "Ode to Napoleon" found its way to you yet? I look at it often and every time it makes me weep. Here are my favorite lines:*

*Is this the man of thousand thrones,*
*Who strew'd our earth with hostile bones,*
*And can he thus survive?*
*Since he, miscalled the Morning Star,*
*Nor man nor fiend hath fall'n so far.*

*But Napoleon will rise again. I feel it in my bones. We await your packets eagerly, but nothing could be as eager as my desire to hold you in my arms!*
*Much, much love, my darling,*
*Your very own Daniel.*

"You see!" said Charlotte. "He'll do it!"

Napoleon waved away an impertinent fly. "Of course he'll do it," he said. "He's under your spell."

"No, he's not. He's under yours! He believes—"

"What is 'fiend'? Is it similar to 'friend'?"

"No! Just the opposite. It means a devil. Like Lucifer. The angel who was cast down from heaven because he challenged God."

He surprised her by smiling. "Like I do," he said, pinching her cheek. "It's time to send your Daniel another letter."

# Chapter 4: Secret Letters

On Friday, March 26, 1816, a messenger boy called at Kew Gardens to tell Daniel that there was a packet for him at the Black Dog. This time there was no George Edwards and no hard man with a squint. All the same he hurried home without drinking his customary bitter and waited until he found a secluded park bench before opening Charlotte's latest. It was dated February 11, 1816.

*My dearest, dearest darling Daniel,*

*How very happy we all were to receive your brave letter! Our new friend has set himself to learn English, from me, can you believe it? He laughed when I told him that he would end up with a Yamstock accent. So I went further and taught him some Yamstock phrases, which he parrots proudly to his entourage, much to their annoyance. They believe I am mocking his imperial dignity. But when I mentioned this to him, he roared with laughter. Said they had no sense of humor, if I understood him correctly. But he was being perfectly serious when he said that you are writing yourself a footnote to history, although I think you deserve much more than that—a whole chapter, at least!*

*A few weeks ago, I ran into your mother at the wharf, where she reads sailors' palms for a penny. She and her girls are well and she sends her love. I'm sure she would write to you if she knew how but is too proud to dictate to someone else, especially me! For the first time, we sat down and talked, which is high time since someday soon, I hope, she will be my mother-in-law. For a woman with no education, she has an extraordinary mind, like yours. But her thinking is all on the occult side, while yours is of course all on the scientific. She asked me a curious question, whether I ever looked at something, especially after dark, thought it to be one thing, often something frightening, and then found it was something else. I said yes, because of course it happens to everyone. Then she told me the most extraordinary thing. She said that first impression we get is reality while the second is a hasty fabrication constructed by reality to hide itself. The trick, she says, is not to blink but to hold on to that first impression, because that's a doorway into the real world. I thought this to be nonsense and was rude enough to tell her so. But the idea stayed with me. Now when I mistake a trick of the light for you, I do my best to hold the impression, which consoles me a little. I do so wish I didn't have to play this silly game and had the real flesh and blood person back here in my arms!*

*I love you so very much,*
*Charlotte*

The next afternoon, dressed in his best, Daniel set out for Mayfair to deliver the slender roll of papers that had been hidden among the herbs. Like the previous one, it was sealed with the imperial French eagle stamped onto a generous blob of red wax.

Although it was not yet evening, the Cock tavern was already noisy and foggy with the fumes of the long-stem clay pipes being puffed and chewed everywhere. If it was true that you could tell a short temper by a short pipe stem, as common knowledge claimed, there were enough angry men present to make a quorum. What with the yapping of dogs playing between the tables and the wailing of a single fiddle being sawed to pieces on a tiny stage,

61

Daniel had to mime that he wanted a beer and point to which kind he wanted. He was taking his first long swallow, because he was thirsty after his long walk from Kew, when he felt a light tap on his shoulder. It was George Edwards, beaked and black eyed, happy as a vulture that had just swooped down on a well-ripened corpse.

"Well met, if a little late," the small man said in his big voice. "You have it?"

Daniel nodded. "I'd forgotten how far Mayfair was from Kew."

"It's never too far to go in pursuit of freedom!" Edwards said. He took Daniel into a little back room in which stood a darkly complexioned man. He was dressed in a blue long coat with trousers to match, which altogether looked very much like a uniform, an impression reinforced by his military bearing. He was slender, above average height, his long face topped with arched eyebrows, which gave the impression that he found everything about the world astonishing. He was quite alone, reading what looked like notes, for his speech perhaps.

"Mr. Thistlewood, I'd like you to meet young Daniel. He's the one from Saint Helena."

Thistlewood's surprised eyebrows arched even higher. Wide brown eyes examined Daniel carefully. "Ah, yes, I've heard all about you! Liberty thanks you for your service. The emperor and I are very good friends, you know."

Edwards nodded in enthusiastic confirmation. "The emperor has sent Mr. Thistlewood a gift, hasn't he, Daniel?"

"Yes," said Daniel. He passed the sealed scroll to Thistlewood, who took it with a polite nod, examined the red eagle seal, and kissed it.

"*Mon empereur,*" Thistlewood said, breaking the seal and unrolling the paper. His eyebrows shot up, even more surprised by life than usual. He reverently rolled up the paper before tucking it away in an inside pocket, so it would be close to his heart, perhaps.

Edwards led the way back through the fuming crowd in the barroom. Behind him Thistlewood shook as many hands as he could, often two at a time. Edwards silenced the sawing fiddler with a tap on the shoulder. To Daniel's surprise it was suddenly very still. Even the dogs stopped yapping. All eyes were on the man who was making his way to the stage.

Thistlewood's voice was loud, and his introductory remarks were long. Then he carved his way into the meat of his speech:

"You should see how they live in America, because I have!" he said, dark eyes wide with wonder. "No man is born great, but there is the opportunity for every man to achieve greatness. The American Revolutionary leader George Washington began life as a humble lumberjack but ended up having the capital city named after him! He was offered the American throne but refused it. Would anyone refuse the throne in England? *Oh, how I wish they would!* If its current occupant spent as much time on statecraft as on his clothes, England would be the best-governed country in the world. No more oligarchs! Britain should be ruled by the people, for the people. A society that keeps its people hungry while its rulers live in luxury is a society that should not exist. A society that takes honest labor away from hungry people and feeds it to machines should not exist. Labor-saving devices? No, labor-stealing devices, I call them!"

On rambled Thistlewood. But Daniel was hardly listening. He was watching Edwards in his dark corner, scribbling away on a long strip of narrow paper that was by

63

now snaking down to the floor. He stopped writing when Thistlewood paused. Began again when he rambled on. Clearly he was taking down everything what was being said, word for word, taking it down in the most inconspicuous way he could, smiling and nodding all the time as if he was drinking at the font of wisdom.

Daniel was exhausted by his eight-mile walk from Mayfair back home to Kew. It was past midnight, but he couldn't sleep. He lay on his right side, sweating in the leaky little loft he shared with two other Kew apprentices, the cold sweat of fear. He turned onto his left side and tried to think of Charlotte. Of mountain walks on their enchanted island. Her wild delight as she skipped down a steep slope inside a rolling bank of mist, arms outstretched, pretending she was flying.

But she wasn't the child he remembered any longer. She was five years older, nineteen already. A woman now, with needs he was so eager to satisfy that he had to wrestle with the devil to resist the temptation of trollops on paydays.

Would they execute her for treason if they found out?

First they would torture her to find out what she knew. Then they would hang her without the consolation of clergy, that chilling phrase. Yamstocks shrieking with laughter as those beautiful feet of hers searched for stairs that weren't there…

"Follow your heart, not your fear." The words came from the Friar's lips. Daniel woke from the shallow dream with his mind made up. He held the night-light to the portrait of an exquisite creature with long, curly blonde locks, a portrait of Charlotte done by Mr. Burchell just three months ago, when his ship stopped at Saint Helena on its way back from the Cape with thousands of specimens.

"She's waiting for you, Daniel, you lucky dog," Mr. Burchell had said. "As you can see, she's worth the wait. Much taller than me. Lithe. High-spirited. The Yamstocks say that she's the most beautiful woman on the island."

First thing tomorrow he would call on Mr. Burchell, who was busy cataloging his African collection. He would tell him everything. Mr. Burchell would know what to do.

William Burchell was in a dusty little room in Kew crammed with specimens animal, vegetable, and mineral. He was working on a sketch of his Cape zebra, *Equus burchelli*, when Daniel knocked faintly on the open door and came in pale and puffy eyed from lack of sleep.

"Daniel!" said the little man in his cultured voice. "How nice to see you, but why so distraught?"

Daniel, whose Yamstock accent tended to return when he was upset, began at the beginning. He told the little botanist about the sealed scroll in the herb packet. About Thistlewood kissing Napoleon's seal. About Edwards making secret notes of Thistlewood's speech.

And then he came to the point that was tormenting him. "Edwards didn't wait to discover what surprised Thistlewood about Napoleon's letter. He seemed, well, not interested and in a hurry. I had hardly had time to sip the beer Edwards bought me when he told me he had other business to attend to and left. I don't know what possessed me, but something did. I followed him, making sure to keep well hidden. He was heading eastward but he didn't go far. Only as far as number four Bow Street. He visited the Runners."

Burchell's eyes widened. He had been listening to Daniel's story with half an ear as he examined the stripes on his zebra, thinking that he hadn't gotten them quite right. Suddenly the boy had his full attention. "What business could Edwards have with the police?" he asked, although he already knew the answer.

"His ribbon of notes, the ones he made on Thistlewood's speech. He handed them over. I saw him do it."

"Very strange."

"I lay awake and thought that through until my head hurt," said Daniel. "Edwards delivers a copy of Thistlewood's speech to the police but doesn't seem to be interested in knowing what's in Napoleon's scroll. Seems to me that could only mean that Edwards knew the police already had a copy of that."

Burchell nodded. "Very astute. But how is that possible? The seal was intact when you delivered it to Thistlewood, you say?"

"Yes, but could it have been broken and then replaced?"

"Yes," said Burchell. "As long as someone took an impression of the seal before breaking it and then made a copy."

"The publican at the Black Dog is too clumsy to do that."

Burchell said, "It wasn't him. My guess is that it was done in Saint Helena."

"But why reseal the correspondence? Why not confiscate it?"

"Because then Napoleon would know his scheme had been penetrated. He would find another courier, and the government would lose access to a priceless wellspring of secret information."

"I'm afraid, Mr. Burchell," said Daniel. "I'm even more afraid for Charlotte."

Burchell sighed. In nature there was such a thing as defensive mimicry. The plant hopper imitates a leaf for protection, he was thinking. Harmless flies imitate stinging wasps. The milk snake imitates the deadly coral snake. And then there was aggressive mimicry, the wolf in sheep's clothing. Nature was full of deception, so why not man?

"Seems to me that Charlotte is being manipulated by the world's greatest manipulator." Burchell said. "She loves adventure, fears nothing. If you refuse to receive her packages, Napoleon's packages, she will find someone else, someone who would then have a hold over her."

"So what am I to do?"

One of the benefits of being educated at Raleigh House Academy was that it gave one some very powerful connections. Burchell was pondering one of these right now, a man who, thanks to his family connections, already occupied an important position in the government, although he was a Liberal. A man who would relish being involved in an intrigue with his hero, the great Napoleon Bonaparte. "I know someone at the Home Office. Someone I can talk to," he said, picking up his brush. "Someone who is on our side."

"Oh, thank you sir! Thank you so much!" said Daniel as he backed out the door.

The little botanist tried to go back to painting stripes on his zebra, but his hand was shaking too much.

Women, were they worth it? Burchell pondered as his rented horse plodded the lengthy way to London and the Home Office.

A woman had broken his heart seven years ago, and he was sure, by now, that it would never heal. The femme fatale was Lucia Green, the niece of that thief Balcombe's wife—he should have been warned by the Balcombe connection, because nothing good could ever come of anything to do with that devious drunk.

The diminutive botanist had paid for Lucia's passage to the island, paid (courtesy of his father) for the most luxurious passage the *Walmer Castle* could provide. And what did she do, the stone-hearted trollop? She had an affair in her fancy stateroom with the ship's captain, a beefy blackguard named Luke Dodds! Unforgivable! But he would have forgiven her, if she'd repented, because Lucia was a passionate young woman and the voyage was long and lonely. But repentant she was not. She simply told him that she'd changed her mind, as if that was a mere trifle, like changing your order in a restaurant from a plate of pigeon to one of pork. While the ship rode at anchor, Lucia stayed with her aunt and was royally entertained by Balcombe, who reveled in his ex-partner's humiliation, even going to the lengths of entertaining the rough seaman in his house! Of course Burchell should have challenged the captain to a duel—he would have, in fact, if he hadn't fallen so ill with despondency that he could barely get out of bed. Would Charlotte break Daniel's heart like Lucia had broken his?

The botanist got back to Kew in the late afternoon and had a supper of boiled bacon washed down with good claret. Then he sent for Daniel and told him the news. "I'm happy to say that rather as I expected, everything is already very much under control. You are instructed to encourage Charlotte to write to you often. You are instructed to continue delivering the scrolls promptly. The government has known about them from the start. You are also instructed to tell no one, no one at all, of the government's penetration of this smuggling scheme, especially not Charlotte. If you obey these instructions, both she and you will be safe."

"But I will be betraying the emperor!" Daniel whispered. "To keep her safe. Won't I?"

"I don't believe you have been betraying him. As usual, he has outthought everyone. I'm told by my friend in the Home Office that he has seduced the government into believing that it has penetrated his smuggling operation. That its agents are reading top-secret correspondence when what they're actually reading is a stew of exaggerations and outright inventions. Fret not, my boy, I am certain you are doing precisely what Napoleon wants you to do."

The expression of relief on Daniel's face was glorious to behold. Burchell jumped up and kissed him on both glowing cheeks. This time Daniel didn't flinch.

That evening Burchell wrote a letter that he sealed within another letter addressed to Henry Porteous. It went out in the convoy carrying no lesser a personage than Sir Hudson Lowe, who was to replace Admiral Cockburn as the governor of Saint Helena and Napoleon's jailer. Burchell had met Hudson Lowe at Holland House, where Lowe was being courted after it was announced that he had been given the Saint Helena assignment, as he called it. A short conversation with him had confirmed the rumors that Lowe was a martinet with the charm of a porcupine. But he was an even harder man than Cockburn, which was why he was appointed. Napoleon would want to know about that as well.

The letter within a letter was entrusted to a young lieutenant on a fast sloop, which would alert the island of the convoy's imminent arrival. The young officer, who had an interest in botany, promised to deliver the letter immediately he made landfall to Henry Porteous, superintendent of the Saint Helena Botanical Gardens, owner of Porteous House, where Napoleon had spent his first flea-bitten night. Henry Porteous, father of Charlotte's best friend, Mary, the man who, as a true Scotsman, wore his kilt whenever there was the least excuse to do so, including his daughter's funeral.

# Chapter 5: Devilish Cunning

Charlotte was at the wharf when the young lieutenant, who didn't know he was smuggling a secret letter for Napoleon inside the letter for the botanist, came ashore on the first longboat. Happy to see such a pretty face after eight weeks at sea, he made a point of approaching her for directions to the botanist Henry Porteous. She laughed, a lovely sound, and said of course she knew where he lived, because he was her uncle, although that wasn't exactly true, and that she would be very happy to walk him to Porteous House. Like almost everyone else, all the officer seemed interested in was Bonaparte, where he was staying, how he passed his time, had she met him, what kind of person he was.

"Depends who you ask," said Charlotte. "We had someone called Raffles here who got permission to see him."

"Not Sir Stamford Raffles!"

"Yes, do you know him?"

"No, but I know *of* him, of course. He's a legend. Founder of Singapore. One of the original promoters of the Zoological Society. How did the two of them get on?"

"Terribly! Napoleon was in one of his high moods, you see. Tore Raffles apart. Raffles told Mr. Porteous afterward that Napoleon was vindictive, had no soul, that he was totally selfish, that his only talent was to enslave mankind, that he looked on everyone as his inferiors, and that all his energy was devoted to himself and his supremacy."

"Is that all true?"

Charlotte laughed. "Not entirely. Raffles also said he was a wild animal, caught but not tamed. That's true. But Raffles said that Napoleon can command respect but never affection, which is not." This took the young officer a moment to digest, which gave her the opportunity to change the subject. "You're not carrying any mail, by any chance?" she asked.

He seemed surprised by the question. "Why, no," he lied. "That will come with the packet ship, with the convoy bringing Sir Hudson Lowe. Should be here by nightfall. Are you expecting something?"

"Yes, a letter from a friend of mine. A botanist. He's apprenticed at Kew. But then, I expect a letter from him on every ship that comes in from England."

"The lucky dog!" said the officer, making it very clear the way he said it that it was not the apprenticeship he was talking about.

Henry Porteous received the letter from Burchell shortly after eleven and made polite botanical conversation with the lieutenant for an hour before bidding him good day. Then he read the note in the outer envelope. It said, "Dear friend, as a special favor, please see that the enclosure is delivered immediately to the emperor. It concerns a matter of the highest importance." There were no salutations.

Henry Porteous walked briskly to the Almond Tree. As he expected, Young Las Cases, the sickly sixteen-year-old son of Napoleon's biographer, was there keeping his sharp ears open for gossip to feed his news-starved father, who was seldom allowed to leave the emperor's side. With the sealed letter, which was addressed simply to *N*, tucked into a secret pocket in case he was searched by the perimeter guards, the boy sweated his way up to Longwood. Napoleon broke the seal and read the letter himself, because it was written in Burchell's impeccable French.

"You are a clever man, Burchell, you have worked it out," he said out loud, because he had fallen into the habit of talking to himself since there was no one else worth talking to on this pile of dung. "Thank you also for confirmation that they are sending me that pinheaded martinet Hudson Lowe as my jailer. Of all the officers in Wellington's army, who will be easier to drive insane? You think you are going to be my keeper, General Sir Hudson Lowe," he growled, "but you are destined to be my liberator!"

Sir Hudson Lowe, KBE, knighted by the prince regent for his service to the nation, was forty-six, red haired and freckled faced, of average height, slim and gaunt thanks to the relentless worm of worry that gnawed at him day and night. Suspicious by instinct, he seldom looked anyone full in the face but instead peered at them out of the corners of eyes that were eager to pounce on every nefarious move from behind their cover of bushy red eyebrows.

Because secret enemies were certain to be watching for any sign of weakness, he stepped ashore on April 14, 1816 with all the swagger of a man who had been a soldier since the age of twelve, who had worked his way up to the position of major general and now, his crowning achievement, the governorship of the Crown Colony of Saint Helena and guardian of Napoleon Bonaparte, the wiliest villain on earth. There were advantages to being famous for your suspicious nature. It had won him this promotion on the recommendation of Wellington himself.

The former governor, Mark Wilks, was there to greet him with his very pretty daughter Laura. Wilks was pleasant enough, Sir Hudson Lowe thought, though only a colonel and far too soft and bookish to put a tyrant like Bonaparte in his place. Also at the wharf touching his hat was Admiral Cockburn, commander of the fleet blockading the island, the man who had eaten President Madison's lunch. Admiral Cockburn had aspired to the promotion, since guarding Bonaparte was much more honorable than guarding Cape Town, his next assignment, but was judged to be too inexperienced an administrator, compared to Sir Hudson Lowe, who had been Wellington's quartermaster and was famous for his fierce eye for detail.

It was a snub that Cockburn planned to avenge.

"When do you mean to see Bonaparte?" the admiral asked Sir Hudson Lowe, to whom he had taken an instant dislike. "You don't want to show hesitation with a man like this, you know."

"I wasn't planning to," said Lowe curtly. "I was planning to beard the rascal first thing tomorrow."

Governor Wilks did his best to come to the rescue. "General Bonaparte can be very irritable, as you can imagine, under the circumstances," he said. "As the admiral knows, he does not normally receive in the mornings. He also insists on setting the day and time."

"Insists!" crowed Cockburn. "I keep my hat on in his presence," he lied, "and sit without asking. In my humble opinion, that criminal doesn't have the right to insist on anything."

Sir Hudson Lowe swallowed the bait. "I was aiming at nine," he said. "Strike while the iron is hot, I say. I've dealt with enough Corsicans in my time to know the type. They respect an iron fist."

"It's been customary for us to request meetings with the general, as a common courtesy, you know," persisted Wilks the bookish ex-governor.

"Courtesy!" said Sir Hudson Lowe. "Did Bonaparte have the courtesy to ask for invitations to Berlin and Moscow?"

"Indeed not," said the ex-governor. "But I must warn you that the prisoner remains a formidable man who has retained every inch of his pride. He is easily…annoyed."

73

"Fah!" spat Lowe. "Sounds like the blackguard needs a whip taken to him! I shall call on him at nine o'clock sharp tomorrow morning. Not a minute before and not a minute after. Please be so kind as to tell him so."

That night Sir Hudson Lowe slept alone in a cramped room in the rambling bungalow that was laughably called the Castle. Or at least tried to sleep, in spite of the predations of mosquitoes that simply ignored the ample net hanging around the bed. Thank God he had left his wife, Lady Susan DeLancey Lowe, on board or he wouldn't have heard the end of it. She was a formidable woman, his wife, especially after the bottle of sherry she drank at bedtime, a necessary supplement to the generous amounts of claret she drank at lunch and dinner. He had remonstrated with her only once about her drinking but regretted it immediately, when she took the opportunity to inform him that she imbibed to console herself for marrying below her station to a stiff back with a limp unmentionable. Should he by any chance have forgotten, she was a DeLancey, who had a New York street named after them, and did he know of any streets named Lowe? Indeed, if her father, Stephen DeLancey, scourge of that traitor Washington, chief justice of the Bahamas, governor of Tobago, had not had his property sequestered by the American thieves, her ample dowry would have secured her a much more suitable arrangement than marriage to a rough, penniless soldier. Why couldn't he be a real man like her brother, Sir William Howe DeLancey, KCB, hero of Waterloo? The dashing young officer everyone called "the American," because, like her, he was born in New York? Plotting with Wellington during the heat of the battle when he was hit by a ricocheting cannonball. Dying in the arms of his bride. A tragedy that was already the stuff of legend. Bonaparte was a murderer, she screeched when the

74

liquor finally mastered her. A common criminal. He deserved to be shot!

"Yes, dearest," Lowe muttered to himself. He scratched and cursed the feral cats screaming in the humid Saint Helena dark. "I hear that Cockburn and that *civilian* Wilks have been soft with him. I won't make the same mistake."

The mosquitoes zinged like bullets past his ears. It was after midnight by his watch when he could bear the torment no longer. He examined the netting with his nightlight. Some villain had gashed the canopy's roof, giving the grateful insects a six-inch portal.

The next morning at a quarter to nine, Governor Lowe, Admiral Cockburn, and an entourage of officers and soldiers emerged from the Jamestown valley onto Deadwood Plain in the midst of a howling tropical downpour. Ten minutes later, wet as drowned rats, they entered the grounds of Longwood, the converted cowshed, where Napoleon had already spent four miserable months. At precisely nine an equerry was sent to bang on the door, which was opened by a liveried servant who summoned a man in a splendid uniform whom Cockburn introduced to Lowe, with a touch of sarcasm, as *Marshal* Bertrand. The marshal told Lowe that the emperor was not receiving visitors, never did in the mornings, as the admiral knew very well, that he was in his bath and that he would not be available to meet the new governor until two tomorrow afternoon. He would be expected then.

Lowe steamed in his sodden uniform. "I feel like plucking the blackguard right out of his tub!" he fumed when the marshal saluted and slammed the door in his face.

"You could certainly do that," said Cockburn, fresh from making his apology about the gash in the mosquito netting, which Lowe had brought up, acidly, to explain the bites on his face. "Although it would have to be on your own authority."

Lowe rehearsed the action in his mind. The redcoats breaking down the bathroom door. Napoleon naked in his bath. What then? Who would haul him out? Who would dare to touch his naked flesh?

A preternatural shiver ran up Lowe's spine. He couldn't do it. "Tomorrow then," he said through clenched teeth. "Precisely at two."

The next day was windy but clear except for the occasional fog bank riding in on the back of the stampeding southeaster. At 2:00 p.m. precisely, the door was knocked on but opened only after an insolent delay. The governor and the admiral entered, the governor first, and were shown into the parlor where they were invited to sit. They kept their hats on.

"We should go in together," said Cockburn in a churchy whisper. "It would be proper for me, as the outgoing military commander, to officially hand him over to your custody."

Lowe was wearing his hardest face, but his stomach was crawling with worms. He nodded.

A door opened, revealing General Gaspard Gourgaud, bristling with medals and Gallic pride. He called out in his best parade-ground voice, "Governor Lowe!"

Lowe's tension released itself into his legs. He sprang up and headed for the open door, the admiral several steps behind him, hurrying to catch up. Through the door Lowe went, and there was the prisoner, short but broad, sitting in the small salon, examining Lowe with mild curiosity, seemingly oblivious to the heated encounter that was going on at the door.

"Let me pass, you villain!" Admiral Cockburn was demanding.

"You were not called!" snapped Gaspard.

"I need to introduce the governor!" Cockburn shouted.

Behind him Lowe heard Gaspard Gourgaud close the door on the admiral's curse. Napoleon looked Lowe full in the face, through him, all the way to the green paper that decorated the walls.

Lowe felt his hand rise to his hat as if it were being levitated by an unstoppable force that to his disgust removed it. He would like to have sat, for his knees suddenly felt weak, but wasn't invited to.

Napoleon was speaking. "I am honored to meet the leader of the Corsican Rangers," he said, chillingly calm, "that band of traitors to Corsica and France."

Lowe felt color fly to his cheeks. "They were loyalists who were doing their duty," said Lowe, "just as I am doing my duty now, General."

The one word Napoleon said was icy as the snows of Russia. "*General?*"

"Indeed. That is how we are instructed to address you."

Still very calm. "The world knows me as the Emperor Napoleon. You are known by no one, but you dare to insult *me*?"

"Sir, *you* do not know *me*. Once you do, you will have a different opinion of my character."

"I know too much about you already. You have never commanded in battle. You have never commanded men of honor. You have done nothing more than conduct skirmishes! Your greatest achievement was being Wellington's quartermaster, his shopkeeper. You are nothing but a clerk!"

*A stiff back with a limp unmentionable!* His wife's drunken accusation struck at Sir Hudson Lowe like a snake. No! He must not allow himself to be flustered. He was facing the wiliest villain in the world. He reminded himself

77

of his heroic race through the ruin this butcher had made of France. Riding alone except for the brave Cossack at his side, taking the news of Napoleon's defeat to London. Received by the prince regent still in his bedroom. Knighted then and there. Endless rounds of congratulation. Sitting next to the prince at dinner that night, answering a thousand eager questions, fighting not to fall asleep in his chair because he hadn't slept in days. A hero, that's what he was!

"Your insults are bombast, *General*," he said. "I *am* a soldier, and you are my prisoner of war."

"You are a hangman sent to execute me!"

"I am your guardian. My duty is to make certain that you do not escape and cause more mischief in the world."

A crude bark of a laugh. "If you are not interested only in my corpse, why do you have the face of a hyena?"

That was enough! Lowe jammed his hat back on his head. "I came to do you the courtesy of giving you the time of day. But you have done nothing but insult me! Good day, sir!"

Napoleon jerked his watch out of his pocket, threw it onto the floor, and stamped it to extinction. "That's what I think of your time of day!" he roared.

Without another word the new governor turned his back, flung open the door, and marched out.

Napoleon stood at the window, hands clenched behind his back, watching Governor Lowe and Admiral Cockburn, both furious although for different reasons, ride away in the rain. In Napoleon's presence you only spoke when spoken to, so Gaspard, who had come through the open door, stood at attention until the emperor's sudden burst of crowing laughter invited him to approach.

"Satisfactory, sire?" he whispered, perplexed by his master's happy mood.

Napoleon spoke without turning round. "Yes. He's my Caliban."

The young general looked alarmed. "Your Majesty, the monster could make our lives a misery."

Napoleon stared at him for a long moment, as if he were considering something. He came to a decision. "Yes, he will crown me with thorns. Send me Rosebud."

Security measures were lax before Governor Lowe, in his righteous fury, tightened his grip. So there were no challenges when Charlotte, wearing a plain dress with a scarf tied round her head, walked up the hill from Jamestown later that afternoon with the washerwomen who were coming to collect Longwood's dirty laundry.

Napoleon was in what passed for a garden, because the rain had been swept away. He was sitting under the best tree near the house, the banyan that threw a thick, moving patch of shade, a lifesaver when the tropical sun burst through. He was listening with half an ear to his young doctor, Barry O'Meara, rattle on cheerfully in French about the benefits of licorice on digestion when he saw the girl approach and stop at a respectful distance. He would use her to strike at the governor while the fool's temper was hot. But first he would feast his eyes on her figure.

She was dressed in a cheap white dress, with a worn white scarf hiding her long blonde hair. Behind her was a grove of gumwoods, leaning away from the wind.

*A beautiful girl, fair complexion, tall, dressed in white, walking in a grove of trees.*

It was a recurring daydream, which had haunted him in quiet moments ever since he first became interested in women. He would like to see those long legs naked! One day he would indulge himself, but he needed her attention at the moment, not her affection. He needed her help in getting him off this black wart disfiguring the shining face of the Atlantic.

"Come!" he called to her, cutting off the doctor's dissertation in midsentence. "Leave us," he said without even looking at him, "but also leave us your prescription pad and a pencil…Rosebud, you look like a peasant!" he said to her before the doctor was out of earshot.

Charlotte's pale complexion was flushed with the excitement that had swept her up the steep path light as a feather. A summons from Napoleon! It put her wildest dreams to shame. "Your Majesty I dressed like this because I wanted to blend in with the women coming for the laundry."

"Bah!" said Napoleon, because the laundry women were all black slaves. "Like a lily blends in with lumps of coal!"

A cheeky flash of defiance lit the emerald eyes. "You did send for me?"

"Yes." He handed her the doctor's pad. "You will write another letter to your boy in Kew, in English of course. First you will write what a chamber pot this island is. Go on, write! Use those very words. Say it even looks like one. Now write that Deadwood Plain, where we are imprisoned, is named so because it is the most desolate part of a desolate rock that makes Hades seem like paradise. Even the weather torments. Fog and rain follow each other with such rapidity that it is impossible to know what clothes to wear. The endless wind pierces even the thickest greatcoat. The rain vanishes in a flash, and the scalding sun leaps out, joyful as a devil in hell, so hot that it steams you alive in your wet clothes. This isn't a climate, it's an assassin! Are you getting all this?"

Charlotte nodded, although she thought it was all a bit of an exaggeration.

"Guarding the portal of this place of horror is our monstrous jailer, recently set loose on us," the torrent of words continued. "He appropriately goes by the name of Lowe. All accounts confirm that he's a cowardly officer turned bully who uses the power given by him by the crown of England to insult and humiliate his captive, who could so easily have fled to America but chose to remain in Europe as the guest, not the prisoner, of Great Britain. This Lowe man besmirches the name of England. A Lilliputian who lords it over a giant. He will certainly drive his noble victim to desperate, even violent, measures to escape his tyranny!"

Napoleon paused to allow Charlotte to finish writing. He took a slender scroll out of his waistcoat pocket. Just like the previous one, it was sealed with the imperial eagle imprinted into the red wax. "Include this among your weeds—any weeds will do. Post it first thing tomorrow."

Neither of them noticed Governor Lowe, back so soon because he was irresistibly drawn to the scene of the crime. He pretended not to be concealing himself behind a bush as he watched Napoleon and a blonde peasant girl talking in the shade of a splendid banyan with long roots hanging from its branches.

"I noticed that tree earlier today, during our visit," he said to Henry Porteous, who had put on his kilt when he was told that the governor required him to ride up to Longwood with him. "That tree will have to come down. Someone could climb up those roots."

"Yes, Sir Hudson," said the Porteous House landlord, who was also the company's gardener and the father of Charlotte's best friend, "although the emperor uses it for reading, almost every day. It's the only decent shade tree on the property."

"That's why it has to come down," said the governor. "See that it's done immediately."

Louis Marchand, Napoleon's valet, eyes, and ears, was sitting at the Almond Tree the next morning sipping his third cup of foul local coffee, which was mostly chicory, when Charlotte finally made her appearance. He watched her hurry with her easy, long strides to the post office to mail her package, watched as she emerged a minute later and walked back up the street on her way to her vegetable stand. As she passed the Almond Tree, she caught his eye and nodded, just perceptibly.

Less than a minute later the fat little postmaster, Cole, emerged and hurried over the road to Balcombe's run-down office. To deliver the packet to Balcombe, Marchand supposed. Almost immediately Balcombe emerged from his office with the postmaster. For a moment they seemed to put their heads together. The postmaster returned to the post office, while Balcombe walked briskly toward the Castle.

Marchand paid his bill. Everything was going according to plan.

After a long wait, Balcombe was shown in by Kay, the government secretary. He found Governor Lowe and Admiral Cockburn, barely on speaking terms since the debacle at Longwood the previous day, sitting as far apart as possible at a heavy black Chinese desk—an addition by the new governor, to add to his gravity, perhaps. The painting of Admiral Cockburn burning Washington had already been removed, leaving the wall yawningly blank. Cockburn introduced Balcombe, who made the mistake of thinking the new governor was reaching out to greet him. An awkward moment followed as Balcombe realized his mistake.

"My secretary says you have something for me."

"Yes, Your Excellency." Balcombe took the packet out of his pocket and put it in Lowe's outstretched hand.

Lowe glanced at it and then glared at Balcombe with his suspicious sideways glance. "Admiral Cockburn is familiarizing me with how things have worked around here," he said. "He has explained who you are and your little…arrangement with him. We are gathered here to determine whether it is worthwhile continuing with it or not." He tossed the packet on the desk as if he thought it was bound to be worthless. "I hear that the Rosebud girl has just posted this?"

Balcombe said, "Yes, Your Excellency. Just minutes ago."

"Well, open it, man," he said to Kay the secretary, who was hovering half a pace behind Balcombe. "We have to determine whether this little venture is worth the trouble."

The secretary undid the packet's clasp, extracted the cover letter then fished out the sealed scroll hiding in the burlap pouch of herbs, laying out all the items in a neat row as if he were performing an autopsy.

"Your Excellency," whispered the secretary, "as you see there's a cover letter. The sealed scroll itself seems to be one sheet of paper, like the last one."

"Which was that list of names," Admiral Cockburn reminded him.

Lowe didn't seem to hear him. "I don't care how many sheets of paper!" he said to the secretary. "Open it, man!"

The secretary broke the seal, for which he had a replacement, unrolled the scroll. His eyes widened. "I can't, Your Excellency," he said, barely audible.

Lowe raised one of his bushy red eyebrows, turned the right side of his face toward the man as if he heard better out of that ear, examining him out of the corners of his eyes. "And why not? Is it written in Hebrew?"

The secretary, who was near retirement and not well, cleared his throat. "No, Your Excellency. It appears to be completely blank—unless they used invisible ink."

Governor Lowe thought he had steeled himself for every eventuality. But not this one. "Invisible ink, that must be it! Try steam. Lemon juice. Green vitriol."

The secretary tried them all, by which time the sheet of paper looked like a wafer-thin slice of moldy cheese. "Your Excellency," he said, "it seems to be what it appears to be. Completely blank."

Lowe was in a frenzy. Balcombe saw the hundred guineas he was due, most of which he had already spent, vanish down the drain.

Admiral Cockburn, although mystified, was doing his best to hide that he was being royally entertained. "I have a possible explanation," he said. "I believe Bonaparte is once again testing the security of this conduit," the admiral said.

"Of course he is!" said Lowe. "Perhaps there are clues in the girl's cover letter." He snatched it up, frowned, turned it on its side. "Damn thing is so cross written to save paper I can't make sense of it." He held it out to the secretary. "Read it, man!"

The secretary took the letter. Voice trembling, he read.

Lowe beat the desk with an angry fist after almost every line. "Blast that girl! That's a damned lie! And so is that!" By the time his secretary had fought his way through Charlotte's epistle, Lowe was apoplectic. "There is no way in damnation I'm going to allow that slander to reach the shores of England!" he shouted.

Admiral Cockburn struggled not to laugh at the preposterousness of the insults. "But we must let it through, Sir Hudson. It's imperative."

"Imperative! Why?"

"Because otherwise there will be no more letters from Napoleon to his accomplices through this conduit. A very promising intelligence operation will be stillborn."

"But these slanderous falsehoods! That I cut down Bonaparte's favorite tree out of spite! Not a grain of truth to it. I cut it down for security reasons. The hanging roots were too close to Bonaparte's window!"

Admiral Cockburn, who couldn't resist a sly gibe, said, "In case Bonaparte climbed one of them?"

Lowe fixed the admiral with his suspicious sideways glance in case he was taking a liberty. "Of course not! It's so a would-be rescuer can't make a surreptitious entry. Almost everything can be twisted into a lie. I'm beginning to think that this intrigue is a terrible idea. I am seriously considering scrapping the whole damn thing."

"Sir Hudson, suffering a little childish ridicule, especially from a slip of a girl, is regrettably the price we have to pay for peering into Bonaparte's bag of tricks," said the admiral. "I'm afraid the government has set its heart on it."

Lowe pondered for a moment. He indicated the soiled scroll. "What about that mess? What do we replace it with?"

The admiral finally indulged himself with a thin smile. "Oh, I'm sure any blank sheet of paper will do."

# Chapter 6: The Vile Poem

Charlotte's letter ridiculing His Excellency Governor Sir Hudson Lowe and a sheet of ordinary blank paper, rolled and sealed with the imperial eagle by Lowe's secretary, arrived at the Black Dog six weeks later, June 2, 1816.

At lunchtime the messenger boy alerted Daniel that a packet was waiting for him. By two Daniel had opened it, chuckled his way through Charlotte's letter, had deposited the dried plant specimens with Mr. Burchell and was on his way to Mayfair and the Cock with the slender scroll sealed with the Napoleonic eagle that he didn't know was blank.

The weather was gloomy. The day was long, but the sun barely came out because this was the year without summer, caused by sunspots or the eruption of a volcano in Indonesia or perhaps nature's sympathy with the shining light of freedom entombed in the fogs of Saint Helena.

George Edwards, stooped and stunted, perched in the tavern's darkest corner. With him, by vivid contrast, was a sparkling young blonde whom Edwards introduced as Polly, a "comrade." Polly acted as if she were already in her cups, although Daniel noticed she didn't do anything more adventurous than occasionally wet her lips in her little glass of claret. He didn't let this deter him from downing a pint of beer in record time, because the road from Kew had been a long one and his spirits needed lifting to catch up with Polly's.

When Edwards asked to see the letter from Charlotte, Daniel was still sober enough to inform the little man that it was too personal to share. Edwards shot a meaningful glance at Polly and excused himself to deliver, he said, the Napoleonic scroll to Mr. Thistlewood.

Daniel, by now in fine spirits, ordered more bitter, then went on to sherry, which inspired him to expound on the romantic beauty of Saint Helena and its reigning queen, Charlotte, mistress of the misty crags. He even showed Polly a small Burchell picture of the love of his life, who Polly agreed was very pretty indeed. It came as no surprise—although in a soberer condition it would have— that the girl calling herself Polly showed not the slightest sign of feminine jealousy at the way Daniel was going on about the charms of another. After he upgraded to brandy, he even read to her from Charlotte's letter, laughing immoderately at what she had written about Napoleon's new jailer, Sir Hudson Lowe.

There came a time for Daniel after which a curtain was drawn over the rest of the evening. The next morning he woke in a cheap lodging house with a frightful headache and without his trousers. His wallet, which he checked first, was still in his pocket though much lighter. His trousers he found on the floor. But his treasure, Charlotte's letter, was gone.

After paying off the landlady, who took his money with a smirk, he headed back on the long journey to Kew, the day just as gloomy as the last one, which perfectly suited his mood. He hadn't gone far, though, when he heard a penny press vendor yelling the headlines of the sheet he was hawking.

"Hot off the press! Napoleon denounces his captors! He's forced to live in a chamber pot! His favorite tree cut down out of spite. Governor a dwarf who lords it over a giant! A disgrace to England! Read all about it!"

Daniel spent his penny. Almost word for word, the news sheet was a list of all the complaints in Charlotte's stolen letter. Across town it was brought to the attention of Lady Holland, doyen of London's premier Liberal political salon, Holland House. Lady Holland, about whom we shall have to say much more later, personally handed a copy to one of her regular guests, the poet Thomas Moore.

"Mr. Moore, you would much oblige me if you could make a poem out of this scandal," she said. "Before he went out to the island, that martinet Hudson Lowe was a guest here many times, in order to persuade him to look more favorably on Napoleon and our cause. Obviously we had no success. He deserves to be made a fool of, don't you think? I mean, his name, Lowe, is perfectly appropriate, isn't it, seeing it so smartly matches his behavior? Perhaps you could start with that."

"I shall, Your Ladyship," said the poet, "although it would be hard to beat Wellington's quip that we sent a man who only knows how to follow orders to guard a man who only knows how to give them!"

Lady Holland favored the poet with a smile. "I'm certain that you will try."

Moore's poem, promptly written, was sniggered over everywhere. As requested it began:

> Sir Hudson Lowe, Sir Hudson Low,
> (By name, and ah! By nature so)...

It arrived in Saint Helena on October 10, 1816, smuggled ashore by a mulatto who performed this service regularly for his master, Napoleon's biographer Emmanuel Las Cases. The biographer's son, known to everybody as Young Las Cases, as usual took delivery of the illicit mail for his father. He chuckled his way through the poem, which was printed on an unsealed broadsheet. Everybody had to read this, it was so delicious! Right there at the Almond Tree, rather foolishly, he made copies in his small, neat handwriting and passed them out to friends and acquaintances. A copy went to Gaspard, who was sitting at a table with Charlotte. They rushed it up to Longwood as fast as Gaspard's horse could take them. He kept reciting lines from the poem in his broken English and screaming his laughter into the wind. He rode recklessly, she thought, to force her to tighten her arms around his waist. She found she enjoyed holding him close.

Napoleon was in his tiny office, sitting behind his tiny desk. Charlotte expected him to laugh when she read the poem to him, translating where necessary. Instead his face instantly became an expressionless mask about which the only animated feature was his deep-set brooding eyes.

"What do you think, Gaspard?" he asked.

Gaspard, standing next to Charlotte with his hat under his arm, and who had by now had time to think things through, was uneasy. "Sire, what a pity it can't be suppressed."

"Suppressed?" Napoleon sat back in his chair. "Why would we want to do that?"

"Because it is going to infuriate the governor, who will strike back at you like the snake he is."

"I thought that—" Charlotte began.

Napoleon cut her off with his bark of a laugh. "*Basta!* Sometimes it's better for women not to think. What's between their legs is much more interesting than what's between their ears."

Charlotte flushed, but she didn't dare contradict him.

"Your Majesty," persevered Gaspard, his mood improved by watching Charlotte being put in her place, "our jailer is a man who will stoop to any depths to make our lives a misery. May I remind you he cut down a perfectly lovely tree because you liked its shade?"

"A triviality. Give me a moment alone with Rosebud, would you? Go saddle her a horse. There's something confidential I need to tell her."

Gaspard choked down his protest and stamped off to the stables as if he were crushing cockroaches, all of them named Rosebud. Being brushed aside by Napoleon in favor of this Yamstock upstart was pushing him perilously close to open revolt.

"Gaspard has a fine head for figures, almost as good as mine," said Napoleon, "and he is brilliant with tactics. But strategy is not his strong suit. He also has a loose tongue. Gaspard can't be trusted with our secret. At least not yet."

Charlotte's emerald eyes clung to Napoleon's for a long second. "Our secret, Your Majesty?"

He gave her that little cupid of a smile, which tipped up at the edges. "That we are urging the governor to make me a martyr." The beautifully manicured hand opened a drawer, took out a sealed scroll, handed it to Charlotte. "Another secret message. Put this in a packet, just like the others. Deliver it to the postmaster this afternoon, early as you can. I'll have Gaspard take you."

On the zigzag path back down to Jamestown, Charlotte reminded herself that there was no such thing as a straight road in Saint Helena. The fist of a god had crumpled the island into a mad mix of rearing mountains and plunging ravines. Every road, every bridle path, every track was crooked just like the crooked path of life.

She was wondering why Napoleon had insisted she post the next packet so urgently, *this afternoon, early as you can*, when it would take six long weeks to reach its destination. There had to be some reason.

Gaspard interrupted her thoughts. "Quite suddenly you seem to have the emperor's ear," he said, making no effort to cloak his jealousy, "while I have nothing but instructions to escort you back into town when any of the servants could have done it."

"He just wanted to make a personal comment or two," she said.

Gaspard laughed bitterly. "He wanted to compliment you on your fresh complexion, long legs, lovely hands, and charming feet, did he?"

Charlotte couldn't resist a faint smile. "Something like that," she lied.

"He likes young women with fair skin who are slender and tall. Did he tell you that?"

Charlotte wished she could strike back with the truth, but of course she couldn't. "What about *your* charms?" she teased, doing her best to sweeten him. "You have become quite the talk of the local ladies since Laura left."

"Ah, Laura, Laura! Now, there was perfection for you. Not so very tall as you are. Very feminine. Very much a lady."

"A governor's daughter and definitely not a Yamstock like me?"

"*Mon Dieu*, no! A flower of the aristocracy."

"Just like the ones you sent to the guillotine?"

Gaspard ignored the spiteful comment. He was reliving the snub Napoleon had given him. "I used to be the only man the emperor would open his heart to. I, who saved his life in Moscow when I fell on the burning fuse of a bomb left by the retreating Russians. Half a million pounds of gunpowder, which would have blown us to perdition!"

"Very commendable," said Charlotte, who had heard this story from him before.

He didn't seem to notice her sarcasm. "And then a second time at Brienne, although he says he didn't see it, when I took a Cossack lance meant for him. I would have died then and there if the lance hadn't glanced off my Legion of Honor medal!"

"Really! How fortunate then that you were awarded one," said Charlotte tartly, because she had heard this story from him also. It had seemed much more heroic the first time he told it.

No doubt sensing that things were going wrong, Gaspard abruptly changed his tack. "I'm sorry," he said, resurrecting his charm. "It's not just him and you and whatever scheme you two are getting up to behind my back that's driving me insane. It's being cooped up on this damn island with the pathetic little entourage, same faces, same stale talk. When we are all together, the emperor ignores me completely—can you believe the man's ingratitude! And when we are alone, all he wants to do is dictate his damn memoirs! I'd prefer to be in solitary confinement, I really would! Especially if you were my only companion," he said with a wicked chuckle. "I tell you what. After we've had a glass of wine at the Almond Tree…I know of a little room near the Castle where we can relax and get to know each other a little better. What do you say?"

What a vain fool he was! It was Charlotte's turn to laugh. "If you're feeling in a romantic mood, Gaspard, and tired of loose women, you should call on my cousin Mary Porteous. I believe she may welcome your attentions."

He pulled his horse to such a sudden halt on the narrow path that for a moment it looked like the startled animal was about to take flight over the three-foot stone wall that guarded the yawning precipice. "Are you trying to say you have no feelings for me? How is such a thing possible? You are little better than a peasant girl! I am Napoleon's greatest officer. His personal aide-de-camp, the man Napoleon chose to deliver his surrender to the prince regent! I am a great man, and you are a wench of absolutely no consequence! You should feel honored to lick the dust off my boots!"

"Depends what you've stepped in."

"You have a mouth like a chamber pot!"

"What do you expect of a Yamstock?"

"You are trying to avoid the issue."

"Gaspard, I'm promised to another, you know that!"

Gaspard shut himself in cold silence the rest of the way down into Jamestown. "Not even a glass of wine?"

"Thank you, but no. I need to check on our stall."

"You choose your vegetables over me!" Gaspard said bitterly. "You and I are no longer on speaking terms!"

There was something in the way Gaspard tied up the horses at the Almond Tree and strode off in the direction of the wharf, something mechanical, that told Charlotte he was acting under the direction of an overwhelming compulsion. What was it? Careful not to be observed, she followed him into a seedy back alley where trollops sold their wares to sailors. He knocked on a door. A black face, a woman's, appeared at the window. The door opened. A large Negro man put a familiar hand on Gaspard's shoulder.

Swept by a storm of emotions, Charlotte headed home before the door closed. She had a packet to prepare. She glanced at the Castle when she passed it, certain that the governor was in there somewhere. He must have read the poem by now. She hoped he liked it. The sarcastic thought lightened her mood.

Sir Hudson Lowe was indeed inside, rereading the poem for the third time.

> Sir Hudson Lowe, Sir Hudson Low,
> (By name, and ah! by nature so)
> As thou art fond of persecutions,
> Perhaps thou'st read, or heard repeated,
> How Captain Gulliver was treated,
> When thrown among the Lilliputians.

By now he almost knew it by heart. It kept running through his head like an annoying jingle, impossible to banish. Bonaparte the giant versus Lowe the Lilliputian! If the scribbler had the courage to set foot in Saint Helena he would be told who was the Lilliputian by the tongue of a horse whip!

Too late now, the damage done. He had to live with the fact that everyone was going to be staring at him with mocking eyes over hands that hid mocking smiles and lips that were mouthing, *Sir Hudson Lowe, Sir Hudson Low.* How could he show his face in public? How could he live with the humiliation of being thought of as a dwarf of a man, weak and ineffectual? He pondered long and hard on how to take his revenge. Someone was going to pay for this. He knew exactly who. But how would he justify the punishment to the government back in London? Unfortunately, Napoleon didn't write the vile rhyme! What he could wreak his vengeance on was the person responsible for distributing it, because he would most certainly find him, sooner or later.

There was knock on the door. A clerk stuck his head in. "Mr. Balcombe is here, Your Excellency. He says he needs to speak with you on an urgent matter."

Like a drowning man sees his life pass before his eyes, Lowe saw all the matters that Balcombe had the authority to say were urgent, but only one stood out. "Well, then, send him in!"

Balcombe entered, mopping the wet tropical heat from his face.

"What is it, Mr. Balcombe?" said Lowe, examining the trader with his suspicious sideways glance that suggested, incorrectly, that he was deaf in one ear.

"Your Excellency, the girl has just posted another one. The fourth." Balcombe said, taking a small packet out of a large inside pocket.

"You have not tampered with it?" Lowe asked, as if the blank scroll in the last packet was somehow Balcombe's doing.

"Of course not, Your Excellency."

"Well, then open it, man!"

Balcombe opened the clasp as cautiously as if the packet was stuffed with explosives then laid it gently on the governor's desk. Lowe removed the girl's letter. It was short, she explained, because Daniel would soon be home, so she was saving the spiciest tidbits of gossip until then. But she would share the tastiest with him: everyone was sniggering about the poem comparing Sir Hudson Lowe with Napoleon.

Lowe flung the girl's letter aside in disgust, broke the scroll's seal, and unrolled the most extraordinary document. It was undated and addressed vaguely to "English Friends." Instead of being blank like the previous one, it was a densely written report of an ongoing operation by the Chilean navy, horrible in its scope and intent.

A flotilla headed by a seventy-four-gun man-of-war and consisting of frigates, gunboats, and swarms of marines, was sailing on Saint Helena. In command was the legendary British commander Captain Cochrane, not for nothing known by the French as the Sea Wolf, who had recently been dismissed from the Royal Navy for stock fraud in spite of his loud claims of innocence and dark threats of revenge. The aim of the operation was to rescue Napoleon, sail him to Chile, then set him up as emperor of South America, which would then forge an alliance with the United States, and fighting as United America, would destroy the British Empire. It was signed *N*, as if this was all that was necessary.

The paper stuck to Lowe's damp fingers. This following so swiftly on the heels of the libelous doggerel! Bonaparte must have laughed his way through the vile rhyme. It had swollen his head so that he couldn't control the impulse to boast to his English minions that he was about to be rescued, not by a ship but by a whole flotilla!

Two punches to the gut on the very same afternoon! It would have broken a lesser man, but not General Sir Hudson Lowe, KCB.

His first thought was to burn the noisome packet, herbs and all. This was overtaken by a moment of doubt during which he considered sending for his aide, Sir Thomas Reade, to ask him what he thought was the best course of action. But rising above this cowardly whisper he heard his wife jeering that Reade was the real governor of Saint Helena. No! He would prove who was in charge!

"You may go," he said to Balcombe. "I shall have my secretary reseal the packet and return it to you for posting within the hour."

Balcombe did not go, instead stood there fiddling awkwardly with his hat. Eventually he found the words he was looking for. "Your Excellency, my creditors are pressing. May I be paid my expenses for this packet, by any chance?"

Red hairs licked out of Lowe's nose like flames out of a furnace. How could the man think of money at a time like this? He scribbled a note to his secretary. "Tell him to come and see me immediately he has paid you off," he snapped at Balcombe, the note of authority back in his voice.

He had decided what his counter to Bonaparte's gloating was going to be. He would make a copy of the scroll then send the original by fast sloop to Whitehall with a cover letter. He would double the lookouts on the mountain peaks. Put the garrison and the frigates on high alert. Man all the batteries. Cancel shore leave. Then he would strike at Bonaparte himself. Instead of the circle of redcoats guarding Longwood closing in at 9:00 p.m. as usual, from now on he would have them swarming Bonaparte's garden by sunset, when the rogue liked to take his evening constitutional. With any luck they would trample his flower beds into the Deadwood dust!

November 22, 1816.

Daniel, in the Black Dog, had just finished reading Charlotte's cover letter for the fourth dangerous package from Saint Helena, which she said would probably be the last. All it reported was that everyone was sniggering about the Sir Hudson Low poem that he must have read by now, that security had been tightened and that Napoleon was being supplied with bad butter and that his milk cows had been confiscated. Her letter was so short, she said, because she was saving the spiciest tidbits of gossip since he would be home so very soon. Then, as if she couldn't wait even that long, Charlotte swept in through the door.

As usual the messenger boy had told Daniel that another packet had arrived. As usual he had gone to the smoky tavern immediately after his taskmasters at Kew released him from work. But it wasn't at all usual for Charlotte to be magically transported from Saint Helena to a tavern in Kew on the heels of a letter that had just spent six weeks on a packet boat battling its way north through the turbulent Atlantic. At first Daniel thought it was the nonsense that his mother had preached to Charlotte, that first impressions were reality, that the bear you saw change in a wink to a bush actually was a bear and that the bush was the illusion. Gypsy nonsense, of course. Except that the Charlotte who walked into the Black Dog remained Charlotte even after he blinked.

Charlotte, as blonde as ever. Charlotte, wearing her hair in ringlets as she always did on special occasions, that familiar lovely spring to her step, waving gaily to him. His heart tried to flee its cage. He nearly cried out with delight.

But it wasn't Charlotte.

"Hello!" said Polly cheerfully, sliding into a chair opposite him. She laughed at his consternation. "Fooled you for a moment, didn't I?"

"What are you doing here, dressed like that?"

Polly ran her fingers through the curls. "Do you like me 'air? I did it like that picture you showed me. Fought you'd like it. Aren't you goin' to kiss me hello? She lets you kiss her, doesn't she, the real Charlotte?"

"That's none of your business," said Daniel, uneasy at this sudden turn of events. "It's nobody's business. Why are you here?"

There was a mischievous twinkle in Polly's blue eyes, not emerald, definitely not Charlotte's. "Mr. Edwards asked me if I'd mind and fetch the secret letter for 'im. Mind! I jumped at the chance of seein' you again." She reached across the table and touched his arm. "Any girl would. She's a lucky lady, your Charlotte. Just 'ow lucky she hasn't found out yet, has she?"

"Of course not, we—" Daniel began and then caught himself. The busy tavern was loud with shouts and laughter, but he leaned forward and whispered to be safe. "I haven't taken the scroll out yet. It's in a bag of dried herbs. Don't want to do all that here."

Polly looked at him with eyes that gave every indication of being adoring. "Of course you can't. I have taken a room, right around the corner, so we can, you know, talk safely for a couple of hours. I have something I need to show you. Oh, you naughty boy. I can read yer mind! No, it's not that! You've seen that already!"

The untidy little room was up some back stairs. It must have been paid for because there wasn't any sign of a landlady. It was furnished with a chair, a tiny table, and a narrow bed. Polly threw herself on the bed with a happy sigh. Daniel sat on the chair and immediately went to work on cutting open the packet, fishing out the scroll, inspecting its large, messy seal. The imperial eagle.

"Everyfing all wight?" Polly asked.

"Yes," said Daniel. He had meant to berate Polly for stealing Charlotte's previous letter that somehow had ended up as the inspiration of a handbill but somehow couldn't get round to it.

"Good!" She waved a sheet of paper at him. "Let's do a swap. This is somefing important. Mr. Thistlewood told me 'imself that he wanted you to read it, didn't he? Come and get it, or don't you dare? I don't bite, you know. 'Cept when I gets excited!"

Daniel approached the bed as if there might be a snake hidden in the greasy sheets. "What is it?"

"A handbill." She moved over, making room for him, patted the bedcover stained with who knew what. "Come on, sit next to me."

Daniel sat as far away from her as the bed's narrowness would allow. He passed her the sealed scroll, took the handbill in exchange.

"Read it out loud," Polly said. "My readin' ain't that good, and I could do wiv' hearing it again."

Daniel could tell at a glance that the handbill was a humble production. The type was crude, and there were frequent spelling mistakes. Every sentence was followed by an exclamation mark. Mr. Burchell would not have approved of the grammar.

"BRITAINS TO ARMS," it was headed and then went on, "The whole country waits the signal from London to fly to arms! Hurry, break into gunsmiths for arms! No rise in the price of bread! No bishops! No aristocrats! No prince regent! Off with their heads! Stand true or be slaves forever! Stand up for freedom on December 2 at Spa Fields!"

"What's this?" said Daniel.

"What it says. It's a call to arms."

"By whom?"

Her eyes were wide with surprise, whether sincere or not, Daniel couldn't tell. "Haven't you 'eard? We 'ad a huge meeting at Spa Fields, over ten thousand of us, just ten days ago. Orator Hunt ranted about us not having the vote and asked His Majesty very nicely to save us from bloodsucking landlords and the like. Then and there we drew up a petition to the prince regent asking 'im to shake up parliament and voted for Orator Hunt to deliver it to His Highness—I mean, His Lowness—in person."

Daniel had heard all about the meeting and how the Regent couldn't arouse his majestic fat self enough to read the petition. Daniel had even discussed it with Mr. Burchell, who said, in his poetic way, that it was just one more cloud of dust thrown up by the fall of that colossus Napoleon. But Daniel had heard nothing of a second meeting just a week away.

"What's going to happen?" he asked rather lamely.

"We're going to storm the Bastille!" said Polly, launching herself at Daniel and assaulting his lips with hers. "Mr. Thistlewood says you need to be there, so you can report it all to Napoleon, man to man!"

Since she was holding her smooth cheek against his, Daniel was forced to speak in a whisper. "The Bastille?"

"The Tower of London, of course."

"This sounds dangerous. We could end up on the gallows."

"It is dangerous." Polly's hot whisper burned his ear. "But you're a man. You've already proved to me that you're a man, but I want you to prove it again."

Her breath in his ear and her hand roving his breeches excited him, but fear of ending up on the noose end of a Tyburn rope worked in the opposite direction. "I can't do it," he said feebly, trying unsuccessfully to push her away. "I leave for Saint Helena in a few days' time. I have to settle my affairs."

"What could be mo' of an affair than this one? That's why Mr. Thistlewood wants you to be there," said Polly, her hand quickly finding what she was looking for.

Daniel groaned, whether in pleasure or pain was difficult to tell.

"Last time you called me Charlotte when you were, you know, finishing," Polly whispered. "You can call me Charlotte again, all the way through this time, I don't mind. Polly isn't me real name, anyways."

After a long morning's walk, begun well before dawn on December 2, 1816, Daniel was finally in Islington, where he found Spa Fields easily because everyone seemed to be hurrying there. In the center of a huge crowd stood a cart decorated with red, white, and, blue banners, the colors of the French Revolution. On the cart stood Mr. Thistlewood and next to him stood Polly, golden curls falling from a pointed red freedom cap decorated with a red, white, and blue cockade. She saw him, perhaps because he was tall, waved and beckoned to him.

Someone with a loud voice was declaiming from the cart, "If they don't give us what we want, shall we not take it?"

"Yes, yes!" roared twenty thousand voices.

"Are you willing to take it?"

To blend in with the throng, Daniel waved his fist and yelled with the rest, "Yes! Yes!"

"Will you go and take it?"

"Yes!"

"If I jump down among you, will you come with me and take it?"

Thousands of voices swore they would. But they didn't.

The speaker leaped off the cart, grabbed the tricolor flag, and set out, Thistlewood at his side. A few hundred followed them, the hotheads, on their way to storm the Tower of London. Liberate it like the Bastille had been liberated in 1789. The rumor flew through their ragged ranks: The aristos are packing their silver! The royal family has already fled London!

"Daniel!" It was Polly, cheeks flushed as red as her liberty cap. Next to her, hopping along like a hungry vulture heading for carrion, was George Edwards. Polly grabbed Daniel's hand. "What are you waiting for? Napoleon will want to hear everyfing! Come on, or we'll miss all the fun!"

There wasn't really much fun to miss. By the time Thistlewood's ragged army reached the city it had dwindled to a band of three dozen, mostly soused with the gin they were drinking to keep going. Revolution was thirsty work. Thistlewood made a long speech in front of the Tower, but their grins never left the guards' faces. Daniel was footsore. He had been walking all day. He needed a cool drink and a bed warmed by Polly. But when he looked for her after Thistlewood stopped bending his ear, she'd slipped away. No ringlets, no freedom cap, no tricolor cockade, no bright blue eyes and shining face.

Gone as if she had never really been there at all.

# Chapter 7: The Incident at the Ball

December 31, 1816.

Sir Hudson Lowe, in full gubernatorial regalia and with a strut in his step, presided over the New Year's ball in the Castle. Faces glowed with admiration as they greeted him. Forgotten was the vile poem. Remembered was the fact that he had locked up Bonaparte's biographer and his son for the part they had played in smuggling in the slanderous insult, and just yesterday, he had packed them off on a boat bound for Cape Town, where they could rot forever in the wilds of Africa for all he cared. It was a warning for anyone who defied Sir Hudson Lowe. It was a message for Bonaparte.

While Lowe was strutting Daniel was busy vomiting his beans and bacon over the side of the storm-tossed brig clawing its way slowly southward toward Saint Helena, where Charlotte was dancing a quadrille and hating every step.

Gaspard had proved he knew how to hold a grudge by cutting her dead for the past two months, ever since Napoleon had confided in her and not him. Ever since she refused to soothe his hurt pride in bed. So she'd arrived at the ball on the arm of Basil Jackson, the handsome young officer who was in charge of the repairs constantly needed at leaky Longwood. She liked Basil, who was twenty, the same age as she was, because he was funny and bright but there was absolutely nothing more to their relationship. She was saving love for marriage and marriage for Daniel, she reminded herself more than once, trying her best to believe it.

Although Gaspard refused to say a word to Charlotte, not even a civil hello, she could feel his eyes boring into her when he thought she wasn't looking. Short a fourth couple for the quadrille, and thinking he might be able to repair fences, Jackson commandeered Gaspard. Clinging to Gaspard's arm tight as a clam, so hopelessly in love that it was quite embarrassing, was plain Mary Porteous, an awkward best friend for Charlotte to have under the circumstances, because she knew that Gaspard was striking at her by stealing Mary's heart.

People were looking so Gaspard couldn't decline the invitation, but he fixed Charlotte with a cold eye that was both contemptuous and bold all the way through the agonizing dance.

Afterward, as a respite from the insufferable Jamestown midsummer heat, Basil led Charlotte out to the garden. Gaspard followed with Mary hanging on his arm.

Gaspard was lecturing an English officer, new to the island. "The emperor?" he said so loudly that he clearly meant to be overheard. "Of course he's not here. He never goes out in public. Why should he?" He glared straight at Charlotte. "Why bother to go out when the pick of the Yamstock trollops, a blonde called Rosebud who doesn't even have the brains to charge for her favors, regularly beats a path to his door!"

Before a thought had time to cross her mind, Charlotte took three long-legged strides and slapped Gaspard's face. The Frenchman raised his right arm to slap Charlotte right back and might have done so if Mary hadn't thrown him off balance by jerking at the arm she was clinging to for dear life. In the heat of battle, Gaspard brushed her off and Mary fell awkwardly, cutting open her lip on the rim of a potted dogwood tree.

"Oh, clumsy me!" said Mary, sitting up and dabbing at her bleeding lip with a handkerchief. "I tripped!"

Gaspard helped her to her feet. "Mary, pardon me, please. I was…" He glared at Charlotte, who glared back at him. "I was distracted."

The night was obviously over for Mary. "Let me walk you home," said Charlotte, although Porteous House was right next door.

"*Mon Dieu*, no! I insist on having the honor."

Mary gave him a bloody smile. "Thank you, Gaspard. Although I don't want to ruin your evening."

"No, mademoiselle, you will not, I assure you. The evening has just begun!"

Later that night Mary told Charlotte what had happened next. "He hurried me here to my room," she whispered. "He was bursting with a strange excitement. First he kissed me fiercely. My cut lip hurt, but he seemed to like that, and soon, very soon, I liked it, too—isn't love peculiar! Then he practically threw me onto my bed. Can you believe it, plain little Mary Porteous from Saint Helena exciting a man used to enjoying the most beautiful women in Europe! Oh, Charlotte, I am oh so divinely happy!"

"Did you..." Charlotte couldn't say the word.

"Of course we did! We've been doing it for ages. We meet secretly in the Valley of the Nymph and make love for hours in the geraniums. So poetic, isn't it?"

The next morning Napoleon had risen as usual at six, taken his tea, had his full-body massage with eau de cologne. "Rub harder," he told Marchand as he did almost every morning, "as if you were rubbing down a donkey." It was during his massage that the valet told him about the incident at the ball and the imminent arrival of Rosebud's fiancé. It preoccupied him while he had lunch at ten and kept distracting him when he dictated his memoirs until late afternoon. Satiated at last by past glories, he had his bath at four and thought about more immediate matters. He was still in his bath at sunset, the coolies who carried water from a nearby stream to keep the boiler going nearly dropping with exhaustion. It was as the moon rose that everything fell into place. In one blinding flash he saw exactly how he was going to set himself free: Gaspard was going to London.

He sent for Rosebud in the morning and told her what she had to do.

"This will test your relationship with your boy Daniel to the limit. But that's what you women like to do, isn't it? Also it will take time because Lowe is a suspicious man. Will you do it for me?"

Her heart was beating like a drum that was marching men into battle. She remembered her father's wish that one of his sons, at least, would fight for Napoleon. Perhaps not. But one of his daughters would!

There were tears in her eyes. She was thinking of the toy with the black hat on the rearing white horse. "Sire, I would be honored."

Daniel came home on a warm day in February, just a month after Napoleon had his secret meeting with Rosebud. Everyone knew about the feud raging between Charlotte and the snooty French general that had been sparked by what happened at the New Year's ball. That stuck-up Frog had the gall to call her a trollop in public. Their Charlotte, the most beautiful girl on the island!

Gaspard was killed by hostile looks whenever he visited Jamestown, which was often, because there was nowhere else to go. Charlotte's brother John, whenever he'd had a drink or two too many, kept threatening to take a knife to "that bantam" as he called him, although not to his face, of course.

Just as often John would tease Charlotte when *tungi*, the local prickly pear liquor, led him by the nose. "Look at her, all prim and proper," he'd crow. "Pretending butter wouldn't melt in her mouth. But watch out, she's a wildcat, that baby sister of mine. At the first ball, she lets that bantam of a Frenchie general kiss her hand, but at the latest she slaps his face! Now that's what we Yamstocks call progress!"

Only Mary, made turncoat by love, had broken ranks at the wharf and stood with the cluster of Frenchmen and British officers, there to meet some foreign dignitary, who had gathered around the fiery young general, resplendent in his full dress uniform, sword hanging ominously at his side.

Charlotte, in a daringly low-cut white cotton dress, her cheeks fanned by the tropical breeze, was the focus of the second, much larger cluster, which included almost the whole of her Yamstock tribe and nearly all of their friends and relatives. Charlotte's mother was there, elbowing her way to the front of the throng. So were her brothers and sisters, her cousins, their spouses, their hordes of snotty, barefoot children. Her brother Henry used the occasion to wear his kilt, as did his mentor, Mr. Porteous.

The most conspicuous absence was dear Uncle Samuel, Daniel's sponsor, who was too ill to attend but who had insisted that Daniel and Charlotte call on him at Horse Pasture Farm the very next day. The other was Daniel's gypsy mother, who lurked somewhere in deep shade, wide eyes fixed on a seagull, which she was seeing as what it really was, a white vulture.

It came as a delicious shock to Charlotte, the way seven years had perfected Daniel. He had grown tall, over six foot, surely, and was dressed from hat to toe as a gentleman. He looked a little apprehensive, it was true, but who could blame him, facing such a large and noisy reception committee. Her heart soared as she broke through the knot of Yamstocks pumping his hand and slapping him on the back.

"Daniel!" she cried out. "Daniel, my love!"
Moments later they were in each other's arms. "Promise

not to leave me, ever again!" she hissed in his ear. "I was so very lonely without you!"

"That's a promise that's easy to keep," Daniel said.

"But you've grown so clever, I'm sure!" said Charlotte. "How are we poor Yamstocks to keep up with you?"

Daniel kissed her full on the lips, a kiss full of promises that lingered almost too long for decorum. But afterwards Charlotte could sense he was distracted. Searching for someone. His mother.

"Is she here?" he asked.

"I thought she would have nothing to do with you after your father found himself a wife."

Daniel said, "It was Father who forbade it. But we met often, secretly. I told no one, not even you."

Charlotte felt a twinge of jealousy. She didn't want to talk about Daniel's mother. After waiting for him for seven years, she felt she deserved his full attention. "She's still very reclusive," was the best Charlotte could do. "Avoids crowds. I've only spoken with her two or three times. Every time she asked about you. I didn't want to worry you about it in my letters, but a lot of the simpler folk still blame her for your father's death."

"That's ridiculous! He died of elephantiasis!"

"Of course. But you know how us Yamstocks are. We don't believe in medical science. We believe in religion and witchcraft in about equal portions. So after your father left her to marry money and then almost immediately fell ill with the worm disease, they blamed her for casting a spell. Oh, let's not talk about this now!"

"I want to see her," Daniel said very simply.

"She'd already seen you. I know she's here, somewhere close, watching. She'll want to meet you alone."

"When? Do you know where she lives? She must have a home. She has children, my half sisters."

"Somewhere up the valley. A shack, I think. Invites no one to see it. She works as a scullery maid in the tavern some nights. She won't want you, a gentleman now, to see her fallen so low."

"She won't work as a maid any longer!"

"She doesn't want charity, that much I know. While you were away Uncle Samuel tried to give her a stipend, in spite of her strange ways, for you and your father's sake. Daniel, things move slowly on Saint Helena. You've been away so long you've forgotten. Your mother will approach you when she's ready. Tonight's the full moon, isn't it?"

"Yes, yes, it is," said Daniel, who had learned how to keep track of the stars and watched the constellations turn upside down on the long voyage to the Southern Hemisphere.

"I think I know when and where she will be waiting for you."

Daniel was about to ask Charlotte how she knew when kilted Henry Porteous, with Charlotte's kilted brother Henry in tow, pushed his way through the crowd to pump Daniel's hand. "So pleased you're here at last, lad," the affable Scotsman said, "and haven't ye grown up bonny? We'll talk business later. The governor, no less, asked me if there may be a position for you in the Botanical Gardens, which means there certainly is. We have so much botany to discuss—boring to everyone but us, eh? Now, you do remember young Henry, don't you?" he said, squeezing the young man's shoulder. "I've adopted him."

"Hello, Henry," said Daniel. "You haven't changed a bit!"

Henry frowned. He didn't like being teased. "Yes, I have! I've grown taller than you!"

109

"Henry's done me the honor of taking my name. Now he's Henry Porteous Knipe, even in official documents. Sounds very grand, doesn't it? It's all arranged," he rushed on in his Scottish brogue. "You're to stay with us at Porteous House until we find you permanent accommodation. The emperor's suite has been made ready—imagine, the very same bed as Napoleon Bonaparte slept in! But that's after you see Governor Lowe. He wants you to call on him at the Castle immediately, before the ladies eat you alive!"

Daniel mumbled his thanks. He was distracted by the little group of officers, most of them French, who were observing him from the distance. One man in particular, who wore the uniform of a general, stared at him with an expression of undisguised hostility.

"Who's the Frenchie with the thunderous look?" he asked Charlotte. "For some reason he seems to have taken a violent dislike to me. I can't imagine why."

"Oh, that's General Gaspard Gourgaud. Stay away from him, dear Daniel. He's a dangerous man."

"Why on earth does he look so angry? I don't even know him!"

"It's a long story," said Charlotte. "Now's not the time to tell it."

Sir Hudson Lowe sat behind his black Chinese desk, which had menacing dragons carved into its legs. In front of it stood Daniel, looking ill at ease. The governor's suspicious sideways glance had unsettled harder men.

The interview began affably enough with the news that there might be a position for Daniel in the Botanical Gardens. Then Governor Lowe got to the point.

"The assistance you provided His Majesty's government in London has proved very valuable. You are instructed to continue to pass on any information that

110

comes your way concerning Bonaparte directly to me, however trivial it might seem to you. The government, through me, gives you every assurance that this is the only way you can keep the girl called Rosebud safe from prosecution. Do I need to mention her real name?"

He didn't.

"There is one further issue of some importance," Governor Lowe went on. "There was an incident at the New Year's ball. Some kind of altercation between your Rosebud girl and General Gaspard Gourgaud. Some sort of jealousy issue. I didn't overhear them myself, but apparently some words were exchanged. Hurtful words. The lady in question, perhaps flushed with wine, did violence to General Gourgaud's face. I must warn you that Gaspard Gourgaud has fought several duels during his distinguished service in the French army and won all of them. I am informed that he is once again itching to satisfy his honor. So be careful not to stir things up." Lowe gave Daniel, who was by this time white as a sheet, a thin smile. "He's killed three men already. It would be a pity if he made it four."

Charlotte wanted to be there in time for moonrise. The ill wind moaned through the crags as she hurried Daniel to the graveyard where his father and the worms that had killed him were intermingled dust. Daniel had told Charlotte nothing, as yet, of Governor Lowe's dire warning or asked her what she'd done at the New Year's ball that had driven General Gaspard Gourgaud into a homicidal fury. What was he supposed to do? Apologize? He didn't even know what for! Because he couldn't fight. He'd held many a spade in his hand but never a sword, much less a loaded pistol. His chances of survival were no better than if he were blindfolded and set up against a wall by a firing squad.

He had to know. "Charlotte, what happened at the ball?"

"Why, we danced, of course."

"Stop tormenting me! You know what I mean. What happened between you and this French general Gaspard?"

"Oh, that!" she said airily, as if it were the most trivial event in a trivial day. "He called me a trollop in public, so I slapped his face."

"Why?"

"Why did I slap his face? I've just told you!"

"Why did he call you a trollop?"

"Because I wouldn't bed him."

"So now he wants to kill *me*?"

She raised an eloquent eyebrow. "He can hardly challenge *me* to a duel, now can he?"

"Charlotte, this isn't a joke. He'll kill me!"

There was a wicked hint of a humor in her green eyes. "A small price to pay for my honor, don't you think?"

"How can you say that?"

"I'm teasing, of course. I won't allow anything to happen to you."

With an effort, Daniel pulled himself together. He couldn't allow her to see how afraid he was. He forced himself to change the subject. "How can you be so certain my mother will be here?" he said.

"Because it was a full moon the night they buried your father. Just hours after his death, because of the condition of his poor body, crawling with those dreadful parasites. She has strange beliefs. You know that better than I do. She comes back every full moon, they say, to pay her respects, by dancing round and round the grave, wailing some strange song. One night I saw her with my own eyes."

The round rising moon was bright, but there was no dancing figure when the graveyard's rusty gate screamed open. Instead, it seemed, Captain Daniel Hamilton's gravestone had a twin that grew as tall as a standing woman. Daniel's mother, Ann Isaack.

Charlotte's breath was hot on his cheek. "Go to her," she said.

Samuel Knipe, Charlotte's rich uncle, did his best to sound cheerful when she and Daniel were shown into his bedroom the next morning. "Oh, what a fine young gentleman you've become!" he wheezed, scraping together his last resources to make a good first impression. "Summoned by the governor the moment you set foot on land like a visiting dignitary, I hear! What did he say to you?"

Daniel told him what he'd told Charlotte. "He welcomed me home. Said there may be a position for me in the Botanical Gardens."

"Botanical Gardens my hat! Governor Lowe wanted to talk about Bonaparte, didn't he?"

Daniel did his best to sound offhand. "Yes, he did. Mostly wanted to know what the man on the street in London was saying about Napoleon. That sort of thing."

"And what did you tell him?"

"The truth," lied Daniel. "How everyone thought Napoleon was getting his just desserts and that the governor was right not to let him get away with his high jinks."

"Splendid! Lowe does keep the poor devil on a tight leash, all right. Some say too tight. Tell me, what did you make of Sir Hudson Lowe?"

"I met him at the New Year's ball," Charlotte cut in. "He has a red face and red hairs growing out of his nose and ears! Goes perfectly with his angry expression!"

Samuel ground out a dry chuckle. "Which I'm sure was in full display when one of his French guests got his face slapped in public by an outraged local lady!"

"I don't want to talk about it!" said Charlotte, a touch of color flying to her cheeks.

"No need to, my dear. Everyone else is. Daniel, do tell me all about yourself. I want to hear more of your fancy new accent! Not a trace of Yamstock in it. Grown up to be quite the dandy!"

"Uncle Samuel," Daniel said, because he'd called him that all his life, although they weren't actually related, as far as he knew, "I'm so sorry to hear about your health."

"Nonsense, my boy, no need for tears. Man shall live threescore years and ten, the Good Book says, and in my case it has already kept its promise!" He patted the bed. "Come and sit by me." Daniel took his hand. It was cold and shriveled and covered with the blemishes of old age. "Welcome to Saint Helena, son. I wish your father had lived to see you grown so fine!" A troubled look crept into the watery eyes. "Have you visited your mother?" he asked.

"Last night. She was at Father's grave."

"I wonder how you knew she would be there," he said with a sly glance at Charlotte.

"I told him she goes there every full moon. She'd certainly be there the full moon her son returned."

Samuel had enough mischief left in him to tease her. "A fine family gathering!" He seemed to be struck by some kind of painful spasm, after which he abruptly changed his tone to one of sadness. "Poor woman, so unjustly blamed for his illness. Your father's physician, Dr. Crout, laughed at the superstition. It was just a bad case of elephantiasis, he said. Picked up in west Africa, probably. But of course the local people blame poor Ann, because of her gypsy heritage." He laughed, which seemed to hurt him, took back his hand, and put it on his chest. For a long

114

moment, he closed his eyes. "But what do you expect from us ignorant islanders?"

Daniel gave him what he hoped was a reassuring smile. "Isolated no longer, Uncle. Because Napoleon has made it the center of the world. That's what I told Governor Lowe when he asked me what they were saying in London."

"What did you make of him?"

"Charlotte's quite right," he said. "He does have red hairs growing out of his nostrils!"

Samuel did his best to smile. "I didn't ask you to come all the way out here to talk about the governor's nose hairs," he said. "I sent for you, Daniel, to keep a promise. Virgin Hall. Of course you know I bought it from your father shortly before his death. But what you don't know is that he sold it to me at a substantial discount on one condition—that if you two should marry, I rent it to you at a rate you can easily afford. I gave him my word of honor."

Virgin Hall, its tropical fruit, its majestic view of Sandy Bay thousands of feet below! Virgin Hall, where, one hot night under a guava tree, Charlotte was very nearly a virgin no longer, her honor preserved only by the appearance of her slave, Molly, who had a suspicious nature and a loud voice that called out, "Miss Charlotte! Where is you, Miss Charlotte?" although she knew perfectly well where Miss Charlotte was and had a very good idea what she and Master Daniel were up to.

They were to have Virgin Hall when they married!

Samuel's plain, unadorned statement could have been the last trump, for the impact it made on Charlotte. "Uncle Samuel!" She embraced the old man and then his old friend's son.

Daniel returned her hug, but his heart wasn't in it. The trailing coat of his thoughts was snagged on the word *honor*. As in "honor that must be satisfied." The wet wing

115

of terror brushed him. A French general, a marksman, wanted to kill him.

No one can be avoided for very long in Jamestown any more than date palms can. Daniel ran into his nemesis the next day at the Almond Tree, where Gaspard was being fawned over by Mary Porteous. Daniel would have pretended not to see him if he could. But Charlotte, arm locked in his, dragged him toward his doom.

"Mary!" she called out, "we have the most wonderful news! Uncle Samuel is going to rent us Virgin Hall!" She pecked the newly made botanist on his rapidly blanching cheek. "But only on condition Daniel marries me! Isn't that delicious?"

Mary looked at Gaspard for permission to speak, but his face had suddenly set like cement neither giving permission nor withholding it. Mary jumped to her feet, kissed Charlotte on the cheek. "Be careful!" she whispered.

Gaspard's eyes remained riveted to Daniel's face. Although he was shaking in his shoes, Daniel forced himself not to look away.

At last the Frenchman spoke. "We have a small matter to settle, monsieur, you and I, but before we do so, you are instructed to call on the emperor with your"—he sneered in Charlotte's direction—"companion. His Majesty hopes this afternoon at four will be convenient. Here are the passes." He held the folded sheets of paper out languidly, pointing them at the cobbles as if they were scraps for a very tame dog. Then, very deliberately, he dropped them. Charlotte gasped. A wave of anger flushed away Daniel's terror. He was about to say something that could have been fatal when Mary hastened to the rescue.

"Gaspard!" she said, "you're so clumsy, always dropping things!" As quickly as her corset would allow she picked up the passes and handed them to Daniel. "There you are!" she went on, much too brightly. "You don't want to keep the emperor waiting!"

Daniel's anger was rapidly on the wane, but he summoned up enough courage to look Gaspard full in the face. The calmness in the Frenchman's eyes brought back the damp wing of fear. It told Daniel that General Gaspard Gourgaud had looked death in the face many times and never blinked.

# Chapter 8: The Duel

Gaspard was nowhere to be seen when they arrived at Longwood. The valet Marchand, who answered the door, told Charlotte that the emperor was in the garden and pointed out where.

"Do I throw myself at his feet?" asked Daniel, nervous as a mouse.

"Of course not, silly. But remember to keep you hat off, whatever you do."

"Ha!" crowed Napoleon, "so this is your stallion, back on the farm at last! Tell me, boy, have you rutted with your filly yet? You can tell me, because, as you can see, I have no one to gossip with. I am as alone as Jonah in the belly of the whale! What say you, Rosebud? Was he worth waiting for? You could have been rutting with Gaspard—I know he wants you. But then, he wants everything on two legs, or even four. I worry about the chastity of my goats. He even asked, very politely, for permission to bugger me! Can you believe such insolence? He is in love with my beautiful hands, you know. Perhaps he's in love with yours, do tell…"

Charlotte and Daniel stood there, rooted to the spot like the gumwoods, as exposed to the storm of words as Deadwood Plain was exposed to the ceaseless southeaster.

The tirade ceased abruptly. "Oh, do say something interesting enough to make me stop talking!" Napoleon said.

"No, Your Majesty," said Charlotte with a blush coloring her cheeks. "We have not…not consummated our relationship."

"Don't stutter, girl, out with it. Nothing but the truth now!"

"When we marry we are going to move into a house called—"

"What house? Where?"

"Sandy Bay, sire. It's called Virgin Hall—"

A coarse Corsican laugh. "Ha! Is that why you guard your virginity? Because you have to be a virgin to move in there?"

"No, Your Majesty—"

"What? Not a virgin?"

"First Daniel has to establish himself."

"Can he talk, this boy of yours?"

"Yes, Your Majesty," said Daniel. "I just don't—"

"Enough!" Napoleon snapped. "Save your pretty speeches for this raging beauty of yours. I used to share in the most intimate pillow talk imaginable. I remember telling Josephine, after one of our bouts, that she had the prettiest little cunny in the world." He looked straight at Charlotte. "Pardon my language, mademoiselle. That wasn't meant for a lady's ear. Please excuse us for a few minutes. I need to have a man-to-man conversation with your young swain."

Charlotte couldn't resist a disapproving sniff, but she did discover a sudden interest in the flower beds that surrounded the lawn.

"Walk with me, Daniel," said Napoleon, hands clasped behind his back, heading in the opposite direction Charlotte had taken. "We have a strategy. It is to goad this fool of a governor, this coarse Caliban of a creature, until he makes the conditions of our imprisonment so harsh that it will provoke an international incident. Do you follow me?"

"Yes, sire. I think—"

Napoleon wasn't interested in what Daniel thought. "When I handed myself over to the English," he charged on, "in exchange for terminating my political career, *hospitality* was the word I used, not *imprisonment,* and especially not incarceration of such unspeakable cruelty." He dropped his voice to a whisper, although the nearest redcoat in the noose that encircled Longwood house night and day was a hundred yards away. "Strategy. I win all my battles with strategy. We will strive to become the victims of cruel and unusual punishment that is specifically forbidden by the Eighth Amendment to the American Constitution. Although America is a French idea, it is not a place I particularly care for. It's raw and savage—so says my brother Joseph, who's over there. I'd prefer to be a prisoner here in Saint Helena than a free man in America!"

Napoleon graced Daniel with his cupid's bow of a smile, made delightful by its upturned corners. "I jest, of course. What I do not jest about is General Gaspard Gourgaud. He is a fearless man and a fine munitions officer, tactically brilliant but with no head for strategy. He complains like a woman about the petty inconveniences caused by our plan, which he knows nothing about, of goading the governor toward the precipice, and God knows this place has enough of those! The truth is that Gaspard does not want his little pleasures taken away. He is self-indulgent, petty, and vain. He is fierce, but it is the fierceness of a rooster! I say it to his face often enough, although I wouldn't repeat that if I were you. Tact is what is required. Tact. Is it true that there is some ill feeling between Rosebud and the general in question? Don't answer, because I know there is. This means that you, Daniel, must watch your step, as you English say. Keep out of Gaspard's way. We are at war. We use both strategy and tactics. Our overarching strategy is to arouse universal contempt for my jailer. Our specific tactic is to fool my jailer into shipping Gaspard to Europe to promote our cause. Of course, it would ruin everything if you shot my messenger." That bark of a laugh admitted the absurdity of the idea. "It would also be inconvenient for us to have to put up with Rosebud's lamentations if perchance Gaspard missed your shoulder and put a ball through your head, wouldn't it?"

"Yes, Your Majesty," mumbled Daniel, whose heart had taken up residence in his boots. "It would."

"Ha! You have a sense of humor! Back to business. I will tell Rosebud to repeat my wildest accusations to you and you alone. Then you must pass these on to my jailer without her knowing it."

"I must deceive her, Majesty?"

"Don't sound so surprised. You've deceived her before with the help of our spy Edweeds."

Although his name was mispronounced, the skeletal vulture George Edwards hopped out of a haunted corner of Daniel's mind and made a birdish bow. "May I know why I have to deceive her, sire?"

"Because Rosebud has no business talking to the governor. Let alone frequently. There would be gossip. Suspicion. You work for the company, in their gardens. You would be expected to discuss horticultural matters with my jailer. If he finds out the truth, that we are intentionally provoking him, there will be retribution against the bringer of false tidings. Painful retribution. A charge of treason, perhaps. A hanging offence. You want to save Rosebud from the rope, don't you?"

"Well, out with it! What did you two talk about?" asked Charlotte as they rode back to town down the winding narrow track from Longwood in a silence that became awkwardly long. "Or are you too overawed to say anything?"

"I was wondering what he said to you first. It was about Gaspard, wasn't it?"

121

"Nothing of consequence," said Charlotte with just a hint of evasiveness. "He wanted my assurance you could be trusted, that's all."

"Well of course he talked and I listened," said Daniel, who was thinking that the only reassuring thing about the interview was that Napoleon had given him an assignment, to pass on gossip, which meant that the emperor expected him to stay alive, at least for a while. "Mostly he talked about you."

"Really! What did he say?"

"He said that he was expecting to see a lot of you at Longwood. That you were bound to pick up wild gossip. That you should discuss it with me before repeating it. In case it was dangerous."

Charlotte didn't try to hide her annoyance. "That's not very flattering. He obviously trusts your judgment more than mine!"

"Don't take it personally. You told me that he thinks that women have more going on between their legs than between their ears."

Charlotte lashed out at Daniel's horse with her riding whip, laughing as Daniel fought to control it. "That's what you think, too!"

Daniel lived on his nerves but the rest of the week passed uneventfully. Charlotte sold fruit and vegetables on her mother's porch. Gaspard took Napoleon's dictation and went on rides with him. Henry Porteous familiarized Daniel with the Botanical Gardens. Daniel avoided Gaspard like the plague. He always found an excuse not to take Charlotte to the Almond Tree. He no longer took the sea air with her down at the wharf. But he knew the reprieve couldn't last for long. There were occasions when he was tempted to get it all over with. To confront Gaspard, take his bullet, and hope it wasn't fatal. But somehow he always changed his mind.

"Surely you're not afraid?" Charlotte asked Daniel suddenly one Sunday as he was planting breadfruit seedlings in the Botanical Gardens.

Daniel knew what she meant but pretended not to. "Of what?"

"Of your own shadow, it seems. You never take me to the Almond Tree anymore."

"As you can see, I'm very busy right now. The breadfruit seeds have to be planted immediately you wash them free from the fruit. They can't be allowed to dry out."

"Too busy to call on me? So busy gardening that I have to come and pull you out like a weed to get you to walk with me?"

"Napoleon's orders!" Daniel said a little too hotly. "He told me to stay out of the general's way until things cool down."

She examined him with her startling emerald eyes. "During your little man-to-man tête-à-tête?"

"Yes."

"But what am I to tell people who say you are hiding under your bed with nothing but your chamber pot for company? Everyone knows about you and Gaspard. How he insulted you at the Almond Tree by dropping our passes at his feet."

"So what do you want me to do? Go charging into a duel with a marksman? I've never fired a pistol in my life. I'm not a bombardier, I'm a botanist!"

Tears swelled in Charlotte's eyes. "I know this is all my fault. But he called me a trollop in front of everybody. Oh, how I wish I had someone to defend my honor!"

Daniel sighed. "All right, then, let's get it over with. We'll go to the Almond. He'll soon be told I'm there."

Charlotte surprised Daniel by kissing him. "Brave darling! Let's do it tomorrow. I'm sure he'll be there at lunchtime."

He was. Charlotte and Daniel had barely started picking at their food in the dining room when General Baron Gaspard Gourgaud walked in. With his red jacket and tight white pantaloons and beak of a hat, he looked every inch the strutting rooster. At his side was young Basil Jackson, first lieutenant, who looked like he was attending a funeral. He exchanged anxious glances with Charlotte, gave her a curt nod. Everyone else was looking at Daniel, not wanting to miss the sight of him running for the door. Unobserved in the kitchen was Daniel's mother, Anne Isaack, scullery maid, who as usual made sure her son didn't know she was there.

Gaspard took a table on the far side of the room. The Almond's occupants seemed not to interest him at all, especially not Charlotte and Daniel. Instead he stared out the open window, apparently deep in thought.

"The usual," said Basil Jackson. The waitress brought their drinks. Two different tropical creations. Besides Jackson's few words, the room, which had been buzzing with loud whispers about Daniel's sudden appearance, was so silent you could hear the two officers sipping their drinks.

It seemed as if an hour passed, although it was only a few minutes, before Gaspard made his move. He raised his nose in the air and sniffed loudly, looking everywhere except for where Daniel sat frozen to his chair.

"Do you smell it?" he asked the silence.

"What?" said Basil Jackson, ill at ease in the role he was being forced to play.

"Fear! I swear this place is reeking with the acrid smell of fear. Now I wonder where it could be coming from. Have you any idea?"

124

"No," said Jackson, moving his empty drink like a chess piece.

"Unless it's coming from outside," said Gaspard. "Or at least it would be if a certain coward had his way!"

A voice came from the opposite side of the room. It was Charlotte. "That's funny! I don't smell fear," she said. "But I do smell a bully. Coming from your side of the room. I wonder who he could be!"

"A pity," said Gaspard, "that they allow loudmouthed harlots onto the premises. This is clearly a place to which a decent man can no longer bring his wife."

"*General*, we all know you bugger Basil Jackson," crowed Charlotte, who seemed to be having the time of her life. "But I never thought you'd admit it in public that he was your wife!"

Gaspard bolted to his feet, and so did Daniel. In five quick strides, they were nose to nose. "Stand aside, coward," he hissed. "There's a face itching to be slapped."

"No!" shouted Daniel, and this time the sound came all the way from his gut.

The details of the duel were arranged in the street just out of earshot of the tavern's clientele, who already had enough gossip to last them a week. It was to be pistols at dawn the next morning in the graveyard behind Saint James's Church so that, Gaspard said, Daniel wouldn't have far to go after he was finished with him. Gaspard would supply the pistols, a fine set that had been well blooded. Lieutenant Basil Jackson would be his second.

Charlotte, who was alarmingly calm through these portentous arrangements, as if duels were fought over her every day, suggested her brother Henry as Daniel's second.

"He has an old pistol," she said as she examined Daniel's stricken face with her large, liquid green eyes, "which he uses to chase rabbits out of the garden. I'm sure that he'll even give you a lesson on how to fire it."

They were hurrying down the high street to inform
Henry of the fateful duty that had just been thrust upon
him. There wasn't a clock anywhere near, but Daniel could
hear one ticking loudly, counting the seconds to tomorrow.
"Rabbits!" he said. "I'm the rabbit, a cornered rabbit, and
I'm going to be shot like one. How can you be so damned
calm? You've murdered me!"
The pain in her eyes was completely convincing.
"You're saving my honor, Daniel. Isn't that worth anything
to you?"

Henry Porteous Knipe, as Charlotte's brother now
styled himself, just a year older than Charlotte, was so
excited by the prospect of being a second at a duel that he
didn't check the flint in his battered old pistol, so the first
time Daniel pulled the trigger it didn't fire.
"Careful!" yelled Henry when Daniel waved the
muzzle in his direction. "Sometimes it takes a few seconds
for the gunpowder to catch. "No," he went on when he had
counted to five. "Flint must be napped. We need to change
it."
So it was quite a while before Daniel got off his
first shot. The recoil numbed his hand. He declined a
second. One more shot tomorrow, and that would be the
end of it. And of him, almost certainly. All he could wish
for was a quick ending. He'd heard of men who received a
bullet in the gut taking days to die.
Daniel couldn't sleep that night. He paced up,
cursing General Gaspard Gourgaud, and paced down,
cursing Charlotte Knipe. How could she do this to him?
Quite clearly she didn't love him anymore, if she ever had.
She was in love with Gaspard. She had set up the duel, he
was sure of it now. She had slapped Gaspard's face at the
ball so that the strutting rooster would be obliged to
challenge him, even though he had absolutely nothing to do

with their quarrel, wasn't even on the island. He was in the Azores when it happened, thousands of miles away! Quite clearly she was trying to flush him out of her life in a way that brought her fame. From now on, she would have the reputation that she was a beauty whom men had fought and died over. This wasn't a duel. It was human sacrifice on the altar of her vanity!

But a force much stronger than his own will, the fear of being called a coward, had Daniel striding manfully into the gray dawn the short distance—oh, too short—to the churchyard where the already dead stirred in their graves, getting ready to welcome him into their silent community.

He had refused breakfast because he'd heard that an empty stomach fares better with a bullet in it than one full of eggs and bacon. It didn't help at all that young Henry, his second, was wearing his kilt as he walked at his side. The kilt he had taken to wearing at weddings and funerals.

Daniel caught himself reading the inscriptions on the cold stones. He wondered what they would write on his. What they should write was: "Here lies a young man in his prime, hounded to his death by a vain and selfish young woman."

The only thing missing from making his misery complete was that there was no sign of the Gallic rooster General Gaspard Gourgaud. The rising sun was just about to sever the throat of the night when the Frenchman's second arrived, Basil Jackson, conspicuously alone and obviously distressed.

"The general sends his sincerest apologies," he said. "He was taken sick late yesterday afternoon. Some kind of food poisoning. Vomited all night. In spite of Dr. O'Meara's orders, he dragged himself to the stables this morning. But he was so weak he couldn't mount his horse. I can't tell you how much he was looking forward to being here and how earnestly he wishes to reschedule as soon as he is strong enough to hold a pistol."

Daniel gaped at Basil Jackson as if he were Jesus Christ riding in on clouds of glory. "Sick?" he said, because that's how he felt. Sick with relief.

"Yes," said Lieutenant Jackson, "but he will give you satisfaction as soon as he stops vomiting, I can assure you of that."

Daniel wanted to say that he was satisfied enough already—or words to that effect—but his response didn't come out right, because he was distracted by a figure that was approaching with long strides out of the dove-gray dawn. It was Charlotte.

"My brave, brave darling!" she whispered as she crushed his lips with hers.

# Chapter 9: Deception

"You are sure Rosebud poisoned you?" Napoleon asked Gaspard.

"Yes, but not personally. Through an agent, that young coward's mother. Everybody knows she's a witch. When she's not casting spells or concocting potions, she works as a scullery maid at the tavern. I will not be drinking at the Almond Tree next time we fight."

"There will be no next time."

"Majesty? Then how will my honor be satisfied? People will say I am a coward."

"All the better. It explains why you hate me."

"Hate you, sire?" A dreadful thought struck Gaspard. "Was it you..."

"I knew of it," said Napoleon. "I know everything that happens on this pile of dung."

"But I don't hate you, sire. I love you."

"Love is war's little sister—she must always take second place. You are a brilliant tactician, but you know nothing of strategy. Let me explain."

They were walking, leaning forward into the southeaster, their hats in their hands, the emperor because he didn't want his famous black hat swept away—he only had forty of them—Gaspard because no one wore a hat in Napoleon's presence. Napoleon reached out and pinched Gaspard's wind-chilled cheek. "You've just had a remarkable change of heart," he said. "Instead of wanting to kill this Daniel boy, you have taken a passionate liking to him. You may bugger him, for all I care—he's certainly young and handsome enough! These are your instructions: you will persuade Daniel that I have besmirched your honor by forbidding you to reschedule the duel. You will tell Daniel that you are tired of my autocratic ways.

Convince him, so he convinces everyone else, that you are seriously thinking of taking revenge on me by siding with my jailer. In fact, you wish you were in England to denounce me to the British government in person. The British will relish your betrayal, because everybody knows that we are so close that I chose you to take the notice of my abdication to the prince regent. Those are your orders."

Gaspard Gourgaud thought of himself as a clever man, but he couldn't work out what was the point of this shameful subterfuge. "Your Majesty, may I know why you want me to pretend to be a traitor?"

The world's master strategist shook his head in wonder. "Must I explain everything? Once you are in London, once you have wormed your way into the soft heart of the English Liberal establishment, you will break out your true colors. You will explain that you had to disguise yourself as a traitor so that my jailer would send you to England. You will reveal to everyone the true horrors of our exile. Once you have set Britain aflame, you will take our message to Europe. Relay it in person to the tsar and the emperor of Austria, my wife Marie-Louise, everyone. Prince Eugene will have money for you. We will be recalled. Our cruel and unusual punishment, our martyrdom on this wind-blasted rock will be over!"

"Sire, you make me feel like Judas," said Gaspard.

Napoleon chuckled. "Don't let it go to your head!"

Charlotte had taken off her shoes because they were walking on the beach. She was pleased that every now and then Daniel glanced at her ankles and naked feet—slender, high arched, even toed—as perfect as her hands. Charming feet.

"You witch, you planned it all, down to the last detail!" he said.

"I didn't plan anything. I did what I was told!"

"By whom?"

"Whom do you think? The emperor, of course."

"Why would Napoleon want to get me killed?"

"That's the last thing he wants. He treasures your connection with Governor Lowe. You were never in any danger. Do you think we would do that to you?"

"Why not? *We* might find it amusing! You know I'm no soldier—I'm a botanist! Why torture me? Don't you think I deserve an answer?"

"The emperor heard Gaspard had challenged you. Gaspard needs to have an excuse to change sides. An excuse that convinces Governor Lowe."

"Change sides? What are you talking about?"

"Not everyone will believe Napoleon has forbidden Gaspard to fight you. Some will accuse him of cowardice. Gaspard fears nothing more than that. It's plausible that he will blame Napoleon for his shame. That this will be enough to turn his love for the emperor into hate."

This plot was so deep that Daniel struggled to find his footing. "But why does Napoleon want Gaspard to pretend to be a traitor?"

"So Governor Lowe will send him to England to testify against Napoleon."

"Then he switches back to Napoleon's side when he gets there?"

"Of course."

Daniel stopped walking to stare at a ship that was breaking out its canvas. "You knew all this? All the time?"

"Yes. Napoleon had me speak to your mother. She had exactly the concoction that was needed."

"But what if Gaspard had not had that drink?"

"Gaspard always has it when he visits the Almond."

"How did he know I was there?"

"Basil Jackson told him."

"How did Basil Jackson know?"

Her emerald eyes were a challenge to the sparkling sea behind her. "I told him."

A wry smile wormed its way onto Daniel's lips. "You are a heartless vixen."

"I must admit it was difficult not to burst out laughing when you and Gaspard were breathing fire at each other."

"Is that why you didn't tell me the duel was a charade? To laugh at me? You have no idea what it's like staring death in the face!"

"Napoleon wouldn't let me tell either you or Gaspard because he needed you both to be completely convincing so the governor will be convinced. Also, he needed to test your courage. He has great plans for you."

He almost forgave her because he felt a flush of pride at having passed the test. "So what's the next step?"

She heard something above the crack and sigh of the waves. "Here it comes, at a gallop."

Lieutenant Basil Jackson rode in a wide circle around them, his horse relishing the soft sand under its hooves. "Hello!" he called out, his fair English cheeks flushed. "A letter for Daniel. From Gaspard." His horse reared when he tried to pass Daniel the note. Although Basil's horse wasn't white, it reminded Charlotte of that famous David painting of Napoleon, in his glory days, leading the charge across the Alps. Daniel managed to get hold of the letter on the third attempt, and with a loud good-bye the messenger spurred his horse onward down the beach.

"Well?" said Charlotte when Daniel just stood there with the letter, which he wanted to hold as much as the hot side of a flaming firebrand. What if Gaspard, the Gallic cock, had decided to disobey his master?

With a last look at Jackson galloping off with wild glee and showing no intention of returning, Daniel broke the seal and started to read.

"What does it say?" Charlotte asked, much too intrigued for Daniel's liking.

The letter was such a short one that he turned it over to make sure he hadn't missed anything on the other side.

"It's an apology of sorts," he said, doing his best to sound casual about it.

"Read it, please!"

"It's what you've just told me," he said.

"Then give it to me!"

Daniel found himself reluctant to part with the letter, as if it were written evidence of a death penalty pardon.

When Charlotte, laughing, squeezed his wrist, he surrendered it. Someone must have done a translation, because the English was perfect, which Gaspard's was not.

"Monsieur Hamilton," she read aloud, affecting a heavy French accent. "My sincerest apologies for being prevented by an acute illness from attending our little affair of honor this morning. Unfortunately the matter has since come to the attention of the emperor, who has forbidden me, in the severest terms, from taking this matter further, even though this stains my good name. Since my challenge was prompted by the behavior of your fiancée, and not yourself, my belief is that you lose no honor in accepting this offer of reconciliation. Because you are a civilian with no experience with arms, I admire your courage in daring to face a man like me, who most probably would have killed you. My hope is that we will become close companions now that I have fallen out of favor with an emperor who does not seem to appreciate that I am in the position to correct the lies he circulates about that good man Sir Hudson Lowe, who is only trying to do his duty. Yours, etc., Gaspard Gourgaud, General."

Charlotte brushed the sand off her feet, slipped on her shoes. "You need to see the governor immediately, so he thinks he is the first one to know about the letter. While you are busy with him, I will be at the Almond Tree. I have to tell everyone the good news."

While Daniel waited for Governor Lowe to find time to see him, Charlotte was mobbed by posturing young officers who feasted on her account of how Napoleon's favorite general, the man who had saved his life more than once, had just turned his coat.

Across the road at the Castle Lowe greeted Daniel with his suspicious sideways glance. "To what do I owe the pleasure?" he said as he went on writing a letter, to make it clear he was a very busy man.

"Your Excellency instructed me to keep you informed on anything relating to the prisoner."

Lowe's goose-feather pen kept scratching away. "I heard you and General Gaspard had a frightful falling out at the Almond Tree yesterday. Scared everyone stiff. Just as well he was struck down last night, by something he ate I suppose, or you would have been a dead man by now."

Daniel didn't linger over the possibility. "He has fallen out with Bonaparte, Your Excellency. He says that Napoleon's forbidding him to reschedule the duel besmirches his honor. He has written me a letter of reconciliation. I have it here."

Now Daniel had Lowe's full attention. "Really? Let me see this letter."

When Lowe finished reading, he shot to his feet as if in the grip of an overwhelming inspiration. He paced like a penned tiger behind his menacing Chinese desk. "I need to hear what he has got to say about Bonaparte with my own ears! I want everyone to hear! Everyone! A dinner party at Plantation House. My full general staff will be there. Prominent locals, like that botanical Scotsman Henry Porteous—he loves to gossip. Purveyor Balcombe—he's got loose lips. And you and your young lady, of course, or is she General Gourgaud's now? It's hard to keep up with her." Lowe flashed something that was very nearly a roguish smile. "She'll be available, I take it?"

"I'm sure Charlotte will be delighted, Your Excellency," Daniel said.

Charlotte had never seen ice, but she felt that icy was a good description of the way she responded to Gaspard effusive greeting at Governor Lowe's hastily arranged Plantation House dinner. They were collaborators now, by imperial decree, but it was difficult to overlook that he had called her a harlot in public.

She was standing with Daniel, who was talking botany with kilted Henry Porteous when Gaspard, of course in full dress uniform, approached. "Ah, *ma chère* Rosebud, you are looking so lovely this evening. Your eyes have lost none of their fire!"

Although Napoleon's instructions to make up with Gaspard rang in her ears, she allowed herself to raise a slightly contemptuous eyebrow. "Thank you, General, although you may call me Charlotte."

"Oh, but I may not," Gaspard said loud enough for Henry Porteous to hear. "The fat spider who stews in his bath all day has spread his web over every inch of the island. The threads are attached to his fingers. He not only knows what everyone says, he knows what everyone thinks. His is a mind that has plotted every intricate detail of sixty mighty battles, that has dominated rooms full of kings and princes. He has ordered us to call you Rosebud, so Rosebud it must be. I hear you came up by ox wagon. So charmingly rustic! If you'd asked I would certainly have arranged for you to be fetched by one of our carriages."

"Actually, I prefer to be drawn by oxen," said Charlotte. "On these treacherous roads they are much more sure-footed and less skittish than horses. It's something you might want to keep in mind."

Gaspard gave her a smile as tight as a vise. "I admire your caution. Saint Helena is indeed treacherous terrain."

A gong sounded, another import from China. A butler announced that dinner was served. Gaspard bowed, Charlotte curtsied, and they went in with the others.

When the last course was dealt with and liquors served, all eyes were on Gaspard raising his glass in a macabre toast. "Here's to the two million men, women, and children he killed!" he said. "The little people who died to make him great!"

"But he claims it was in a noble cause," said Governor Lowe, cunningly playing devil's advocate. "Bringing equality to the world."

"Nonsense, Your Excellency, with respect," Gaspard said. "That's what his sycophants would have you believe. Once the scales have fallen from one's eyes, one realizes that he's no more an egalitarian than the tyrant of Timbuktu. He gave the crowns of Europe to his family, handed them out like trophies. The day his son was born, he made the whelp king of Rome, when his only accomplishment was that he knew how to suck on his wet nurse's teat!"

Lowe, who wanted to maintain a demeanor of high seriousness, didn't laugh with the rest. "What about the men who followed him into exile?" he asked. "He must have qualities to attract fine volunteers like you to such a faraway place."

"Volunteers! He bribed us to keep him company with reminders of how much money we could make writing books about him! Wouldn't take no for an answer. While we were still on the *Bellerophon*, one of the wives, the elegant Madame Bertrand, no less, barged into Napoleon's cabin and begged him to let her husband off the leash. Napoleon refused. So the poor, distraught woman rushed back to her cabin and tried to throw herself out the window, she was in such a state of despair. Unfortunately, she got stuck and we tried to pull her back, but someone else yelled, 'Let her go! Let her go!' We were all at one another's throats, even then."

"One of the ogre's victims was my brother, Sir William Howe DeLancey," said Lady Susan Lowe, maudlin with drink. "Shattered by a cannonball."

"DeLancey, the hero of Waterloo?" said Gaspard, whose glass was being refilled for the twentieth time. "Of course I've heard of him, my lady. That cannonball was meant for Wellington, who was right at his side. He gave his life for his general!"

Lady Lowe drained her glass. She gave Gaspard a sly smile. "Would you do that for your emperor?"

"There was a time when I would. When I did. Twice I saved his life. But whenever I remind him, he becomes irritated. Says he can't remember! Can you believe such monstrous ingratitude? He treats me a like a dog!"

"What about the lies he circulates abroad concerning the governor?" ventured Daniel, keeping his tone low and respectful. "Everyone in England believes them."

Gaspard turned up his hands. "Lies? At Longwood? How can they be lies when everything is done strictly according to the dictates of the Code Napoleon?"

Lowe allowed himself a chuckle. "That's rich," he said.

Gaspard appeared to be having the time of his life. "He calls you Caliban after the deformed monster in Shakespeare's play. He intentionally misunderstands all your communications. He draws up lists of demands he knows perfectly well you can't accede to. He makes up promises he pretends come from you and then claims you have broken them. And it's not only you whom the monster abuses—it is us, his staff. He treats us with contempt, as if he were still master of Europe and we are minions barely fit to polish his boots. He is a lunatic who won't accept that the horse of history has thrown him and galloped off into the future."

"What about his absurd obsession with being called emperor?" Lady Lowe cut in. "I'm told that a few weeks ago he received a letter addressed to General Bonaparte. He advised the messenger to go to Egypt, because that's where *General* Bonaparte was last heard of, at the Battle of the Pyramids!"

This offering was swept on its way by another gale of drunken laughter. "Water!" cried Gaspard. "Your mentioning Egypt reminds me of water, at least the lack of it. Every day he wallows in water that is hand carried two miles from the nearest spring, even though we have hardly enough at Longwood to boil our vegetables. No wonder he insists on always shaving himself, otherwise one of us would certainly have cut his throat by now!"

Henry Porteous, whose kilt kept riding up and who was hiding his bare knees under the tablecloth, thought it high time he made a contribution that sailed with the prevailing wind. "He's putting on weight, Bonaparte complains, because he's not allowed to take exercise. That's not true either, is it?"

"More lies!" crowed Gaspard. "He's allowed to ride within a twelve-mile perimeter, but he claims to everyone who will listen that he is kept cooped up day and night in a damp, drafty dungeon of a house with a leaky ceiling. He isn't. He's as fat as a Chinese pig because he eats like one. It's hard not to burst out laughing when you watch him walk. It's something between a swagger and a waddle."

Daniel said nothing, merely following the center of attention with his calm brown eyes as it flitted round the table. Charlotte, who had been cut off the few times she'd tried to speak, raised her voice. Something Napoleon's doctor, Barry O'Meara, had said popped into her mind. It was out of her mouth before she could stop it.

"Sir Hudson, I've heard a rumor that you are refusing Napoleon leeches to drain his hemorrhoids. I would have thought General Gaspard Gourgaud the perfect man to set the record straight on that point."

The stunned silence was broken by Lady Lowe's tipsy giggle.

"Another damn lie!" shouted Lowe so angrily that it had to be the truth.

# Chapter 10: Virgin Hall

"The fool swallowed it?" said Napoleon.

"He loved every word," said Charlotte. "I haven't seen the governor smile before."

The emperor, who rose at six, was already halfway through his *petite levée* when Charlotte arrived. Everything being done in the same order as before, as if he were at the Tuileries, Malmaison, Fontainebleau, Rambouillet, or Saint-Cloud instead of this ruined shack on a barren plain on a flyspeck of an island in the middle of nowhere.

He was standing at the window, shaving. His valet Marchand was holding the mirror, and a second valet held a tray with soap and water. The dogs barked. She was with the household servants, head hidden in a dirty scarf. The sleepy soldiers, who had heard nothing more sinister during the long, gusty night than the scream of a feral cat, hardly glanced at her. She entered the house through the back door, keeping her scarf on until she was shown into the imperial presence.

"That boy of yours, Daniel, is doing some excellent work for us, as are you. You both deserve to be rewarded."

"There is no need. We do it for freedom."

Napoleon glanced at her with such a quick movement that he nearly nicked himself with the razor. Cupid's bow arched on his lips and then was gone when its arrow was discharged at her. "You mentioned that when you marry you are going to rent a farm called Virgin Hall in Sandy Bay?" he said, handing the cutthroat to Marchand.

"Yes. On his deathbed Daniel's father sold it to my uncle Samuel."

"For how much?"

"Two thousand pounds."

"Do you recommend the place?"

"Oh, yes! It has spectacular views and anything will grow there."

"Take a message to Balcombe."

Charlotte delivered it on the way home. William Balcombe wasn't alone at the Briars, because he had Bacchus for company. Business was bad, had been bad since the black market dried up with the lifting of the embargo at the end of the war. He was sinking into a deep hole of debt, and how could a man dig himself out of a hole without lifting a glass?

"Papa's not well," said Betsy, subdued for a change. "Who is the message from?"

"The neighbor," said Charlotte, trying unsuccessfully not to sound too important.

"Boney!" crowed the brat. "Why didn't you say so?"

"I just did, didn't I?"

"Papa's in his study," said Betsy, transitioning into a whisper, "but as I said…"

"I think this message will make him feel better."

Betsy, who had grown into a willowy, not unattractive sixteen-year-old, looked doubtful but did show Charlotte in.

Balcombe was unshaven, and although the Briars was in a protected valley his hair looked like it had been attacked by Longwood's southeaster. He was beyond pretense about his drinking, a bottle of brandy and a half-full glass within easy reach on the desktop.

Charlotte said, "The emperor has a request."

"Napoleon? What does he want this time?" he rambled. "He knows that every request has to go through Governor Lowe, and Lowe says that everything has to go through London, so it takes four months to get permission to sneeze."

141

"He wants you to buy him Virgin Hall from my uncle Samuel."

"What for? They will never let him move out there. Too close to Sandy Bay. Governor Lowe would be terrified that someone will rescue him."

"I don't think he plans to move to Virgin Hall."

"Why does he want to buy it, then? A sudden urge to speculate in land?"

"He didn't say."

"Any idea what he wants to pay?"

"Uncle bought it from Daniel's father for two thousand pounds."

A crafty look crept like a thief into Balcombe's bloodshot eyes. "You don't happen to know, just between the two of us, how Napoleon intends to pay for it? He puts it about that he doesn't have a brass farthing. He had to sell his silver plate last year just to get by."

"Mr. Balcombe," she said, allowing a whiff of impatience to show, "I'm sure you know that the emperor smuggled out millions of gold napoleons on the *Northumberland*. He sold off his imperial plate to pretend he was penniless, to drum up sympathy in Europe."

Balcombe didn't dispute it. He'd heard that Napoleon's valet Louis Marchand had split a fortune into money belts that were worn by just about everyone in Bonaparte's party. He could tell by the itching of his palms that he was about to get his hands on a life-saving chunk of French gold.

Samuel Knipe, although very ill, received Balcombe, now sober, when he called on him the next morning.

After the usual pleasantries, Balcombe said, "I have a client who wishes to buy Virgin Hall."

The old man gazed at Balcombe with watery eyes as if he didn't quite understand him. "Virgin Hall?" he said eventually. "I can't sell it. I promised to rent it to Daniel."

"Daniel!" said Balcombe, springing at the idea. "Exactly! My client wants to buy it for Daniel—buy it, not rent it—because the boy has been of such great help in certain private matters. A secret gift."

Samuel still had enough of his business acumen left to be confused. "But why buy it for Daniel if I plan to rent it to him for next to nothing, as a wedding present?"

"A wedding present?"

"He must marry Charlotte," wheezed Samuel. "To get the property."

"But Samuel, Daniel's got too much going on in his life right now, with his botanical duties and whatnot. Also, he's so young, barely in his middling twenties. He's not established. No need to force him into marriage. Let my client give Virgin Hall to him. You have so many heirs who are depending on you. This way there will be more money for them when…when the time comes."

This tactless reminder of his imminent demise took the wind out of Samuel's sails. He lay back on his pillows, clearly thinking things over. Balcombe didn't interrupt him. "This client of yours, he's French, isn't he?" the old man asked eventually.

"That I may not reveal, save to say that there are indeed high matters at stake here, matters that will advance both Daniel's and Charlotte's prospects."

Samuel sighed. "Agreed, then. I have no intention of making a profit on this sale. It is a family affair. So long as Daniel is named as owner in the title deed, I shall sell it for what I paid. Two thousand pounds."

"Done!" said Balcombe without the slightest hesitation.

That afternoon Gaspard called on Balcombe's shabby office in town, which didn't have many callers these days. "The emperor believes you have a price for Virgin Hall," he said.

"Yes. I got it for a bargain. Three thousand pounds."

Gaspard savored the amount for a moment. "*Three* thousand it is. But the sale must be confidential," he said.

"Of course. I will take care of all the paperwork, General. You know you can rely on me."

"We know," said Gaspard. He turned sharply on his heel, leaving Balcombe shuffling papers to decide which of his creditors he would pay off first.

"Balcombe sold his soul for a mere one thousand pounds!" Gaspard crowed when he returned to Napoleon with the news.

Napoleon walked to the window, took a pinch of snuff, clasped his hands behind his back, and stared at the rain drumming on the low roof. "Souls are cheap in Saint Helena."

The leaky ceiling admitted a large drop of water that hit him on the nose and teared its way down his cheek. He didn't flinch. "Gaspard, I need you to take Daniel swimming," he said.

Close to noon a few days later Daniel, who had just left Charlotte selling peaches and potatoes in her mother's front porch store, was walking up to the Botanical Gardens when Gaspard with a saddled horse in tow thundered past him, took a wide turn in the street, to the consternation of the resident dogs, and then thundered right back.

Daniel had seen the Frenchman only once, at the Almond Tree, since the drunken dinner at Plantation House when Charlotte had brought up the painful matter of the missing leeches. He had been polite but hardly effusive.

Now he radiated bonhomie. "Daniel, *mon ami*," he crowed, his large Gallic nose in the air and an even larger grin on his lips. "I have found you at last! Walking is good for the constitution, but I'm sure you will make a more suitable impression on the ladies when seated on a horse! See"—he gestured at the little nag—"I have brought you one! The emperor has heard your knowledge of the local plants is absolutely prodigious, so he sent me to learn from you. What do you say we ride up into the mountains for an hour or two? I have lunch and a bottle of good wine in my saddlebag."

Daniel looked at the slavering beast he was being offered. At least it was less threatening than a duel, but threatening all the same. He'd ridden with Charlotte as a child, but going mounted was not how apprentices at Kew got around. "I'm afraid I'm not that much of a horseman," he said, trying to divine what lay behind the Frenchman's surprise invitation.

"Nonsense! This horse is as quiet as a lamb, quite boring, in fact, a big favorite with the weaker sex. Hop on. If you don't like it, you can always fall off!"

Daniel ran excuses through his mind. That he had urgent business. An appointment. A shipment of plants to inventory. But it seemed the Gaspard was reading his thoughts. "Come on, be a devil. I'm so sick of the stale conversation at Longwood. You can't imagine how boring it is. Everyone gets on everyone else's nerves. The emperor is in one of his black moods. He's sheer hell. Almost as bad as when he's elated. Your company will be like a breath of fresh air. We'll talk about London. You can tell me all about the English ladies. You are so…so presentable that I'm sure there were dozens of those. And I'll tell you war stories—I certainly have hundreds of those. We got off to a bad start, you and I. Someone nearly got killed. Let's turn to a fresh page, what do you say? Please say yes!"

145

Daniel didn't dare say anything else.

"What did you talk about?" Charlotte asked Daniel as they sipped sherry at the Almond Tree that evening.

"Except for answering a few botanical questions, all I did was listen. He's only thirty-four, but he's had an extraordinary life already."

"Really?" said Charlotte, not liking the hint of hero worship in his voice.

The object of their conversation walked up with Mary Porteous beaming proudly on his arm. For an hour Charlotte had to listen, with growing irritation, to Gaspard describing his battles, in which he always, for some unfathomable reason, played the central role. What made matters worse was that he said nothing to her, directing his graphic descriptions at Mary and Daniel, whose face increasingly wore the same adoring expression as Mary's did.

It wasn't that Gaspard was ignoring her. Just the opposite. She had the distinct impression the whole point of his heroic monologue was aimed at her. He was crowing about the fact that he had captivated both of the people closest to her. It was his way of taking revenge on her for refusing to go to that little room near the wharf with him.

Every day that passed, and days soon passed into months, was another twist of the rack.

"It's such pleasant weather, Daniel. Shall we go up Sister's Walk this afternoon?" Charlotte would ask.

"Dearest, I'd love to. But I've promised Gaspard"— yes, Daniel was calling the villain by his first name now— "to go riding to Sandy Bay." Or: "Nothing I'd like better, but Gaspard has borrowed one of Napoleon's pistols for me. Imagine that! A pistol that's been fired by the emperor himself right in my hand!" Or: "Gaspard has been invited to Plantation House for tea and insists I go along with him.

He's keen to show the governor that these days he prefers English company."

"Am I not invited as well?"

"I will have to ask Gaspard if that would be suitable."

"Don't bother," Charlotte said. "I promised Mother I'd feed our rotten fruit to the pigs this afternoon." It was difficult to keep the bitterness out of her voice. Napoleon had warned her that the battle to get Gaspard sent on his mission to England would not be won easily, that it would strain her relationship with Daniel. She hadn't realized how much.

On September 21, 1817 an earthquake, although modest in magnitude, shook the island. It did nothing to shake it awake. Charlotte sold vegetables and fruit. Daniel attended to his garden. They pretended to be in love but the long shadow of Gaspard fell between them like a chasm.

It wasn't until February that matters came to a head. Gaspard called on Porteous House and told Mary that he and Daniel were going to exercise with sabers that afternoon at a little pool called Nymph's Pond, which was near Longwood. He also told Mary, in his bullying way with her, to bring Rosebud, as Daniel very much wanted to show her how much progress he'd made in the manly arts.

Mary's homely face was so alive with excitement that Charlotte couldn't say no.

Because the island was very quiet away from Jamestown, except for the sighing of the wind, they heard the clang of the swords a mile away. The martial athletes were at work on each other on the banks of the little pool. Both had their shirts off, their fine young bodies shiny with sweat. Gaspard touched his forehead with his saber in salute. Daniel, a quick learner, did likewise. The younger man hadn't quite recovered his stance when Gaspard darted a surprise stab at him, which he was only just able to parry.

Ten minutes later Gaspard called it a day. Daniel looked as exhausted as he looked happy. "I don't know about you," said the general, "but if the ladies will excuse us, I'm dying for a swim."

"Does that mean we have to withdraw?" asked Charlotte.

"What on earth are you hinting at? Of course you must withdraw," said Daniel with a giggle that sounded almost girlish, Charlotte thought. "We'll come find you when we're done."

"Nonsense. You're welcome to watch," said Gaspard, loosening his trousers. "I'm a great believer in heroic nudity. All the athletes competed totally naked in the ancient Olympic Games, you know!"

"Spare me!" Mary put her hands over her eyes but peeped through her fingers as if hinting that she couldn't resist a look at what Gaspard was about to reveal, then raced off into the woods, shrieking with laughter.

Of course Charlotte couldn't stay. She followed Mary, although at a more sedate pace. She found her resting on a mossy bank, her ample bosom heaving from the exertion of her narrow escape from the spectacle of heroic nudity. There they sat, too hidden to see, but close enough to hear the men splashing and laughing.

Suddenly the laughing stopped and it fell quiet except for the croaking of the frogs. "What's the matter?" whispered Mary. "We'd better take a look in case they've drowned."

But they hadn't drowned. Far worse. Their nude bodies were embracing in the shallows. Daniel had his back to them, but Gaspard was peering over Daniel's shoulder, smiling triumphantly at them.

Charlotte was sure the men, if you could call them that, heard her gasp of horror. She didn't care. Longwood was just ten minutes away. She would tell Napoleon what

148

he could do with his strategy! It was strategic for Gaspard and Daniel to appear to be friends. But lovers! Never!

"What's the matter?" Napoleon asked when she was shown into his presence, her eyes awash with emerald tears that had been welling up for months.

"Daniel. Gaspard has stolen him away from me!"

His haunted eyes examined her. "Tell me."

He listened attentively, a disconcerting smile toying with his lips. When she finished he let loose his bray of a laugh. "What? Did Gaspard actually bugger the boy?"

"I didn't wait to see. He's gone far beyond just pretending to be friends with Daniel, as you instructed. He's been seducing him with his endless boasting. Now Daniel adores the monster!"

Napoleon laughed again. "I've never heard of a strategy working too well!"

"Well, this one is, Your Majesty."

A crafty look crept into the deep set eyes. "Did Gaspard know you were watching?"

"Yes! He smirked at me!"

"Ha! That's the explanation right there!"

"Your Majesty?"

"Gaspard was mixing business with pleasure. Where's your female intuition? Gaspard is in love with you! Deliciously and hopelessly besotted. He's accustomed to having any woman he wants. He wants you all the more because you have refused him. What he's doing is taking his revenge. Let him bugger you instead, and he will leave your precious Daniel alone! You are provoking him."

"You honestly think—"

"Of course you are! You're a woman. You can't resist." A stray thought seemed to strike him. "Oh, Josephine!" he sighed. "How can you abandon me in this wasteland?"

"Your Majesty, I am not provoking him. I am being civil to him for your sake, because that's what you asked me to do. It's a sacrifice."

"Sacrifice!" Napoleon thundered. "Let me tell you what sacrifice is! It's fifty thousand fine young men turned into stinking corpses in just one day. Riderless horses trying to outrun their own dragging entrails." He paused and, standing very still, hands clasped behind his back, gazed out the window at the gum trees bowing in obedience to the perpetual gale. Charlotte didn't dare interrupt him.

Eventually he spoke. "You are beautiful. In spite of your modest birth, Gaspard will be proud to have you on his arm. When our strategy succeeds, when my jailer sends Gaspard to England, and that will be soon—the matter is being settled as we speak—I want you to go with him."

The ill wind was howling so loudly that Charlotte thought she'd misheard. "Your Majesty?"

"Gaspard is magnificent, but he is erratic. He needs to be supervised. He needs to be led around like a chimpanzee on a chain. Who better to do that than a woman he's in love with? Think of it as an act of revenge for his attempt to seduce Daniel."

An awful thought struck Charlotte, that the incident at Nymph's Pond had been Napoleon's idea. "Your Majesty—"

He knew what she was about to say but didn't allow her to go on. "I want you to make sure Gaspard speaks to the right people about how I am forced to live. I want you to corroborate everything he says, to add observations of your own. When you return to me, I expect a full report."

For a long moment Charlotte was speechless, overwhelmed by the exultation of having just been vaulted onto the galloping charger of history. "You want me to spy on him?"

"Yes. Beauty is the best disguise. It will take you everywhere, where even Gaspard cannot go. It will help you deliver a letter for me. This one."

When she took the letter, she noticed, once again, how impeccably manicured he kept the fingers that had once pulled the strings of a mighty empire, unblemished except for the dusting of snuff between thumb and forefinger. The letter was sealed with the imperial eagle, just like the scrolls had been. She turned it over. There was no address on it. All that was written there was one word in Napoleon's scrawl.

*Byron.*

"You must deliver it to him in person," Napoleon said.

There was an urgency to her words, the loud whisper of a collaborator. "Your Majesty, the newspapers say Byron has left England. He's in Europe—Italy, I think."

"So was I!" said Napoleon. "I won my first great victory there, Montenotte in '96. If you cannot deliver it to Byron in person, destroy it. Unopened. It is for his eyes only. Do you understand?"

"Yes."

"You are also to deliver a verbal message to Lady Holland, hostess to England's Liberal establishment."

"Yes, Your Majesty."

Napoleon lowered his voice, although the only living thing within earshot was the lamenting wind. "My jailer has instructed Dr. O'Meara, my own doctor, to murder me."

Charlotte held Napoleon's gaze. She knew the jovial Irish doctor well. He loved to talk, and she was very happy to listen. He had laughed when he told her that anecdote about the hemorrhoid-hungry leeches, which had later caused such a sensation when she had mentioned it at

Sir Hudson Lowe's dinner. Trying to turn this kindly man into an assassin? Unspeakable !
"If that leaked out!" she said.
"Of course. It's a bigger mountain of gunpowder than the Russians tried to blow me up with when I called on the Kremlin. The revelation must be a mighty explosion, not a feeble series of damp squibs. That's why Gaspard can't be trusted with it, why no one can, except for you. It must be delivered to Lady Holland as a secret that she must keep secret at all costs. Only then will she put all her energy into betraying it."

After their Grecian tableau at Nymph's Pond, Gaspard had parted company with Daniel at the Botanical Gardens. As arranged young Basil Jackson, whom Gaspard had moved in with a few days before, supposedly because he could no longer stand the sight of Napoleon, kept a seat for him at the Almond Tree. Gaspard was on his second fruit cocktail laced with *tungi* when Marchand, chief valet and keeper of the imperial purse, passed by with a curt nod and continued on to the run-down offices of Balcombe, Fowler, and Cole. When Balcombe heard Marchand was outside asking to see him, he found inspiration in the bottle of brandy he kept in his drawer, because he knew Marchand was a hard man and so he needed to be at his best.

The bag Marchand fished out of his pocket made a pleasant chinking sound when he dropped it on the desk. "As agreed with General Gaspard, the equivalent of three thousand English pounds in gold napoleons for Virgin Hall," he said. "You have the title deed?"

"Yes, and as requested I have made young Daniel Hamilton the new owner," said Balcombe, "although, as requested, Daniel is not to know at this time. Is that still so?"

152

"Yes. The house is to be a gift. When the time comes."

"May I know why?" said Balcombe.

Marchand, who was a master at imitating his betters, ignored the question as he ran his eyes over the title deed. "It says here, 'in full and sufficient payment,' but it does not say the amount."

The brandy began to work its magic, so Balcombe was ready with the riposte. "That's the custom here in Saint Helena. It's thought to be vulgar to specify amounts."

"How extraordinary," said the valet, "for the island is vulgar in every other way. Gossip, for example. Gossip has it that Samuel Knipe sold Virgin Hall for two thousand pounds, not three."

Balcombe's mouth was suddenly very dry. He itched to wet it with another medicinal dose. "There may have been the matter of a commission, but I don't recall the details." He tried to brush off Marchand with a superior smile, but what limped onto his lips was crippled and sickly. "As I'm sure you can appreciate, I have so many large transactions passing through this office that the details of the small ones tend to escape me."

"Really?" said Napoleon's valet, looking around at the peeling wallpaper. "And here I was thinking that your business was slow! Never mind, the buyer has instructed me to ignore wagging tongues in exchange for your doing him a favor."

Balcombe of course knew perfectly well who the buyer was. "A favor? Certainly, if it's in my power."

"It certainly is," Marchand said taking a bundle of sealed letters out of his pocket. "These are letters the buyer urgently needs delivered to London. The *Dragon* sails this evening . I believe your company has been supplying her?"

"Indeed. I go on board frequently. The captain is a friend."

"Is he reliable?"

"Very!"

"That's what we heard. And to ensure security, you would hand the letters over to him personally?"

"Of course."

"And immediately," said the valet. "A longboat is waiting for you."

Marchand left with the title deed and headed for the Almond Tree. He touched his hat to Gaspard and nodded as he passed by. Gaspard paid his bill and walked over the road to the Castle, where he demanded to see the governor immediately because he was bringing urgent news.

"Urgent?" said Governor Lowe when Gaspard was shown in.

"Letters, Your Excellency, inflammatory letters from Napoleon denouncing you to the Liberals in England. Balcombe is about to deliver them to the *Dragon*."

Lowe narrowed his eyes. "How do you know?"

"Although I am estranged from *General* Bonaparte, I still have my sources. His valet Marchand is in my pocket."

The governor examined Gaspard carefully with his sideways look. The young general's uniform was becoming noticeably threadbare, but he still knew how to stand to attention. "You have moved in with young Basil Jackson, I believe?"

"Yes, Your Excellency, a few days ago. I can no longer stand Napoleon or his French entourage. They sicken me. I prefer British company."

"That's why you have become close friends with Daniel Hamilton, I suppose."

"Yes, Your Excellency. I have grown to like the boy. He proved his courage by accepting my challenge to a duel. Just as well I didn't kill him. He's helping me improve my English."

A ghost of a smile made a fleeting appearance on Lowe's thin lips. "I hear you want to go to London to denounce Bonaparte. What I don't know is whether I can trust you."

"That's why I'm here, sir. To earn your trust."

"Tell me more about the letters."

Neither Balcombe nor the letters he carried reached the *Dragon*. The longboat carrying both purveyor and package was visited by harbor police before it even cast off, police who seemed to know exactly what they were looking for. Balcombe, in spite of his loud protests, was arrested and thrown into prison, where he shared a cell with a drunken sailor who was as desperate for a drink as he was.

While Balcombe was doing his best to shut his ears to the drunken old salt's demented rants, Sir Hudson Lowe was reading the confiscated letters. They were a nightmare revisited. The more Lowe read, the more furious he became. The worst thing was that they were not downright falsehoods. They were half-truths spiced with lies, a treat that would be caviar to England's Liberal circles. How fortunate that General Gaspard Gourgaud had tipped him off! How brave of the young cockerel to march into his office and betray his emperor! He had just proved himself. The *emperor* must already have a price on Gaspard's head. The cockerel had to be protected, kept alive so he could set the record straight in England. So he could testify to the vast web of lies being spun by the black spider lurking in that dark, damp house on Deadwood Plain! He must arrange it so Gaspard Gourgaud started right at the top, with Holland House, Liberal England's Vatican, presided over by Lord and Lady Holland, who worshipped the French Satan and invited the cream of Liberal society to worship with them. Dangerous traitors the Hollands were, traitors who would go to any lengths to promote the interests of their dark master, Napoleon.

Lowe knew all he needed to know about the Hollands from personal experience. When they heard that Lowe was to be Napoleon's jailer, they had tried to overawe Lowe by inviting him, a simple officer, to their heady functions. He had rubbed shoulders with the likes of Talleyrand and Wellington and that degenerate Lord Byron, no less! Not once but eight times he was invited to walk the hallowed halls of Holland House, basking in the obsequious attention of the mighty, everyone by word or sigh begging him to loosen the bite of the shackles binding his prisoner-to-be.

They were wasting their time. When he got to Saint Helena, he had done the opposite. He had tightened Napoleon's shackles. The beast had escaped from captivity once, from polite confinement on the island of Elba. A hundred days of war followed that had cost Europe another fifty thousand brave young men. Bonaparte must not be allowed to kill again!

Lowe consigned the lying letters to the flames. His toes curled with pleasure inside his boots as he imagined the faces of the Bonapartist sheep hearing the truth about Napoleon from Napoleon's favorite general! At the same moment, Lowe heard the whistle of an assassin's bullet, felt the stab of the knife in the back, the spreading agony of deadly poison in the gut. The brave young general had already been poisoned once. The sooner this apostle for the cause of peace was sent off this treacherous rock to spread the truth in England the better. Lowe would command the *Dragon* to sweep him to safety!

In the grip of a frenzied decision, Lowe hurried up the steps to a balcony with a view of the sea. But the *Dragon*, which had long ago set sail, was nothing more than a white fleck on the horizon.

Lowe took his fury out on Balcombe, still in prison. The failed trader was soon reduced to a tearful wreck.

"What is the next passenger ship going home?" Lowe asked him, his voice seething with contempt.

Balcombe pulled himself together with a painful effort, looked Lowe in the eye. "Should be the *Winchelsea*, Your Excellency. She's due in soon."

"You will settle your affairs, and you and your family will be aboard her. You are fortunate I am not indicting you for treason."

Balcombe's resolution deserted him with alarming speed. "Please, Sir Hudson," he begged, "I have helped the government once. With the matter of the smuggled scrolls."

"By demanding money for exposing that Rosebud wench's poisonous letters? Hardly patriotism."

Balcombe didn't contest the point. "May I at least say, for my family's sake, that we are leaving because of my wife's illness? It is true that her hepatitis is being aggravated by our long stay in this tropical climate."

To protract the villain's agony, Lowe made a point of giving the request lengthy consideration. Eventually he said, "Yes, you may say that."

Balcombe was so pathetically grateful that it inspired Lowe with another brilliant idea. "In fact, I will go a step farther. I am going to supply you with lively company. General Gaspard Gourgaud."

# Chapter 11: Mission to England

Only the southeaster flies faster than gossip in Saint Helena. Charlotte, on her way back from Longwood late that afternoon, heard all about Gaspard's betrayal and poor Mr. Balcombe's exile before she found Daniel sequestered in the Botanical Gardens.

"Did you enjoy your swim in Nymph's Pond this morning?" said Charlotte, as cool as the fresh mountain water must have been.

"Well enough," Daniel said with a cheerful laugh. "Except Gaspard tried to embrace me—can you believe it! The man's a goat!"

"Embrace you? You're teasing me!"

"You didn't see? Mary did."

She searched his eyes. "And exactly what did Mary see?"

"We were standing there, ankle deep, drying off, when Gaspard pretended a biting fly had landed on my back. He made as if he was going to slap it, but instead he threw both arms around me and blubbered something about passion into my ear. I pushed him away, of course."

"Of course!" said Charlotte—somewhat archly, Daniel thought.

"He apologized immediately, said he was really sorry. But he wasn't really—that was obvious. Don't tell Mary, but you could have run a flag up his mast, if you know what I mean! I went looking for you. Found Mary had locked herself in her bedroom. I asked her where you were, through the door, but all that did was make her howl all the louder. Where have you been? Even your mother didn't know."

"I was upset too, seeing you in flagrante. So I went to see Boney. For advice."

"And opened your heart to him, I suppose. Do tell, what did the great man say?"

"Not much. He seemed to know all about it. He had more important matters on his mind."

"I should hope so."

"You obviously haven't heard. It's the talk of the Almond Tree. Governor Lowe is sending Gaspard to England."

Daniel stared at her in blank amazement. "What?"

"Poor Mr. Balcombe has been caught trying to smuggle out a batch of Napoleon's letters. They say he's been exiled. Everybody's saying it was Gaspard who tipped off the governor, because he was seen going into the Castle before Mr. Balcombe's arrest, and then a couple of hours later Gaspard was given permission to go back to Europe."

"Well, I'll be damned," said Daniel, clearly astonished by the news.

"There's more, my darling," she said. "I know this is going to hurt because if it doesn't you wouldn't love me. When Gaspard goes Boney wants me to go with him."

Daniel stared at her, sure she was teasing and then sure she wasn't. "With him?" he croaked.

"The Balcombes will be sailing on the same boat as Gaspard, they say. The story will be put about that I'm to be the Balcombe girls' companion."

"No one will believe that! Everybody knows you hate the Balcombe girls, and that includes Governor Lowe."

"Lowe will be told that the real reason I want to go is that I'm eloping with Gaspard. The governor will like to hear that, because he thinks it will hurt Boney."

For a long moment, Daniel was speechless. "Charlotte, how can you? We have only just reunited. Now you want to abandon me?"

"Darling you must know it's the last thing I want to do. It's tearing my heart in two. But I must do this for Boney, he needs me to go. It will only be for a few months, I promise. What's that in a lifetime together? Boney says Gaspard needs someone to keep an eye on him, to anchor him, someone presentable who can accompany him everywhere. A Saint Helena native who can confirm what he says about the island is the truth."

They held each other's eyes, his troubled, hers filling with tears. "Do you want to go?" Daniel asked.

"I must! Boney's helpless. He's depending on me! I feel it's my duty. Please say yes because I won't go if you say no!"

"And you'll make me regret it forever after. You can't wait to spread your wings, can you? And since when have you needed my permission to do anything you please?"

She threw her arms around him, kissed him so hard it hurt. "Oh, I do love you so much!"


"Eloping with a young French general! You can't do that! What about Daniel?" piped Samuel Knipe in a voice that was growing weaker by the month.

Charlotte was alone with her frail uncle, who was propped up in what everyone was already calling his deathbed. "Uncle Samuel, I'm only *pretending* to elope with him, to pull the wool over the governor's eyes! Daniel understands. I detest Gaspard Gourgaud, but the emperor wants me to help him get the news out. It's only for a month or two, I promise. You'll be better by the time I get back."

Samuel had more strength in his wits than in his body. "Nonsense, I'll probably be dead. Exactly why does he need your help?"

Charlotte looked at the drawn, wrinkled face, tying to divine how much her uncle knew and how much she needed to tell him. "To confirm that Governor Lowe is a cruel tyrant, of course."

"You seem to be fishing in very troubled waters," the old man said with a sigh. His thoughts drifted. A smile courted his thin lips. "You will rub shoulders with the aristocracy," he rambled. "Visit stately homes. Attend grand receptions. Just think, a Knipe might even be presented to the prince regent!" He held out his skeletal hand. It was cold to the touch. "You will have the honor of our name in your hands. I will make sure you have enough money to be dependent on no one. But I do worry about Daniel. What does he think of all this…this espionage? When will you return to him? I want you to marry and live together at Virgin Hall. It's what I promised Daniel's father."

"Soon, very soon. As soon as I've done my duty. Daniel understands that."

There were tears in her uncle's eyes. "Soon, then. Or I'm afraid it will not be soon enough for me."

"What?" screeched Mary, thrusting four fingers of her right hand into her mouth. She'd confined herself to bed, looked awful, hair unbrushed, face unwashed except by a perpetual stream of tears.

Charlotte had put off giving her the news. Told everyone likely to see Mary to do the same. But eventually one of the black chambermaids had whispered just enough to get Mary screaming, and so here she was, facing the fury of the storm.

"Why are *you* going with him? Why not *me*? You're running off together, aren't you? This excuse that the reason you're going is to chaperone the Balcombe brats is just a damnable lie, isn't it? You're eloping with the man

I love, with the only man I've ever loved. How could you do this to me? You, of all people, my very best friend, my only friend in the world, betraying me! You have no idea what it's like to be in love with someone who you know is too good for you. Go fetch Gaspard—I want to hear this from his own lips! Coldly, heartlessly abandoning me and running off with you! Go fetch him, because if he doesn't come to me I will most certainly go to him."

Charlotte was surprised how calm she felt, like she heard it was in the eye of a hurricane, as she walked a slippery tightrope of lies. "You and I, two young Yamstock girls," she said to Mary, "have been caught up in great matters. We are mere pawns in a game. I hate Gaspard for insulting me in public, calling me horrible names—you know that. But the governor needs someone to keep an eye on him. To make sure he accomplishes his mission. Can Mr. Balcombe keep an eye on Gaspard in London? Of course he can't!"

"Why not? Is there something wrong with Gaspard like there's obviously something wrong with me?" said Mary, choking on a sob.

"Because Gaspard needs to travel in the best social circles to get his message out. Mr. Balcombe is a trader. Little better than a shopkeeper. He won't be admitted anywhere."

"But you will, that's what you're saying, isn't it? Why not me? It's because I'm not beautiful like you, isn't it? Not beautiful!" she howled.

"No, it's not that," Charlotte lied. "The governor doesn't know you. He knows me."

"It's Gaspard I'm talking about, not the governor. Why is Gaspard abandoning me?"

"Because he's a soldier who has to do his duty," was the best Charlotte could come up with.

"You're not telling me the truth. It's not the governor! It's Boney, isn't it? He's behind all of this!"

Charlotte couldn't tell Mary that she'd stumbled onto the truth. "It's best if Gaspard explains it all to you. Mary, I know you think he's the only man on earth right now. But he's not. If Gaspard doesn't return, you will find someone else, I promise you. The island is full of dashing young officers."

But it wasn't the prospect of finding someone new that prompted Mary Porteous to jump out of bed and pull on her shoes. "Where is he? Your fiancé!"

"Gaspard's not my—"

"Tell me!"

"Gaspard is at Basil Jackson's, as far as I know."

"Then that's where I'm going."

"You can't go out in public like that! Put on a fresh dress. At least do your face and your hair!"

"No! I want everyone to see what you two have done to me! How could you, Charlotte? You of all people, how could you?" Abruptly, the defiant mood fled. Mary threw herself back onto her bed. She pulled the bedcovers over her even though she was still wearing her shoes. "Leave me, Jezebel," she whispered, turning her face to the wall. "I never wish to see either of you ever again."


Charlotte called with Gaspard at Porteous House the next day, ready to explain almost everything to Mary. She sent word that she didn't want to see them. Charlotte called on her every day that followed but always got the same answer. She and Gaspard tried again the morning the ship sailed, but she was not receiving visitors. Mary didn't emerge from her bedroom until she got news that the *Winchelsea* had set sail with Charlotte, Gaspard, and the Balcombes on board. It was March 18, 1818, just three

163

weeks after the memorable events at Nymph's Pond. She hurried up Ladder Hill and watched until the boat sank below the horizon. It wasn't the plaintive cry of a bird swooping down from the cliffs that reared above Jamestown. It was Mary Porteous screaming as she fell.

By sunset the news, told in whispers, was everywhere. She had been at least three months pregnant.

# Chapter 12: Ship of Fools

Charlotte felt a heartstring snap as the last of the little island disappeared down the gullet of the vast ocean, taking Daniel with it. Dearest Daniel! He had been so magnificently brave about her departure.

"It's only fair," he'd quipped, although there were tears in his eyes. "First I go to London and leave you here. Then you go to London and leave me here."

"Darling it will be for just a few months, not seven years. All the same I shall miss you so very much, you know that!"

"Oh, no, you won't. You'll arrive in London at the height of the Season. There will be dances and receptions every night. You will be on the arm of Napoleon's most dashing general. You won't have time to think of us poor Yamstocks!"

He was only half joking, she knew that. "My darling I will come back soon, very soon, I promise. As soon as Gaspard has spun Boney's web and caught a cartload of fat Liberals in it!"

He'd gazed at her then, a wistful look, as if he had lost her already. "Charlotte, don't come back for my sake. I love you too much to be second best, yours only because you feel you owe yourself to me. I can't bear the thought of you living a life of regret, looking at a mere botanist at breakfast when you could have been looking at a baron or an earl."

The pretty little speech stung Charlotte, because she knew there was an awful truth lurking there.


The Honorable East India Company's ship the *Winchelsea*, 1,331 tons, the southeaster filling her sails, plowed northward on her six-week journey to England. Charlotte's hands tightened on the rail as the boat heeled. Her thoughts drifted.

The day before the ship set sail, Napoleon had sent for her. He was alone in his tiny study when Marchand showed her in, sitting at his tiny desk. For what seemed to be a long time he examined her without speaking. A rat scampered across the floor. He ignored it.

"What time do you sail?" Napoleon's interrogation begun.

"Tomorrow afternoon, Your Majesty."

"At least you will have Betsy Balcombe for company," he teased, because he knew Charlotte couldn't stand the brat. "She calls us Boney. Did you know that?"

"Yes, Your M—"

"Since you are closer than a friend, you may call me that, too." A quick smile revealed his tiny licorice-stained teeth. "Betsy, ah, Betsy! We played games, you know, two years ago. Blind man's buff. She was too young to be afraid." He sighed, flicked away a fly. "For her sake we regret we had to sacrifice her father to win Gaspard's freedom. A casualty of war. Mrs. Balcombe will school you in manners, because you have so few. You must disguise yourself as a lady."

"I'll do my best, Your Majesty. I mean, Boney."

"Ha! Boney. How delicious that sounds coming out of your mouth." His expression changed in an instant to one of infinite longing. Charlotte was swimming in his eyes. "Rosebud, you must come back, even if you don't succeed. Especially if you don't succeed. I don't think I can survive on this cursed rock without you."

"Are you savoring your escape?" It was Gaspard grasping the rail next to her, dressed in faded regimentals that bristled with slightly corroded medals.

"Not really," Charlotte said. "Because now I am your captive."

"If only I were yours!" He smirked. "With hands as beautiful as yours holding me tight, I would be the most willing captive on earth."

Charlotte did her best to mask her irritation at the innuendo. "Gaspard we are yoked to the same plow. It would be best if we repaired our relationship so we cut a straight furrow."

He laughed at the rustic metaphor. "I see I've unnerved you enough to bring out the Yamstock in you. But alas, I'm not an ox. I'm an ordnance officer. All I know is how to blow up things!"

"You also know how to provoke."

Gaspard seemed to need a respite from the game they were playing. "Peace! I come waving an olive branch."

"Which is?"

"I have fallen in love."

Charlotte felt a prick of annoyance when her heart beat faster. "Not with me, I hope!"

"Certainly not."

She gazed at him to see if he were making another fruitless attempt at being humorous, but his raised eyebrow did nothing more than invite the obvious question. "All right, with whom?"

"Betsy Balcombe."

"Gaspard, seriously, she's a child!"

"She's not. She's sixteen."

"Forgotten about Mary so soon?"

"As you know perfectly well, it is Mary who pursues me. She clings to me like a vine. She's probably

167

gone and stowed herself away in the bilges and will emerge triumphant at bedtime."

"So you cut her loose?"

"As you know perfectly well, I tried to let her down gently, but she refused to see me. Also, mademoiselle, she refused to see you."

"Can you blame her, after your disgusting overtures to Daniel?"

"Your relationship with him recovered from that amusing incident rather quickly, if I may say so."

"Because he was the innocent party. Passion, indeed! He knows nothing of passion. He's an innocent. Have you no shame?"

Gaspard examined his nails as if he wanted to make sure there was no gunpowder under them. "A sense of shame is an expensive quality. It requires sacrifices that often aren't worth making. However, I wager that I have a more highly developed sense of shame than you have a sense of honesty. Quite frankly, beauty has made you the most accomplished liar I've ever met. The way you pretended you wanted Daniel to fight me. That was masterful!"


The morning after Saint Helena was swallowed by the South Atlantic, Charlotte sat on the forward deck with Balcombe and his wife, already much improved by the sea air, and Betsy, who was keeping an ardent eye open for Gaspard.

"How many social classes are there on Saint Helena?" Balcombe asked her.

"Three, I suppose," said Charlotte. "Slaves, us Yamstocks, and you English."

"Well, in England there are at least nine!" piped Betsy.

168

"Impossible!" said Charlotte. "How could you possibly keep track of what class you were in?"

"You don't need to remember," said Mrs. Balcombe. "Because if you don't keep in your place, you will soon be put there."

Betsy was suddenly so absorbed in playing the teacher that she missed the magnificent sight of General Baron Gaspard Gourgaud strutting onto the deck. "Paupers, poor things, are right at the bottom."

"And then come the working poor," said her mother. "Above them are servants. Then craftsmen and tradesmen."

"And then the middle classes, such as teachers and doctors and business owners," said her father.

"So you Balcombes are middle class?" said Charlotte, who already knew the answer to that question.

Mr. Balcombe glanced at Mrs. Balcombe for support. "No, we're more like the next class up. The gentry," he said. "At least in Saint Helena we were gentry, because we owned an estate."

At this Mrs. Balcombe shook her head. "If it hadn't been for my illness…we're in transition now, until we find our feet. But we do have some fine connections. We're expecting Mr. Balcombe to go into government."

"Above gentry comes the aristocracy," persevered Betsy.

"So Sir Hudson Lowe is an aristocrat?" asked Charlotte, who would have thought much less of the aristocracy if he were.

"Oh, dear, no!" said Mrs. Balcombe with a sniff. "He's just a knight. You have to have a hereditary title to be an aristocrat. A noble bloodline."

"Then comes royalty," Mr. Balcombe came in quickly as if he wanted to get this business over with.

"And right at the top of the heap sits Prinny," said Betsy. "Which is what *le bon ton* calls the prince regent."

Charlotte was distracted by a flying fish sailing above the waves. "The *ton*?"

"Oh, dear," said Mrs. Balcombe. "I see we really are going to have to start at the beginning. *Le bon ton* is what society calls itself."

"And Charlotte you are completely *ton* deaf!" said Betsy with a silly giggle.

"I've actually met Prinny, you know. More than once," said Balcombe, not trying to hide the pride in his voice. "When I was a boy. In fact, my brother still serves him as an equerry."

"It was all because of a terrible accident!" Betsy trilled, because she had just caught sight of Gaspard, who touched his hat to her with what came very close to a leer. "Tell her, Daddy, I've quite forgotten how it goes!"

Balcombe shifted in his chair, clearly made uncomfortable by Gaspard's appearance.

"Tell her, William," Mrs. Balcombe said. "She might as well know."

Balcombe sighed. "All right, then, it was a mishap, a dreadful one. You see, my father was the captain of a frigate in the early days of the French Revolution. One night, in a dreadful fog, he was run down by the prince regent's yacht just off Brighton. He went down with his ship."

"I'm so sorry to hear that," said Charlotte. She'd heard the old rumor that William Balcombe, like so many others, was the illegitimate son of the prince regent, a rumor he was slow to deny. But she hadn't heard the story that Prinny had killed his father.

"The prince regent was devastated, of course," said Mrs. Balcombe, who, Charlotte knew, was much more intelligent than her husband. "This happened in 1789, you see, the year the Bastille fell in Paris. It gave the impression that Prinny was like one of those French aristocrats who ran over peasants for sport. He went to great lengths to make amends."

"He adopted my brother and me," said Balcombe, trying his best to sound offhand.

"I think *adopted* is too strong a word, dear," said Mrs. Balcombe.

"Perhaps. But Prinny extended what's called the king's bounty to us. We were given a royal education. We even spent time at Carlton House—that's the prince's London residence, you know. He appointed his private secretary, Sir Thomas Tyrwhitt, as our guardian. I will do Sir Thomas the courtesy of waiting on him the moment we arrive in London." He smiled at the happy thought.

The slow weeks passed as the *Winchelsea* plowed northward. Gaspard fought off boredom by making everyone's lives a misery. Hoping to make Charlotte jealous, he flirted brazenly with Betsy, pressing his suit with such ardor that Charlotte feared for the girl's virginity. Although Balcombe was no soldier (although he had fought at the Battle of the Nile as a midshipman, he kept reminding everyone), he had to fortify himself with brandy to warn Gaspard to keep his distance. Gaspard of course immediately challenged Balcombe to a duel, which the captain fortunately forbade, threatening, not very seriously, to clap both gentlemen in irons if they pressed the matter any further. Betsy got the worst of the falling-out. For four long days, she was locked in her cabin, from which her heartbroken laments could be heard almost anywhere downwind.

Charlotte pretended that it was for the sake of her mission that she was being more than civil to Gaspard, but she had to admit that she was flattered by the attentions of the most dashing bachelor aboard, a handsome young man who trailed clouds of his master's glory behind him.

"You'd better keep your distance," Gaspard teased. "Balcombe nearly fought me for flirting with his daughter. Imagine what he'll do if I become over familiar with his new lapdog!"

"Gaspard," she shot back, "I am no one's lapdog! You know perfectly well that it's a chore having to memorize all this pointless nonsense the boring Balcombes are stuffing down my throat. For example, I have no intention of sitting out the next two dances just because I have turned down some drunken lecher who has asked me to stand up with him!"

"That's because you have no breeding, mademoiselle," said Gaspard with a twinkle in his eye.

"Of course," said Charlotte, "a fiddler's son, brought up in the household of a comedian, would know all about breeding! But this British brand of breeding I can do without. Another example: you have to keep your friends of different ranks from meeting! Another: you have to know whom you shake hands with and whom you don't."

"A fine rule, mademoiselle," said Gaspard with a smirk. "You never know where some hands have been."

The mournful cry of a seagull flapping through the rigging distracted them. It seemed like it was trying to deliver a message. "Must be near land," said Gaspard. "A small island, perhaps."

"Oh, how I wish that small island were England!" Charlotte said. "Because I'm in a tearing hurry to practice my dos and don'ts. Whom to address by their first names and whom by their last. But what I won't be practicing is not wandering about at a reception on my own just because I'm a woman. That's a rule I certainly intend to break! If it wasn't for the emperor's instructions, I would have nothing to do with all this manners nonsense. I don't need manners to go to the Hollands and tell them the truth about how the emperor is being treated."

Gaspard laughed as if this were the most delightful of jokes. "You honestly expect the cream of English society to receive a peasant girl like you because she claims to have a few tidbits of gossip about an exiled emperor?"

"I have more than just tidbits," said Charlotte, sounding ominous.

"Such as your gem that Governor Lowe won't give Napoleon leeches to drain his hemorrhoids?" said Gaspard, letting his sarcasm show.

Charlotte looked away to follow the path of another flying fish. She must watch her tongue. She shouldn't even hint at the dark secret Napoleon had confided to her. That secret was for Lady Holland's ears only. Gaspard couldn't be trusted with anything to do with Dr. O'Meara, Charlotte knew. Gaspard hated the garrulous young doctor, because he was so close to the emperor, almost as close as he was, closer perhaps. O'Meara had told her, with a hearty laugh, that Gaspard had even challenged him to a duel, although somewhat halfheartedly because he knew Napoleon would never allow it. The doctor had accepted, he said, so long as they fought it out with scalpels! Gaspard had stamped off in a huff, and the matter went no further.

Charlotte fought off the silly fantasy of two well-muscled men, shirts off, slashing at each other with razors. Fighting over her, as two men had almost done already. "How about the fact that Napoleon's guards at Longwood sell tickets to passengers who want to peep at him?" she said.

The young general's gray eyes gazed thoughtfully into hers. He really was a remarkably handsome man, she thought. Brave as well. He made something melt inside her.

"Charlotte, this is a military campaign. Take it seriously."

173

"I am," she said. "You're the general. What's our strategy?"

"I don't know how much the emperor told you. My first move, as soon as we land, is for me to see Bathurst, the war minister, and reassure him that Napoleon has been spreading lies about his treatment on the island. That in fact he has everything he needs and that Governor Lowe is doing his best to make him comfortable."

Charlotte slipped off her shoes and wriggled her bare toes, gratified that this seemed to unsettle Gaspard. "A big fat lie. And then what?"

"And then, Miss Pretty Toes, as soon as I have convinced Minister Bathurst that I strongly support Lowe, he will most certainly want me to repeat everything I've told him to Lord Holland and all the rest of the pro-Napoleonic lobby, to set them straight."

The emerald eyes looked him full in the face until, to his annoyance, he began to feel uncomfortable, perhaps because he felt guilty about so openly admiring her naked feet. "But will they listen to you?" she asked.

"Are you saying they'd rather listen to you?"

"They'll look and then they'll listen. Men are that way with me, as you very well know! That's why the emperor sent me."

"Damn your impudence!" Gaspard spat and worked off his irritation by stalking off and winking brazenly at Betsy, recently released from her cabin, right in front of her father who pretended not to see it.

Who did Charlotte think she was, Gaspard debated with himself. She was nothing more than a Yamstock peasant who had been puffed up by Napoleon's attention until she actually believed she was destined to play an important part on the world's stage. How laughable! Pathetic, really. Gaspard had seen the emperor make puppets out of kings and princes, playing them in such a masterful way that they believed it was destiny, not Napoleon, pulling their strings.

He would take his revenge. It might take a little time, a glass or two of wine, but sooner or later he would conquer her like he had conquered her best friend, Mary. Napoleon had conquered emperors, and he had helped him do it. But Gaspard believed his own specialty was conquering women. He liked a spirited resistance, in love and war, it made the moment of surrender more exquisite. This pretty young upstart was no longer under Napoleon's protection. She was at his mercy. Soon she would grovel at his feet like her friend had done, begging to be ravished again and again!

She did have beautiful feet…

Charlotte slipped her shoes back on. She walked over to where the Balcombes, husband and wife, sat in a sullen heap, stewing in the unpleasantness that had sent Betsy howling back to her cabin. As soon as she had pulled herself together and come back on deck, she did her best to intimidate Charlotte with the size of London.

"When I first saw Jamestown, I laughed out loud!" she crowed. "What's its population, do you think?"

"Depends," said Charlotte, "on how many ships are in."

"I meant permanent population, silly. How many? Guess."

"A thousand," Charlotte said.

"A thousand!" Betsy hooted. "There are more than a million people in London! It's the largest city in Europe by far!"

"Even bigger than Paris?"

"Paris is only half the size!"

"It must have been quite a shock for the emperor to…" Charlotte trailed off and tried to hide her eyes in *Pride and Prejudice*, which she was reading for the third time at Mrs. Balcombe's insistence, even though she found it frivolous. Had these women nothing better to do than fuss about getting a husband? Where was the intrigue in their miserable little lives? Where was the Napoleonic grandeur?

"Boney!" said Betsy triumphantly, as if she'd just made the most remarkable discovery. "You're thinking of him again, aren't you?" She lowered her voice to a conspiratorial tone. "You're involved in some deep and dangerous plot to rescue him, aren't you? You and Gaspard, always putting your heads together! Oh, I hate Gaspard so much! He's much vainer than Mr. Darcy," she said through a sudden shower of tears, "and I hate Papa even more for all his interfering! I'm sick of you all. I'm going back to my cabin! There's a cockroach under my bunk I'm becoming very good friends with!"

Charlotte laughed and went back to Mr. Darcy. The wind went back to inching the *Winchelsea* toward London.

# Chapter 13: A Rosebud in Regency London

The carriage dropped Balcombe off in front of the Palace of Westminster. He turned his back on it, gazed instead at the tidy Thames sweeping the great city's refuse down to the sea. Somewhere in this ancient building, the home of legends, was the office of Sir Thomas Tyrwhitt, private secretary to the prince regent, gentleman usher of the black rod. For a moment he imagined the honorable gentleman beating his ebony rod three times on the door of the Commons, and when the door was obediently swung open inviting the honorable gentlemen to follow him across the threshold to the House of Lords.

But the only instrument he had to ease his entry into Black Rod's presence was the flask in his pocket. He took a swallow of the brandy and turned to face the edifice.

He was kept waiting for over an hour. By the time the skeletal clerk, who looked like he'd been on a fast for forty years, showed him into the great man's presence, the flask was empty. Ten minutes later, perhaps less, Balcombe was back on the bank of the Thames. Sir Thomas had said he would see to it that a notice appeared in *The Times* that said Mr. William Balcombe, provisioner to the Emperor Napoleon on Saint Helena, had returned home and was exploring the possibility of taking up a suitable mercantile position in London.

"It's not much, William," Sir Thomas said, "but I do have it on authority that you were involved in some irregularity or other on the island. Until Sir Hudson Lowe clears your name, it will be difficult to find you a position, in government, anyway. I'm sure you understand my position."

Balcombe did. He went to the nearest tavern and got quite drunk.

Gaspard had better luck. He polished his medals, dressed in his least threadbare regimentals, and walked the two miles from his totally suitable lodgings near Brunswick Square (paid for by the British government) to the mighty edifice in Whitehall that housed the War Office. For a while he watched a troop of redcoats marching on the parade ground. How much rather he would be doing humble drills than this treachery Napoleon had lured him into!

The sergeant guarding the entrance to the War Office, one of the departments in the huge Palladian edifice, eyed Gaspard's well-worn jacket with faint disapproval. "Who now?"

"General Gaspard Gourgaud. Lord Bathurst is expecting me."

"Is he now?" said the insolent redcoat. "Very odd, because Lord Bathurst is not in today." He ran his finger down a roster. "You'd be seeing his undersecretary. But I don't see anyone called Go-Go anywhere. What exactly is your business?"

Gaspard flushed with fury. He'd never been treated like this in his life. "Napoleon!" he barked. "Now I'm sure you've heard of him!"

That one word was enough. The sergeant's eyes widened in awe. "Bonaparte! I fought him three times and lost every one. Now there was a real general for you! We loved him even though he was killing us in droves. Go-Go, you said? Ah, here you are! General Baron Gaspard Go-Go. Do you know him sir? Napoleon?"

"Of course!" said Gaspard irritably, "I am his aide-de-camp. May I go through now? I am already late."

"Right away, General." The veteran of three lost battles rang for an attendant. "What's he like? In person, I mean?"

Gaspard, who had turned to watch a detachment of horse guards trot by on the parade ground, ignored the impertinent question.

The undersecretary turned out to be a clean-shaven, balding, urbane young man in his mid thirties. At a side desk sat a clerk, looking straight ahead, pen poised, ready to take notes but not presuming to be seen.

"General Gaspard Gourgaud," the undersecretary said with a tiny bow. "Lord Bathurst has asked me to offer you his apologies. He's been called away on important matters of state."

"I wish I'd been informed," said Gaspard, still fuming. Was the man trying to infer that his business with Lord Bathurst wasn't important?

The undersecretary gave him an amiable smile. "My apologies," he said, slipping into faultless French. "His Lordship is most interested in everything you have to say." He nodded in the general direction of the clerk. "Everything you say will be written down and passed on to His Lordship." He waved Gaspard to a chair and sat down himself. "Now tell me, what is your major concern?"

"Nothing, really," said Gaspard with a bite of sarcasm, "except that Bonaparte plans to escape to America, where he will take up arms with that warmonger President Monroe. He talks of nothing else. The Americans will build a mighty navy and sail for Europe. That gutless puppet Louis XVIII you have put on the throne of France will flee. Austria and Russia will take up arms with Bonaparte. Within five years he will rule one half of the world and his American ally will rule the other half!"

The clerk's pen scratched away in the deathly silence that followed. When the undersecretary got the wind back in his sails, he said, "You have heard him voice this plan?"

"Of course. He talks of nothing else. We live in the same house. He dictates his memoirs to me, lies and all. I am closer to him than anyone else on earth. But he has no friends, only followers. He is a wild animal caught in a trap, slavering and snapping its jaws."

"But I hear that he has an entourage, a court of sorts, that strives to follow imperial etiquette at meals and such. Isn't that so?"

"An entourage! There's only one reason he has any hangers-on. They intend to make their fortunes writing books about him! He knows this, berates us about it. He looks down on all mankind as his inferiors, you see. I saved his life at Brienne and in Moscow, where I foiled a Russian plot to blow him up with a huge cache of gunpowder. But does he thank me for it? No! He treats me like his dog! He treats everyone like a dog. He shaves himself because he fears his barber will cut his throat!"

The undersecretary frowned. "Is that why you have come over to our cause—personal animosity?"

"There's nothing personal in it. I have turned to you because twenty years of conflict is enough. Unleash Napoleon and you unleash the dogs of war. Let him continue to rot in hell!"

The undersecretary, whose name was Henry Goulburn and who would go on to greater things, raised an eyebrow. "Hell? Saint Helena is that bad?"

Gaspard corrected himself. "No, it's a very pleasant island, tropical but fanned by the southeast trade winds that blow all year. Much too good for the tyrant, in my opinion. His accommodations are spacious; food and drink are so plentiful that his butler runs a thriving black market with all the surplus wine we can't drink. The selfish monster spends most of his day wallowing in a hot bath, in water that has to be carried miles from the nearest spring. He uses so much water for this swinish indulgence that the soldiers in the guard camp don't have enough to make their tea!"

On went Gaspard, stimulated by invention, pausing only to make sure the clerk was getting everything down. When he saw the undersecretary beginning to fidget, he ended his recitation. "I could go on for hours, because Bonaparte is the most cunning rascal in the world. But surely you don't need more to persuade you that the beast must be kept chained to his rock?"

"It isn't the war minister that needs to be persuaded, it's Holland and his hangers-on. We have your testament now, but it would be so much more persuasive if you delivered these facts in person to Lord Holland and the rest of the Liberal lobby."

"That would be my pleasure!" said Gaspard, trying to keep the crow of triumph out of his voice.

"Excellent! I shall speak to the minister this evening and strongly recommend your plan of action. I am sure a communication will pass as early as tomorrow between my superior and Lord Holland. Expect an early invitation to the decadent splendors of Holland House!"

Very satisfied with himself, Gaspard took the air by walking south along the embankment to spit on the Houses of Parliament. The English boasted that they embodied the wisdom of the ages, but they had fallen for a simple ruse. The expression on the undersecretary's face assured him that very soon he would be whispering what he thought was the vile truth of Napoleon's behavior to the fine feathers that adorned the Liberal wing of British politics. He turned back north, and on his way, as he was about to strike away from the river, a spring in his step, a commotion outside a tavern caught his eye. Someone was being poured, not very ceremoniously, into a cab, which took off at a trot.

He could have sworn its incapacitated passenger was Balcombe.

As the Balcombes were low on funds, they were staying in a comfortable terraced house with Lucia, Mrs. Balcombe's niece, the siren who had broken Mr. Burchell's heart. This was where the letter addressed to Charlotte had come late the previous afternoon. The envelope was plain but slightly scented. The message was one line of hurried scrawl: "Go shopping for a suitable dress in Bond Street tomorrow morning." It was signed, "Lady H."

"A Bond Street dress!" said Mrs. Balcombe with a tight little laugh. "How does Her Ladyship expect us to pay for that?"

"Uncle Samuel gave me money."

"I know that, dear, but it won't get you very far on Bond Street."

"Can I at least go and take a look?"

The expression on the pretty face was so eager that Mrs. Balcombe couldn't say no. "Why not?" she said. "I'm sure the girls will love an outing."

So while Gaspard was lying through his teeth in the War Office and Balcombe floating his in a tavern nearby, Charlotte was savoring the enchantments of London's most fashionable arcade, where those who already had everything went to shop.

"Aunt Jane, you are to stay as long as you like," Lucia said as they walked along. "Luke won't be back from the Indies for months, and it's just little Lucia, me, and the nanny in that big house. Honestly, I could do with the company."

"You are too kind, Lucia," said Mrs. Balcombe, "but I'm sure Mr. Balcombe is securing a position with the government as we speak, and we will probably need accommodations nearer Whitehall. Betsy, what do you think you're doing?"

Mrs. Balcombe's abrupt change of tone distracted Charlotte from the splendid sights in shop windows and the splendid people who were looking at them. The brash sixteen-year-old had put on a disdainful expression and was walking with a most unladylike strut.

"Look!" said the brat, as a knot of exquisitely dressed but very bored-looking young men, with their hands stuffed deep into their pockets and toothpicks rolling around in their mouths, strolled toward them with a languid swagger. "It's called the Bond Street Roll. Beau Brummell used to do it, and so did Lord Byron. It's what all the fancy gents do when they promenade down Bond Street!"

Byron, the world's second most dangerous man! The name on the letter written in Napoleon's scrawl. How often had she looked at it? She'd even kissed it once, late at night, in a fit of pure depravity. How much simpler if she could just have bumped into him, swaggering down Bond Street on his way to take boxing lessons with Gentleman John Jackson at number thirteen! But Byron was in Italy— in Venice, she'd heard—and that seemed almost as far away as Saint Helena. The delivery of the letter from Napoleon would most probably never take place.

"Gentlemen may walk like that, perhaps, but certainly not ladies," said Betsy's mother. "Can't you walk like Charlotte? She fits right in!"

Betsy immediately changed her walk to a mocking, mincing step with exaggerated swaying of her hips, although that was not the way Charlotte walked at all. She dabbed at her nose with an imaginary handkerchief, which suggested she was trying to drown out the offensive smells of ordinary life. "Is this better?"

Charlotte ignored her and went back to her principal objective: dress shops populated with gorgeous creations, looking for something—something fashionable, emerald green to go with her eyes. Green. Napoleon's favorite color. She found one that clung to the body and featured the daringly low, more natural waistline that had suddenly become all the rage among the fashionable Bond Street ladies. It had short sleeves to show off the arms and a plunging neckline to show off other assets.

The shop assistant sniffed as she examined the homemade Saint Helena dress Charlotte was wearing. "So you and your mistress have the same measurements, then?" she asked.

Charlotte did not dignify the slight by noticing it. "It's for me."

"But miss, it's offered at fifty pounds!"

Mrs. Balcombe laughed nervously. "Ridiculous! Charlotte, we need to go elsewhere. This shop is grotesquely overpriced."

"Can't I just try it on?"

"Charlotte, that's not done. You don't try on clothes you can't afford," said Mrs. Balcombe.

"I think it will suit the young lady handsomely," said a man who had just walked into the shop. He was tall and well dressed, with curly black hair and blue eyes as sharp as broken glass. "Let her try it on if she wants to," he said.

The shop assistant recognized authority when she saw it. Her attitude changed instantly. "Certainly, sir."

Ten minutes later, because there were a few nips and tucks to be made, Charlotte emerged, radiant, from the dressing room. Her face fell when she saw that the tall stranger was no longer there.

"The gentleman had to leave," said the shop assistant.

"He paid for the dress," whispered Lucia. "All of it! He wouldn't take no for an answer. He said he was acting on behalf of your friend in Saint Helena. He came right out with the name of the island. I could hardly believe my ears. He must have been following us."

"Of course he's been following us. I noticed him get out of the carriage right behind ours," piped Betsy. "It was very fancy!"

"He left you a note," said Mrs. Balcombe. "Of course I had to read it for propriety's sake." She handed Charlotte a neatly folded sheet of paper. On it, in a hasty scrawl, were the words: *With the compliments of Lady Holland.*

# Chapter 14: Holland House

The invitation arrived by messenger the day after Gaspard had spoken with the undersecretary and Mr. Balcombe had been deposited, still swaying, at the front door of Lucia's house in Cheapside.

The nanny, who did what she could to help out when two-year-old Lucia was napping, interrupted Charlotte who was in the living room reading Byron's "Manfred." "Miss, there's a messenger asking for you. I think he has an invitation."

The boy couldn't have been more than twelve. In spite of his fine blue livery, he needed a good wash. "Miss Nip?"

"Knipe," Charlotte corrected him.

"This is for you."

Charlotte took the envelope from the grubby hand. It had her name and Lucia's address written on it and was sealed with some sort of mythological creature, perhaps a griffin.

The boy hovered in a way that suggested he was waiting for a tip. She gave him a penny. "Fank you, miss. I am to tell you that I have already delivered an invitation to the French general and that a carriage will be calling for you. The general said he would wait for it 'ere with you."

She opened the envelope, careful not to break the handsome seal. *Lord and Lady Holland request the pleasure of your company for dinner at Holland House on Monday, the fourth of May, at 4:00 p.m.*, it read. Under the type, written in ink by a loud hand, was the note: "Wear the dress!"

Gaspard, in well-worn regimentals, arrived early. He sat and made awkward conversation with Mr. Balcombe

186

over a sherry while he waited for Charlotte, who was busy dressing upstairs, and the carriage.

"So you never actually spoke to Lord Bathurst?" asked Balcombe, a little reassured by the news that he wasn't the only one to get short shrift.

"There was no need," said Gaspard. "I told his man enough. I will no doubt talk with Lord Holland this evening. I take it your meeting was a failure?" he added spitefully.

"On the contrary, it went well," lied Balcombe. "Tyrwhitt is like a father to me. He has been my guardian since I was ten. Appointed by the prince regent himself. However, my sudden arrival here in London due to my wife's illness came as a surprise."

"There's no need to pretend that you left the island because of your wife's health, Mr. Balcombe," said Gaspard. "You fell in combat, you know that. What you may not know is that those letters you were given—defamatory letters, all of them—we composed them for Governor Lowe's consumption. Oh, how the emperor laughed when we wrote them together!" Gaspard leaned forward in his chair, lowered his voice to a whisper. "You see, it was I who told Lowe that you were trying to smuggle them out. It was a ruse to convince the idiot that I had turned traitor, that I was now his man, not Napoleon's. That it was safe to send me to London!"

Even Gaspard's battle-hardened heart softened when he saw the stricken look on Balcombe's face.

"Governor Lowe promised to say…my wife's illness," was all Balcombe managed to get out.

"Love and war!" said Gaspard with a light laugh, as if that resolved a trivial issue.

Charlotte was having her hair curled by Lucia, who would have given anything to change places with her. "Of course I haven't met Lady Holland," Lucia said with a trace

187

of bitterness, "but I have *heard* all about her—hold still, you want to be kissed by a prince, not a hot curling iron. She's a scandalous woman."

Even with her limited exposure to fashionable life, Charlotte had learned that the more besmirched your reputation, the more eager you were to besmirch someone else's. What Lucia had done to poor Mr. Burchell in Saint Helena, abandoning him at the church door, so to speak, was outrageous. But here she was about to let loose a broadside aimed at the honor of her hostess-to-be, Charlotte was sure.

"Scandalous?" she asked. "In what way?"

"To begin with she's a hypocrite," said Lucia twirling the curling iron which had turned Charlotte's long, wavy blonde hair into spirals. "She pretends to her liberal hangers-on that she's a firebrand for slave emancipation, when her father is the biggest slave owner in Jamaica!"

"Really? I heard he farmed sugarcane."

"Ha! And who do you suppose cuts and stacks the cane? Squirrels?"

"She was married young, wasn't she?"

"Age fifteen. To an indolent aristocrat more than twenty years older than she was. Well, he couldn't have been *that* indolent, because they had five children."

"She divorced him, didn't she?"

"Hold still! Yes. She fell for Liberal Lord Holland, or he fell for her, when she was traveling alone in Europe. Traveling alone? A woman of quality? Unbelievable! Not only did they have an affair, but in an excess of Liberalism, Lord Holland got her pregnant. Oh, what a scandal! There was nearly a duel. They married two days after the divorce. Of course Lady Holland was shunned by society, so she just went ahead and created a society all of her own, half of them titled Liberals, half penniless poets."

"Byron"—Charlotte was annoyed when she detected a tiny tremor in her voice when she said the name—"was a guest, wasn't he?"

"Practically lived there! Until he was banished from England, two years ago. Did that find its way to Saint Helena? I'd be surprised if it didn't. All people seem to do there is gossip, because there's nothing else to keep them occupied. I ought to know."

Charlotte allowed a few seconds for that comment to creep under the carpet. "Byron. Something to do with incest with his sister?"

"No, much worse than that, I'm told. Something unmentionable. Ask Lady Holland. I'm sure she'll have no problem mentioning it."

From outside came the clatter of a carriage drawing up, a nervous whinnying of horses. Charlotte rushed to the open window. The carriage was gilded, the griffin coat of arms on the door. It was time for her to step onto the stage.

Holland House, with its red brick turrets and soaring arches, was a fairy-tale castle when sunset lit it on fire. The carriage carrying Charlotte and Gaspard joined the queue of elegant conveyances, many of them resplendent with coats of arms, waiting to deposit their distinguished passengers at the front portal.

As Charlotte and Gaspard stepped out of their carriage, the full orchestra assembled in the garden struck up a slow triumphal march, full of heady vainglory.

"Handel," said Gaspard, standing even straighter. "They're playing it for us, in honor of the emperor."

Every eye was turned on them. There was even a flutter of applause. Once again Charlotte felt a delicious tingle running up the back of her neck, a magical sensation she had first felt when Napoleon noticed her at Porteous House in Saint Helena, that little island that now seemed so very far away. Here she was, being cheered on her way to the front door of a famous palace when her parents wouldn't have been welcome at the back!

"I think you're right, they're playing it for us," said Charlotte when she recognized the tall, handsome man, now in naval uniform, who had paid for the dress she was wearing. She had seen him signal the bandleader to strike up.

He approached them with a wide, very white smile. "Thomas Johnson," he said. "Charlotte Knipe. General Gaspard Gourgaud. Welcome to Holland House!"

"And thank you for the dress," said Charlotte as he pressed his lips to her gloved hand. How she wished she didn't have to wear gloves so he could see her hands naked!

"You must thank Lady Holland. May I say how splendid you look in it? You have quite stolen the center of attention!"

"I believe they have a new statue of the emperor. I would like to see it," said Gaspard, who was annoyed by the rapt expression on Charlotte's face.

"It's in the Portuguese garden," he said, waving in the direction of a large hedge maze. "Ask anyone. I'd show it to you myself, but I have strict instructions from Her Ladyship to inform her the minute you arrived."

The bust was bronze. The sculptor had somehow captured Napoleon's calm ferocity. It stood on a polished granite pillar with a short Greek inscription carved into it.

"What does it say?" asked Charlotte.

Gaspard frowned and narrowed his eyes, but Charlotte got the distinct impression that he had about as little Greek as she did—which was none at all.

"He is not dead," said someone behind them, who sounded like he was talking in a dream. The voice belonged to a fat little man with a plump pink face who was jauntily dressed in a maroon jacket with blue trim. "That's how it begins. Do you want me to read you the whole thing? Of course you do." He blew his nose on the handkerchief he carried like a flag of surrender, because everything about him from the stoop of his narrow shoulders, bent knees, his shuffle when he walked a few feet closer, suggested a deep-seated and insatiable indolence. He recited the inscription in a melodious voice, his eyes closed with pleasure:

> He is not dead, he breathes the air
> In lands beyond the deep,
> Some distant sea-girt island where
> Harsh men the hero keep.

"It's a line from Homer's *Odyssey*, you know. It refers to the isle of Ogygia, where Odysseus was marooned. Code for Saint Helena, of course. And we don't need to venture a guess as to whom the harsh jailer is, do we? Hudson Lowe, of course, who is the subject of poetry himself!"

"Of course," said Charlotte.

The nose on the friendly pink face was blown again. "And you? You have an unfamiliar accent. Where do you hail from?"

"Saint Helena."

"Yes!" said the little tub of lard, delighted that Charlotte had entered his magic realm. "You are a Nereid from the enchanted isle! Oh, how splendid this all is!" The little man closed his eyes, as if he could see better that way, waved his handkerchief around as if he were cleaning a misted window. "Enchanting!"

Gaspard's boots creaked as he impatiently shifted his weight. "Where will we find Lord Holland?" he said.

"It's Lady Holland you need to find, monsieur. She rules this magic realm!"

191

"I'm Charlotte Knipe, and this is General Gaspard Gourgaud," Charlotte said.

The odd little man waved his handkerchief in farewell. "Coleridge," he said with a lazy little bow, "at your service. Samuel Taylor Coleridge."

They found Henry Richard Vassall-Fox, third Baron Holland, holding court in his hall, which was bigger than Saint James, the largest church in Saint Helena. His Lordship, standing at the center of a knot of sycophants, was resting a hand on the shoulder of a man dressed like a Roman senator. It was a bronze cast of Lord Holland's famous uncle, Liberal firebrand Charles James Fox. Suddenly Lord Holland lost his audience. All eyes, including his, were devouring the girl in the emerald dress who approached with a threadbare French officer of some sort.

"Who is this feast of femininity?" asked His Lordship rhetorically. "You must be Napoleon's girl, surely?"

"Charlotte Knipe, Your Lordship."

"Knipe," said Holland. "That's an unusual name."

"Not on Saint Helena, Your Lordship," said Charlotte. "There it's quite common."

"Common? Really? And that accent of yours?"

Charlotte smiled. "That's even more common, sir. It's Yamstock. Means we're descended from yams. Yams are our national food, you see. Or at least they used to be."

"Yamstock? How droll! I've never had a yam in my life. I shall immediately order my gardeners to plant some in your honor. Tell me, does Napoleon eat them?"

"I don't think so, Your Lordship. General Gaspard Gourgaud would know," she said, nodding to Gaspard, who, she sensed correctly, was by this time breathing fire at being ignored.

"Ah, General Gaspard Gourgaud! What an honor. I believe that you fired the last volley of cannon at Waterloo. Is that so?"

Gaspard, somewhat mollified by the remark, made a shallow bow. "Yes, Your Lordship. I believe I have that distinction."

"Splendid! Napoleon said something amusing about cannons. What was it? Oh, yes, he said the most honorable way for two gentlemen to become acquainted is to exchange cannonballs instead of greeting cards!"

When the wine-fueled titter from his hangers-on subsided, Holland abruptly adopted a more serious tone, and the faces surrounding him obediently adopted a more serious expression. "But tell me, how is the emperor being treated? One hears so many conflicting accounts."

"Monsignor, if we could talk privately," said Gaspard.

"Oh, certainly," said Holland, "if we have to." Reluctantly he relinquished the support of his uncle's bronze shoulder. "This way."

Holland, a short, broad man hobbled by a gouty ankle, escorted Charlotte and Gaspard across the vast reception room. Up a grand staircase they went, into his lavish private study. A footman in a well-powdered wig lit a seven-stemmed candelabra on an ebony table before backing out the door and closing it softly behind him.

"Well, now," said His Lordship with an unselfconscious display of his uneven yellow teeth, "what's the big secret?"

"I told the War Office what it wanted to hear."

"Which is?"

"That Napoleon is living in the lap of luxury. That he lords it over everyone. Treats us all like dogs. He plans to escape to America and raise an army, which will rub the British Empire off the map."

The color drained from Lord Holland's gouty face. "You blackguard! We hoped you were coming to England to get the emperor's conditions improved. But you have done exactly the opposite!"

Gaspard raised his long nose and aimed down it like a marksman. "With respect, Your Lordship, I am merely following the emperor's instructions. You see, he wants to be treated worse, not better."

"What? Has he gone mad?"

"No. He wants freedom, not comfort. He is martyring himself. He wants the British government, through Governor Lowe, to treat him so badly that it causes an international scandal of such proportion that the British government will be forced to unchain him."

"So you fed the War Office lies that seem to confirm Napoleon is a dangerous monster?"

"Yes. Otherwise the War Office would never have allowed me to visit you."

"And the moment you're here, you switch sides and reveal how Napoleon is made to suffer?"

"Yes. The emperor ordered me to inform you, in case you become aware of any…exaggerations."

Holland gazed at the candles while he thought this over. "Very elaborate," he said. He raised his eyes to Charlotte, who he could see was becoming increasingly restless. "And you, Miss Knipe, where do you fit into this labyrinthine plot?"

"I have a private message from the emperor for Lady Holland," said Charlotte.

"Thanking her for the books and the sugared prunes?" said Lord Holland with a sly smile.

Charlotte ignored the attempt at humor. "The emperor has instructed me to help with the whispering campaign."

"A whispering campaign. The diabolical cunning of the man! He knows that there's no sound in London that carries farther than a confidential whisper. Try one out on me, would you?"

"He is forced to live in an unfurnished dank hovel," Gaspard jumped in, "fed stale bread spread with rancid butter, given the choice of drinking either sour wine or muddy water. Imagine the horror. The flame of the Enlightenment extinguished by perpetual fog!"

Holland looked visibly shocked. "This is certainly not what we hear from the War Office."

"The redcoats sell tickets to people who want to take a peep at the emperor," Charlotte said. "They treat him like a circus freak."

"I can see my guests are about to be royally entertained. Don't worry, none of them will tattle to the War Office. At least not until tomorrow!"

Without any warning the door burst open, and a woman in a regal velvet gown with a truncated peacock's feather presiding over her lumpy turban barreled in. "Henry!" she said in a loud voice. "How typically selfish of you! You have stolen our guests of honor. Everybody is dying to hear all about Napoleon straight from the lips his favorite general!"

"Dearest—"

"Don't dare dearest me! You're a selfish old squirrel forever hoarding the best nuts for yourself! Stand up, girl," she said, ignoring Gaspard, who had jumped to his feet and bowed crisply. "I want to look at that dress. After all, I paid for it!"

It seemed every word that dropped from Her Ladyship's lips was spiced with pepper. "First of all, I love the color. Green is the emperor's favorite, because it is the symbol of spring, of rebirth. But I suppose you chose it because it matches your eyes. And what a daringly low

195

waist! Unlike the empire line, it emphasizes the natural female hourglass waist. I certainly hope it doesn't catch on, or all of us old biddies will have to go back to squeezing ourselves into corsets!"

"May I present General Gourgaud," Charlotte said.

"General Baron Gaspard Gourgaud!" exclaimed Lady Holland as if she had just noticed him. "What an honor to meet you. Everyone knows how you saved the emperor's life two—or was it three times? Our most deeply felt thanks for that. But come, Charlotte, diplomatic strategy is way above our shallow little heads. We must allow the men to delve into such deep matters. My guests are straining at the leash to devour you. Come along, we mustn't keep them waiting! You see, the silly things believe you are the emperor's mistress and that you have a buffet of naughty Napoleonic tidbits for them."

Charlotte had the distinct impression that behind the mask of an overbearing harridan was an extremely cool and intelligent player. "Yes, Your Ladyship. I mean, I do have some information. Scraps, really."

"Well, then, tallyho, let's throw them to the hounds!"

Although Charlotte could feel eyes eating her up, their owners were too well-bred to swamp her. Instead they waited their turn for Lady Holland to make the introductions before barraging her with questions.

"Is it true the emperor had to sell his imperial silver to feed his servants?"

"Tragically, yes. Fresh food is very expensive on the island. Ordinary people live on potatoes and salt beef."

"What are his accommodations like? Is it true that his house is nothing but a rambling cowshed?"

"Yes. Unfortunately the roof leaks, which feeds the mildew, and the mildew feeds on just about everything else. His servants do their best to hide it by hanging fabric on the walls and ceilings. But it has to be scraped off books and boots. Playing cards have to be dried in the oven before every game!"

"How dreadful!" Lady Holland crowed. "And talking of dreadful, what about Sir Hudson Lowe? We have heard his surname, Lowe, is most appropriate:

> Sir Hudson Lowe, Sir Hudson Low,
> (By name, and ay! By nature so...)

Everybody knows that rhyme!"

"He is both malicious and vindictive," said Charlotte. "The emperor had a favorite tree. He used to like reading in its shade, so Sir Hudson cut it down. Now wot you all tink 'bout dat?" she said in Yamstock before she could catch herself.

This announcement, barbarous accent and all, was drowned by Lady Holland's indignant cry. "What? Does that brute of a governor think Napoleon is a monkey?"

Charlotte smiled, happy at the impression she was making. "Certainly not, my lady. The rats swarming everywhere in the house are the only creatures who come and go as they please."

This got a little laugh. One of the ladies, very pretty, took advantage of the frivolous moment. "What kind of perfume does Napoleon prefer his ladies to wear? He's fond of eau de cologne, isn't he?"

"For himself," said Charlotte. "After his bath he is rubbed down with it. But as far as women are concerned, he prefers them to smell of nothing at all. He has a very sharp nose, you see." When this comment caused the exchange of embarrassed looks, she hurried on. "He can't bear the smell of fresh paint, for example. It makes him quite ill."

"What about his meals? We've heard that he still dines very grandly."

"He does his best to keep up appearances," said Charlotte, "but his entourage says that his dinners today are a parody of what they were in the great palaces of Europe."

"Although I'm told his servants are properly dressed," said Lady Holland.

"Yes, they are, in green and silver livery, worn every day, so it has become badly frayed. The governor complains about what he calls unnecessary luxury. When we left the servants hadn't even been paid for over two months, poor things!"

"What a disgrace! But you say the food is at least properly served?"

"I think so," said Charlotte, warming to her theme. "The routine is always the same, at least on the few occasions I've been invited to dine. On the stroke of seven, the door to the dining room is thrown open by the majordomo, also dressed in green and silver. He announces, in a very loud voice, 'Your Majesty's dinner is served.' Then the emperor leads his guests into the little dining room. His chair, at the head of the table of course, is pulled out for him by his two valets, who take up permanent posts behind it. Only when he is seated does anyone else do the same. And no one dares to say a word unless Napoleon asks them a question, and he seldom asks a question because he's too busy bolting down his meat. So the room is silent as a morgue!"

"How extraordinary!" said Lady Holland, gazing across the vast expanse of the gilt chamber, to where Gaspard was standing surrounded by a bevy of bare-shouldered young women, some of whom had their waistlines as daringly low as Charlotte's. "I do declare that your dashing young escort is attracting bees like a honey pot. Not since the happy days of Lord Byron have I seen the ladies so swarm a man."

"I'm sorry to have missed Lord Byron," said Charlotte.

Lady Holland raised a manicured eyebrow. "In that case you will be interested in seeing my inner sanctum. Come."

Greeted with bows and curtsies all the way, Her Ladyship showed Charlotte to her private drawing room. A hovering footman opened the door. The chairs and the sofa were covered in gold brocade. The walls were adorned with drawings and paintings, many of them oval miniatures.

Lady Holland said, "My household gods. Napoleon on the right wall. Byron on the left. The gods of liberty and license, I call them. Go on. Feast your eyes."

Charlotte examined Napoleon's wall first, a graphic record of his astonishing career. Napoleon backed by Pyramids. The famous one of him crossing the Alps, white horse rearing, face grave, hand pointing the way to glory. Napoleon's triumphant entry into Berlin through the Brandenburg Gate. Napoleon presiding over conquered kings. Cannons blazing and cavalry charging at the battle of Austerlitz. Crowning himself emperor. Miniatures, caricatures. The swirl of that mighty life swept Charlotte away. And not only did this man know her, but she was on a mission for him. She was a player in his drama, a rider in the mighty cavalcade of history!

A caricature caught her eye. It depicted a beautiful woman, naked except for her fan, dancing behind a gauze curtain while Napoleon, in full military uniform, watched.

"The woman is Josephine," Her Ladyship explained. "Do you dance for him, Charlotte? Everybody thinks so, you know."

"No, Your Ladyship. I suppose the emperor has more important matters on his mind," she said, gazing at a reclining statue, done in the classical style, of a beautiful young woman who was naked except for the wispy drape around her waist.

"Really? What could be more important than love except more of it? That's what the lady who posed for that statue believed. The original, waxed marble, is life-size, but this gives you a good idea. Notice the apple in her hand. Paris awarded it to her because he judged her to be the most beautiful woman in the world. *Venus Victorious.* You know who the model is, don't you?"

Charlotte had seen the face before, in a print, but not the figure. "It's Pauline, I think. Napoleon's sister."

"In the flesh, so to speak. The most beautiful woman of our time, they say. Although I'm sure your admirers will beg to differ. Manners of a kitten, morals of an alley cat. Wellington, who ought to know, calls her a heartless little devil, because she bedded everything in uniform, especially vigorous young officers. Left a string of broken hearts in her wake. Harmonious voice, though, and that air of well-bred indifference. Easy for her, because she really didn't care for anyone besides her brother. Perfect pair they make, don't they? Lord of War and Lady of Love. Pauline suggested they get married, like the pharaohs who were always marrying their sisters. She told him that she was already bathing in asses' milk, like Cleopatra, which she was—still is, no doubt—carried naked to her bath by a giant black Negro. Oh, I can go for hours about her little peccadilloes, but I won't. Except to say that when Pauline was asked whether she felt uncomfortable posing in the nude, she answered, not in the least, the room was heated!"

Lady Holland, who had been giving Charlotte sharp looks to see how she was taking all this, chuckled with glee when Charlotte laughed. "Now it's Byron's turn. As you can see, dozens of pictures of him—he is, of course, justifiably proud of his face and is happy to sit for just about anyone. Characters and scenes from his poems, mostly miniatures. He presented them to me when he left, one short step ahead of the law. At first I refused them, but he insisted. Said they'd be seized by the bailiffs if I didn't take them. You see, his affairs were in a terrible mess."

Charlotte couldn't resist the question, although she had the strong feeling it was indelicate. "Why was he exiled?"

Lady Holland paused, and when she answered it wasn't much louder than a whisper. "You have an important and very private message for me, from Napoleon, I have been told."

"Yes, Your Ladyship."

"Then it is only fair I share a secret with you. But you must promise to keep it to yourself, because it is a hanging crime in England, and as much as I enjoy having Byron hanging around, as the Americans say, I would hate it to be at the end of a rope."

Charlotte smiled dutifully at the grisly joke. "I promise."

"Like so many libertines before him, Lord Byron has a passion for boys."

Charlotte kept her eyes fixed on a miniature of the poet, which showed off his troubled gaze and swollen, enticing lips. "Yes, my lady," she whispered, "I can believe that."

"But he was too much of a show off to keep this vice private. He dressed up his female conquests as pages and paraded them in public. Poor Lady Caroline Lamb was one of them. He met her here, you know. Now she's locked away in the country, a slave to brandy and opium."

Charlotte would like to have filled in the silence that followed this announcement but couldn't tear her eyes away from the seductive monster's portrait.

201

"And now," said Lady Holland, softly as someone reluctantly waking up a child, "it is your turn to tell."

"Dr. Barry O'Meara has had instructions."

"Napoleon's physician?"

Charlotte wasn't surprised Lady Holland knew who Dr. O'Meara was. She seemed to know everything about everybody. "Sir Hudson Lowe has ordered him to assassinate Napoleon."

This, at last, took Lady Holland by surprise, because there was a short intake of breath. "Napoleon told you this?"

"Yes. He said it was for your ears only and that he wanted you to keep it a secret until O'Meara is in London to confirm it. Then it can be sung from the rooftops."

"Let me understand you clearly, girl. That blackguard Hudson Lowe instructed Napoleon's own doctor to break his Hippocratic oath and not just harm the emperor but actually murder him?"

"Yes."

"Unspeakable! And you have told no one of this?"

"No."

"Keep it that way," Lady Holland whispered fiercely, as if, in that instant, the pictures on the walls had grown hostile ears.


The gilded carriage came for them at midnight.

"Well, Rosebud," said Gaspard, who was by this time slurring his words, "do you think they swallowed all the *merde* I fed them?"

They had done well. Even after Lady Holland had introduced them to the most important Liberals in the vast room, Charlotte, with Gaspard in tow, had continued to seek out fresh pairs of ears.

*Lead him around like a chimpanzee on a chain.*

They made a charming couple—the beautiful island girl, surely Napoleon's mistress, and the handsome young French general, Napoleon's aide-de-camp, who wore his threadbare uniform like a badge of honor.

"Yes, Gaspard," she said. "You make a good liar."

"And you make a better one, because it is impossible to believe that anything that comes out of your lovely mouth is a lie. That impudent Captain Johnson was one of your most ardent victims, I noticed. He took up so much of your time I began to think I was going to have to take him outside and kill him. Fortunately he took the hint and disappeared."

Swashbuckling Captain Johnson's attention had been most welcome, but he had indeed left suddenly, without saying good-bye. Had Gaspard threatened him? Why did she find that exciting? Two handsome men fighting over her while Napoleon's bust looked on… What an abandoned hussy she'd become! What about Daniel standing bravely in the graveyard at dawn, waiting for certain death? When had she last thought of him?

Impetuous thoughts carried her away faster than the carriage hurrying her home through the empty London streets. "Lady Holland says that not since Byron has a man been such a magnet to the ladies as you, Gaspard. You even caught my eye!"

She reined herself in too late. Her heart sank when she saw the expression on Gaspard's face soften.

"At last, my Rosebud!" he sighed passionately. "I see flattering company has made you shed some of your thorns. The time has come to kiss and make up, don't you think?"

"Gaspard, I meant I was proud of you."

"Oh, you meant far more than that, admit it!" he said, moving closer. His leg touched hers. She shrank from him, but he had her trapped against the door, strong fingers digging into her bare shoulder.

"No, Gaspard! We serve the same master, that's all! You know I'm engaged to Daniel!"

"That invert! I could have buggered him at that mountain pond if I'd wanted to! The time has come for you to have a real man!"

She smelled the brandy on his lips as they hunted for hers. "Coachman!" Charlotte screamed. "Please stop!"

Even before the carriage ground to a halt, she had thrown open the door.

"What is it, milady?" said the footman, catching the door.

"I am feeling ill. I need fresh air."

The footman glanced at Gaspard but made sure not to hold his angry gaze. "You're welcome to take my seat up top, milady. I'll ride on the tailboard."

The coachman was the taciturn type, but when he saw Charlotte shiver, because in her haste she had forgotten her shawl, he offered her a damp raincoat.

By the time the carriage drew up at Lucia's, she'd rehearsed something conciliatory to say to Gaspard, but the carriage door remained stubbornly shut. She glanced in the window. Gaspard was sprawled across the seat, snoring softly.

# Chapter 15: A Dark Day in Kew Gardens

*May 5, 1818*
*Dearest Daniel,*

*I can't believe how we have become mirror images of each other, just the way you said! Here I am writing a letter to you from London, which you will read in Saint Helena instead of the other way round!*

*Please forgive me for not writing sooner. We have been in London for five whole days, but I have not had a moment to put pen to paper. What a huge, exciting city this is! If you hadn't been here yourself, you could never have conceived how far it is beyond the wildest dreams of people who know nothing except our remote, romantic little island!*

*Let me begin with our hostess, Lucia Green, now Lucia Dodds, of course. She is already thirty, although she has kept the good looks of the twenty-year-old who captured and then broke poor Mr. Burchell's heart. She has an adorable two-year-old daughter also called Lucia, who has helped keep her mother more or less on the straight and narrow.*

*I say, "more or less," because I am a naughty gossip who has absolutely no proof that my hostess seeks consolation for her husband's being away at sea. All I know for certain is that, like most ladies, she has an absolute infatuation with Lord Byron and makes me take turns reading his poetry with her almost every evening. She even claims, with a little bit of a blush, I noticed, that she met him once or twice before his wicked ways got him exiled two years ago. The mad and dangerous man, I hear, has so far ravished more than two hundred women, so who's to say that Lucia wasn't one of them? Oh, I really am awful!*

*My only excuse is that I'm still a little light-headed from my visit to Holland House last night. Daniel, you can't believe the grandeur of the place, the brilliance of the company! So I would make a good impression on her illustrious guests, Lady Holland, who is totally besotted with Napoleon, bought me this lovely green dress, which makes my best Saint Helena weeds look shoddily homemade, which is, of course, what they are.*

*So there we were, yours truly and General Gaspard, the center of attention of the cream of Liberal London society, who inundated us with questions about the emperor down to the smallest details of his everyday life—what he ate, who shaved him, and even what perfume he preferred on women!*

*Then, precisely at midnight, a gilded four-horse carriage called for us. You'll laugh at me, but there was a moment when I expected it to turn into a pumpkin pulled by mice! Since there are no secrets between us, I have to report that there was an embarrassing incident in the carriage on the way home. Poor Gaspard, much the worse for drink, tried to kiss me. I soon put him in his place and traveled the rest of the way outside with the coachman, even though I nearly froze off my pretty toes, as you keep calling them!*

*Tomorrow I will visit Kew Gardens, your old haunt, because Mr. Burchell has invited me to spend the day with him. He says he has "sensitive" news for me. But of course you will be the main topic of conversation, just as surely as Lucia's name won't even come up!*

*Sent to you with a sigh,*
*Your Charlotte.*


The little botanist had not aged well in the eight years since she and Daniel had seen him off on his expedition to southern Africa, where he hoped, perhaps, to shake off the pain of Lucia's loss. Always a slender man, he had shrunk even smaller, so that his clothes hung loose on his little frame.

"Charlotte, what a beauty you've become!" he said, sounding jolly enough in spite of the hint of deep melancholy in his eyes. "How old were you when I last saw you?"

"Fourteen. It was eight years ago."

"And so it was, so it was," he said. "You were my favorite pupil."

"Taught me to speak proper," Charlotte teased.

"Indeed, though I suspect you still talk a good Yamstock when you're in the mood."

"Yamstock? Wot dat?"

Mr. Burchell laughed in a way that told Charlotte he was out of practice. "Come, enough small talk. Time for the grand tour." He showed off the gardens, had something to say about almost every plant, but she detected a guardedness, a reluctance to meet her eyes, a gloominess that drew him to trees with dark histories. But he had nothing to say, not even a hint, of the sensitive news she had come all this way to hear.

"Here we have an alder. Its wood turns red after being freshly cut, so the old people thought it bled. Here's a black mulberry, which was planted in prison yards. The nursery rhyme 'Here we go round the mulberry bush' refers to the inmates trudging round and round in a circle, which was all the exercise the poor devils got."

Charlotte felt something had to be said that might open the door. "I know the two of you don't often speak, but Lucia sends her regards. She has a two-year-old girl, you know."

Burchell winced as if he had been struck in the face. "Really? A girl? What's her name? What does she look like?"

"She's also Lucia. She's inherited her mother's eyes and her coloring. I'm sure she'll grow up to be a lovely girl."

"Of course she will, with a heart hard as stone," said Burchell. But he seemed to want to talk about anything rather than Lucia, even the sensitive news Charlotte was dying to hear. "Well, there's no point in putting it off, I suppose. Let's sit." He led the way to a lonely bench crouched in the deep shade of a chestnut tree. For nearly a minute, he was silent, moving his hands as if he was trying to wash them.

"What is it, Mr. Burchell? Please tell me!" Charlotte said.

"I hesitate, because I don't know how to break this to you. It's tragic news…Daniel…"

"Daniel! What's the matter with him?"

"Daniel's fine. The news is not. He asked me to break it to you in person. It's about your very dear friend Mary Porteous. You must be strong. For the emperor's sake."

"Mary!"

"She's passed on, Charlotte."

"When?" she asked, but she knew the answer. It had to be shortly after the *Winchelsea* sailed for the news to have reached London so soon.

"She was watching from Ladder Hill cliff. When the ship disappeared, she must have stepped too close to the edge. They heard a scream."

Charlotte was crying so  hard she could scarcely speak. "Mary! My poor Mary! It was an accident. Tell me it was an accident!"

She held his eyes. What was it she saw in them? There was something hiding behind the compassion.

"Charlotte, you deserve to know. Everybody else on the island does. She was pregnant."

Tears of grief turned instantly to tears of anger. "Gaspard! He did it to her! I never want to see him again, ever! Oh it was all my fault! I should have broken down her bedroom door. Told her everything."

Now that the deed was done, Burchell seemed to recover his composure. "You couldn't do that. You're on a mission. A terrible shock but you must do your duty. I hear you have passed…certain information concerning the emperor's doctor on to Lady Holland and that your mission is nearing completion."

"Oh, I wish it *were*! I want to go home. To visit Mary's grave. To be with my darling Daniel. But I have to go to Italy, to Venice. To deliver a letter."

"I know," said Burchell gently. "You have a message for Lord Byron."

Charlotte sniffed down her tears. Concentrated on the moment. "How do know all this?"

"Lady Holland."

"You know her?"

"I help her with her gardens. She has arranged your passage to Venice. You will be escorted by the British consul, no less. Her Ladyship has even chosen a suitable disguise for you."

In spite of the tragedy of the moment, Charlotte noticed that the hint of an impish smile was creeping stealthily onto Burchell's lips. "What kind of disguise?" she said.

"She wants you to dress as a page."

# Chapter 16: Voyage to Venice

Lady Holland sent Charlotte a hairdresser to crop her hair. She sent a tailor to measure her for her page boy tunics, to be worn with tights, and a cobbler to make her shoes and a fine pair of riding boots. Then she sent word that Charlotte was to attend her *in costume*.

Her Ladyship, laid up in bed with arthritis, viewed the results with obvious satisfaction. "A hand on your hip, chin tilted up just a little. Now walk across the room and back. Just a little strut in your step. Yes! Fortunately, you are an athletic young woman—the tights show off your fine, long legs. You will most certainly pass for a slightly effeminate boy. I am sure Lord Byron will greet you with open arms."

Charlotte was examining herself in the full-length mirror attached to the wall at the foot of Lady Holland's bed, wondering what being met with open arms entailed. "Thank you, Your Ladyship, although all I have to do is deliver a letter. A postman could do that!"

"Oh, you are quite wrong, my dear. You are carrying a very special letter from the emperor, which Lord Byron is to read while you are in his presence. You are also on a mission for me."

Charlotte reluctantly turned her back on the remarkably fine image, she had to admit, that stared at her from the mirror. "A mission, Your Ladyship?"

"Yes. You are to use all your wiles to persuade Byron to write an epic poem about Napoleon, just like 'Childe Harold' is an epic poem about himself. You see, Byron calls himself the 'Napoleon of Rhyme.' So urge him to prove it by winning the sympathy of the world for Napoleon's cause. Byron, more than anyone, has the power to arouse public opinion to such a pitch that our jealous government is shamed into freeing the imperial eagle from his cage. Damn it, Charlotte, seduce the man if you have to!"

Charlotte suddenly felt it difficult to hold her proud pose as the weight of this unladylike proposal settled on her shoulders. "Your Ladyship, I'm not sure I can do that!"

"Of course you can, my dear *Charles*, for Charles you must be until Byron turns you back into a woman. You have the beauty, you are inexperienced, but you have wit, and most of all you know Napoleon. Byron is convinced that he is surrounded on all fronts by mental dwarfs. He respects only his idol, the emperor. He has nothing but contempt for the rest of humanity. Even the most dazzling luminaries are faint stars blinded by the brilliance of his moon and Napoleon's sun. Byron will feast on your anecdotes about the emperor's private life. He will be salivating to feast on you as well. Make him pay a high price for your favors! Make him write that poem, the more epic the better!"

Charlotte felt a flush burn her cheeks, whether prompted by shame or excitement she wasn't sure. "Your Ladyship makes me feel like a courtesan."

"Napoleon! Byron! Don't these names make your head spin? And what's wrong with being a courtesan in the halls of greatness? So was Theodora, and she rose to be empress of Rome. Free Napoleon and perhaps he will make you empress of Europe!"

Although the words were nonsense they haunted her through the frenzy of her hurried departure. Nonsense as dizzying as the pitching of the fast clipper that was carrying Charlotte around the boot of Italy as it headed for Venice, her cabin trunk full of costumes, some of them for a page, others for a princess.

211

Charlotte's traveling companion, the British consul in Venice on his way back to Italy, had introduced himself at the docks. "Richard Hoppner," he said with a foppish twirl to his scented handkerchief as he made his bow, "very much at your service. Lady Holland said—"

"Yes, she told me that you were kind enough to be my—" Charlotte had nearly said *chaperon* but caught herself in time, because she was dressed as a page, Lady Holland had insisted on it, so Charlotte could practice the impersonation on the ship. "To be my traveling companion."

The consul was fresh faced, barely thirty, slightly effeminate. He smiled sweetly. "Yes, well, it just so happened that I was returning to Venice after receiving fresh instructions from the government. Lady Holland, who knows absolutely everybody, remarked on the happy coincidence when I was calling on her the other evening, to update her on Byron, of course. It's why I am honored to be the occasional guest at Holland House whenever I'm back from Italy."

"It's very kind of you," said Charlotte. "Although I hope I won't bore you with all my questions!"

The British consul waved his handkerchief in a circle, as if he was in pursuit of an elusive idea. "You don't perchance have a sister?" he said with a twinkle in his eye. "Because the other night I saw the most beautiful young lady at Holland House. Quite the center of attention, she was. Escorted by one of Napoleon's generals, no less, that frightening chap Gaspard Gourgaud, who has a nasty reputation for being perpetually in pursuit of his next duel."

Charlotte dismissed the topic with a laugh. "That must have been someone else," she said.

"Is Lord Byron really bad and dangerous to know?" Charlotte asked the British consul that evening when the ship's captain finally excused himself and they were alone in the tiny officers' mess.

"Oh, yes, he is the very devil, although you mustn't believe everything Lady Caroline Lamb says. She's madder than he is!"

She smiled, mysteriously she hoped. "Lady Holland said Byron drove Lady Caroline to it—madness, I mean."

"Yes, by seducing her into his twilight. He enchanted her."

"Did he love her?"

"Certainly. He loves everyone, for a short time."

"Even Napoleon?"

This caught the consul by surprise. "Napoleon is the exception, because His Lordship believes that Napoleon is as great a man as he is."

Charlotte laughed, swirled her beer in what she thought was a manly fashion, and swallowed some of it, although she hated the bitter taste. "That's absurd! Napoleon commanded a million men. Perhaps he will do so again. From what I hear, Byron can't even command himself!"

"His Lordship commands an army of the mind. He commands more heads than Napoleon does feet."

Charlotte was enjoying the game. "Napoleon rose from nothing. His father was a backstreet lawyer in backward Corsica. Byron was born a lord!"

"Oh, no, he wasn't," countered the consul. "He's the son of a penniless wastrel, a mere army captain they called mad Jack Byron, who slit his throat when his debts finally caught up with him. His Lordship was only two when his father died. He was brought up by his mother, an absolutely repulsive harridan with aristocratic pretentions. His Lordship stuck pins into her arms because he hated how fat they were, the story goes. He's disgusted by fat to this day, especially his own. Goes for days fasting on hard biscuit and soda water."

"Am I too fat?" Charlotte asked, stretching out her legs.

The consul's eyes widened. "Not at all, and you know it! Your tights show your legs off to perfection. I must warn you, His Lordship has a naughty fascination with lithe young men. Picked it up in a Greek monastery."

"Interesting," said Charlotte ambiguously. "But if his father wasn't a lord, how did Byron become one?"

"Divine intervention! He and his mother were cooped up in cheap lodgings in Aberdeen when his great-uncle, someone he didn't know at all, finally did the right thing and died. When the genealogists did their work, they found that the lonely, clubfooted boy of ten was now the sixth Baron Byron, master of Newstead Abbey, a medieval monastery, which dates back six hundred years and came with vast acreage worth a very large fortune."

The ship, struck by a rogue cross wave, heeled. "Whoops!" Charlotte said, laying a slender hand face down on the table to regain her balance. "Sounds like a fairy story where a magic castle appears overnight."

The British consul waved his handkerchief. "More like a horror story. The great-uncle had let the estate run down, you see. Oh, you'll love this part. His favorite pastime was playing with his tame crickets. Let them run all over his naked body because he liked their tickle."

Charlotte made an unladylike sound and broke into Yamstock. "Dat so disgustin'!"

"My, my! What is that accent? You sound like a different person!"

She pouted. "Yamstock. It's what we old Saint Helena families speak like. It be the raal me. You lick it?"

The consul cleared his throat as he searched for the right words. "Ah, perhaps I would, if I got used to it. But I doubt I would ever like it less than a bed crawling with crickets!"

Charlotte laughed as she pictured the grotesque sight, but her thoughts were soon elsewhere, wandering the ruins of Newstead Abbey. "Did he fix it up? The abbey?"

"Yes and no—that's always the case with His Lordship. He had some of the rooms superbly furnished but didn't bother to fix the roof, so the expensive antique carpets are ruined and the beautiful new wallpaper is peeling off the walls. The great hall is a shooting gallery now, the grand dining room used for fencing practice. He prefers the abbey ruined, you see. More romantic that way. A memento of a vanished age. Ghostly processions of chanting monks carrying candles, lightning-blasted towers, ravens screeching as they swoop through cracked arches and over gardens run wild. A celebration of death and decay." He threw Charlotte a quick, clever look. "That's why it's so famous, you see. The inspiration for Gothic writers everywhere. For example, Thomas Peacock's *Nightmare Abbey*. Just published. Have you read it?"

Charlotte shook her head, missing the familiar swish of her long blonde hair. Her lapse into Yamstock had made her think of Daniel and what he could have done with the wild gardens of Byron's haunted ruin. Out of nowhere she felt the lash of a sudden flush. Daniel Hamilton and Lord Byron in the same sentence! Preposterous! But why was it preposterous? And where did that errant thought come from?

The consul interrupted her disturbing thoughts. "How about Mary Shelley's *Frankenstein*? Or hasn't the book found its way to nowhere yet?"

Charlotte tried to clear her head and defend her home all at the same time. "Saint Helena isn't exactly nowhere!"

215

"I was teasing, *Charles*. In fact, right now your island is the navel of the world. But we were talking about *Frankenstein*, or at least I was."

"What's *Frankenstein* about?"

"The creation of a superman out of dead body parts, sparked to life with electricity like Galvani's frog legs or something. Just published, anonymously. But, aha! I just happen to know the author. She's Mary Shelley, wife of the poet. It was all Lord Byron's idea, you see. Came to him at his chalet on Lake Geneva. This was in June, just two years ago, 1816, the year without a summer, damn awful weather. Something to do with a volcano in the East Indies poisoning the atmosphere. Incessant rain, too foul to go outside. Surely Saint Helena was affected?"

"Not really. The trade wind, the southeaster, blows away everything."

"That so?" said the consul. "Anyway, His Lordship had just arrived in Switzerland in Napoleon's carriage—"

Charlotte clutched at the word. "Napoleon's?"

"Proves how much he's obsessed with the emperor, how much he wants to be mistaken for him. He had an exact copy of Napoleon's campaign carriage made, the one that delivered him to destruction at Waterloo. A pull-out bed so comfortable he overslept and so lost the battle— that's at least what they say."

"I thought it was exactly the opposite. He couldn't sleep because of his hemorrhoids."

"Hemorrhoids? Where did you hear that?"

"Oh, just Saint Helena gossip. Tell me about the carriage."

"The original's in Madame Tussaud's now. Lord Byron took the replica with him when he crossed the Channel. It's dark blue, convertible, the roof folds down on both sides, just like Napoleon's. All the amenities, kitchen, dining room, desk that can be drawn out, en suite bathroom

216

with outside access for easy emptying of chamber pots. A real monster, so heavy it needs six horses to get it up a hill. I don't know why I'm telling you all this, because I'm sure he'll take you for a spin." The consul batted his right eye in a big, theatrical wink. "He absolutely loves to be seen chasing around in it with someone beautiful at his side."

"Really?" said Charlotte, her heart missing a beat.

"Take my word for it," said the consul, downing his brandy, his eyes riveted to Charlotte's face, watching her imagine the experience of riding through the Swiss Alps in Napoleon's carriage with Lord Byron at her side, his scarf blowing in the wind...He could see the poor girl's head was swimming like a cork in a whirlpool.

"Anyway," he went on, "getting back to *Frankenstein*, Lord Byron suggested they have a competition to see who could tell the scariest ghost story. He set the tone by reciting some verses from Coleridge's 'Christabel,' which he knew by heart—he really has the most astonishing memory:

> Beneath the lamp the lady bowed,
> And slowly rolled her eyes around...

"And so on. Now you have heard of Coleridge, haven't you, *Charles*?"

"Yes. In fact, I met him. At Holland House. He translated the epitaph on Napoleon's bust for me."

"Oh, I beg your pardon!" teased the consul, by now a little drunk. "I forget that you're the lass from nowhere who's been everywhere."

Charlotte arched an eyebrow. "Lass? So we are no longer going with the pretense?"

"Lady Holland had to tell me so I wouldn't make a faux pas. Pity, really. You see, I have to admit that like

Lord Byron, I enjoy male company now and then, if you know what I mean."

Charlotte faked surprise. "I thought Lord Byron was obsessed with women!"

"He is, but that's only half of it! Why do you think he's in Venice? You see, since Napoleon legalized homoerotic love in most Italian states, including Venice, it's become the hub of the liberated way of life. The Venetian carnival, held during the New Year season, is an absolute dream. Delightful young men and maids in costumes and masks so you can't tell them apart and don't want to. Hermes, Eros, Pan, and Harlequin everywhere. Minotaurs, demons. Six weeks of nonstop carnival. Quite enough to wear you out. After drinking the cup dry after his first carnival, last year, His Lordship collapsed into one of his famous sulks and wrote this:

> So, we'll go no more a roving
> So late into the night,
> Though the heart be still as loving,
> And the moon be still as bright.

The consul raised an approving eyebrow above a surprised smile when Charlotte took over:

> Though the night was made for loving,
> And the day returns too soon,
> Yet we'll go no more a roving
> By the light of the moon

"Well said, young *sir*. You've just shot up in my estimation."

"Was I ranked so low?"

"I jest, of course. We are shipmates, passing the time with trivialities. Now, where was I?"

218

*"Frankenstein."*

"Oh, yes. Well, to cut a long story short"—the consul was one of those people who made that promise often but never kept it—"most of them came up with nothing. Even His Lordship turned out only a couple of verses. Shelley told a weird tale about a woman who had eyes instead of nipples. Panicked by his own story, he grabbed a candle and ran shrieking out of the room to check on Mary—they weren't married yet, living in sin, you see. Free love, they call it these days. All Napoleon's fault. Everyone was very young then. Mary only eighteen, Shelley twenty-three, Byron a very old twenty-eight, all driven delirious by large doses of laudanum."

Charlotte leaned forward, an arm propping up her chin, one of her prettiest gestures. She was warming to the young consul. "Laudanum?"

"You haven't heard of it? How old-fashioned Saint Helena must be! Opium dissolved in alcohol. It's all the rage with the smart set. Anyway, to cut a long story short, every morning LB—that's what his close friends call Lord Byron—asked Mary if she'd thought of a story, and every morning she confessed she hadn't. One night she was thinking about the human leg and arm bones that His Lordship had dug up from a mass burial site, leftovers from an ancient battle, and kept under his bed to give him Gothic dreams."

"Human bones?"

"Of course! Kept telling everyone he had 'a leg and a wing,' as if they were parts of a chicken."

"Strange sense of humor."

"Strange? Yes, I suppose so. His Lordship is fascinated by 'glorious bones,' as he calls them. Scratched over the Waterloo battlefield on his way to Switzerland but found it had been picked clean. Anyway, he managed to buy some bones near Lake Geneva when his Napoleonic

219

carriage eventually delivered him there. They were the leftovers of soldiers the Swiss had slaughtered in the fifteenth century in some massacre or other. Made knife handles out of them. They're famous for their knives, you know. Anyway, to cut a long story short, Mary Shelley, at the stroke of midnight, had a waking dream where the bones under Byron's bed grew back their flesh. Someone who looked very much like Shelley was digging up more body parts and stitching them together to make a creature. The whole horrible scene was lit by huge flashes of lightning. Poor Mary jumped out of bed with a scream in her throat and *Frankenstein* in her head."

"*Frankenstein.* Was that the monster's name?"

"No, Victor Frankenstein was the scientist. The book's subtitled *The New Prometheus*. It's all very incestuous, because Byron was writing his 'Prometheus' poem at the time. Now you do know who Prometheus is, don't you?"

"He's chained to a lonely mountain peak, and a vulture feeds on his liver because he gave away the secret of fire to humans. Napoleon keeps saying that he is the modern Prometheus and that the fire he gave to us mortals is the Enlightenment."

There was suddenly a cautious look of respect in the consul's eyes. "And he is. Oh, how wonderful it must be to actually know him! You have no idea how lucky you are! Then I suppose he's read the poems he inspired Lord Byron to write about him?"

Charlotte smiled just enough to show a flash of teeth between her full lips. "He thinks every poem is about him. He calls Saint Helena his rock, Sir Hudson Lowe his vulture, and giving man the gift of liberty his sin."

The consul called for another brandy. Charlotte declined another beer. "All quite fascinating!" he said. "There are those who've read Mary's book who say that

Napoleon's not Prometheus. He's Victor Frankenstein stitching together Europe to make a monster such as the world has never seen."

"That's nonsense!"

"Read it and tell me what you think. His Lordship told me to bring him a copy. It hasn't made its way to Venice yet, as far as I know. It's a long tome, three volumes. Whatever you do, be careful not to blot it. His Lordship is awfully fussy about little things like smudges."

# Chapter 17: Mad, Bad Byron

Venice, the watery city. Charlotte could tell why Byron liked it. It was a decadent ruin. It looked like it was on the point of sinking beneath the waves like Atlantis.

"He wants to meet you tonight," the consul told her. "There's a fancy dress ball at the Fenice." He gave her his sweet, slightly shy smile. "That should be suitable, shouldn't it, seeing you're already in costume?"

"He's in that much of a hurry? I was hoping for a hot bath!"

"Oh, he's always in a tearing hurry when he isn't prostrate with melancholy. You'll see soon enough. Of course there's time for a bath. Nothing naughty starts before ten at night in Venice!"

The embassy was on a canal, like just about every building in this liquid city. The sour face of the consul's wife contrasted oddly with the sweetness of the consul's. "This is our guest, Miss Charlotte Knipe, who is to be called Charles for the moment to humor His Lordship. Charles this is my wife, Isabelle. She's Swiss," he said as if that explained everything.

"Delighted," said Isabelle, although she didn't look delighted at all. A child cried somewhere in a back room. "Oh, dear, she's probably wet herself again. Please excuse me. Her nanny is out shopping."

"You have a child?" said Charlotte.

"Yes and no," said the wife. "I've been taking care of her, but she's not mine. She's Lord Byron's. Her name's Allegra, although she isn't cheerful at all, poor thing."

"I thought his daughter's name was Augusta," said Charlotte.

"That's his legitimate child," said Isabelle over her shoulder. "Allegra is one of his many bastards. Her mother

222

is Mary Shelley's stepsister. A loose trollop, if ever there was one. She's besotted with His Lordship, but he avoids her like the plague. Not because she's loose. They all believe in free love, him and the Shelleys and all the oh so romantic poets. The type of free love that relies on someone else to pay."

The Fenice was vast. It could seat two thousand, the consul told Charlotte. But the seats had been covered up by a wooden floor built level with the stage, where an orchestra was playing Vivaldi. Charlotte had changed into a fresh page's uniform and wore a feathery bird mask the consul had lent her. Fortunately his wife couldn't be with them because the nanny had better things to do in bed with someone or other, *as usual*, the sour Switzer complained.

After walking Charlotte around the floor and greeting several people he somehow recognized in spite of their masks, the consul took her up to a large box decorated with lavish drapes and full-length mirrors. Byron's box. It was empty.

"He shouldn't be long," the consul said. "I'll be right outside. He wants to meet you alone."

Charlotte was terrified. She felt her shoulders nudging her ears, forced them down. She wasn't doing this for herself. She was doing it for Napoleon, she had to remind herself. She'd greet Byron, say something polite about his poetry, give him the letter, and leave. As the minutes dragged by, she nearly did leave, several times, but somehow she couldn't get her legs to move.

"Bugger him, dis all be crazy!" she whispered to herself in the full-length mirror. Somewhere behind her a curtain swished open. A figure appeared in the mirror. Even its mask was black.

She didn't turn, couldn't.

"A mask in a mirror," a voice caressed. "What lives behind the mask?"

Once again she felt that eerie tingling sensation at the back of her neck she'd first felt when Napoleon had looked her full in the face back at Porteous House in Saint Helena. Without giving it any forethought whatsoever, she found herself swept up into the game. "You know who I am," she said, turning. "I am the messenger."

"You have the message?"

She reached into a pocket, produced the letter that she'd kissed more than she should have. "Here it is."

He approached her with a quick sideways gait that was at the same time deliciously sinister and predatory, took the letter from her, impatiently tore it open. It couldn't have said very much, because he didn't do much more than glance at it before sliding it into his breast pocket, envelope and all.

"It orders me see your face," he said sounding almost regretful. "Although I'm sure that will reveal nothing. The letter says that beauty is the best disguise."

Charlotte slipped her mask up onto her short-cropped hair, where it sat like an oddly contrived cap. His approving smile, although followed by a pout on his full, almost feminine lips, gave her courage to go on.

She said, "I'm sure the letter says you are also to show me your face."

"Are you certain you want to look on the face of the devil?" he teased.

"Yes. If he looks like his portraits."

"Ha!" That pout again, and with a movement so sudden that it startled her, he tore off his black highwayman's mask.

His face was ivory pale, his forehead noble, his nose as neatly chiseled as a Greek statue of Adonis, but it was the eyes that ruled his face. They were bright blue, prominent and alive with a wild recklessness that no picture could capture. Byron was the finest-looking man Charlotte had ever seen.

They were still examining each other, Charlotte stunned and silent, when the mirrored door burst open and a slender creature dressed as a woman came in. "Oh, pardon me," the intruder said with a feminine wriggle but in a voice only just too deep to be female. "I'm obviously in the wrong place. I'm looking for the *masked* ball."

Byron slipped his mask back on, and so did Charlotte. "My apologies, Carissima, for abandoning you. This young gentleman had an urgent letter for me. All the way from Saint Helena."

"How exciting!" said the creature, taking possession of Byron's arm. "He's most certainly welcome to deliver a packet to me any time he wants!"

The magic went out of the moment as the British consul appeared. "Am I interrupting anything?" he asked.

"Hello, Hoppner," Byron said. "On cue, as usual. The message has been delivered, but the messenger must be fatigued from his long journey, I am sure." He looked down his perfect nose at Charlotte. "Do you ride?" he asked.

"Yes, Your Lordship," she said.

"Then we shall have a merry race of it on the Lido tomorrow, what do you say? The consul will escort you to where the horses will be waiting. Same time, same place, hey, Richard, waking the dead?"

"Certainly, Your Lordship."

Byron gave her a smirk, a pout, and a slight bow before allowing the gay to lead him away.


It was mid afternoon the next day when the gondola arrived at the canal entrance of the consulate. The consul didn't need to give the gondolier instructions.

"What did His Lordship mean by 'waking the dead'?" Charlotte asked when they got underway on the watery street of the floating city.

The consul laughed. "He is mysterious, isn't he? It's where the grooms wait for us with the horses. Used to be a Jewish cemetery until Napoleon leveled it to make room for a gun battery in '96. Wish he'd cleaned up after himself, because all those broken shards play havoc with horses' hooves."

Byron was sitting on a toppled tombstone. He looked bright and intensely alive. Two horses, held by handsome young men in tights, pawed the sand. Without a word the poet leaped into the saddle and took off down the beach.

"He's like that," said the consul with a grin. "He wants to challenge everybody at everything."

It was a wild ride along the Adriatic side of the long sandbar that was the Lido, mad, exhilarating fun for Charlotte to be free as a seagull after two weeks' confinement on a small ship at sea. Just her, the poet, and two good horses neighing with pleasure as they took in great lungfuls of cool, salty air. Forward and expert in the saddle, she caught up with him in less than a minute, swept past him with a whoop, and then, out of courtesy, slowed to let him take the lead again. She hoped he would stop for a breather, for a moment she could treasure for the rest of her life: the Venetian afternoon she had walked along the skirt of the flirtatious wavelets listening to the most famous poet in the world whisper love lines in her ear.

But Byron didn't spare his horse. When he reached the remains of an ancient jetty staggering into the sea, he spun it around so roughly it reared up onto its hindquarters.

"You ride well for a woman," he yelled into the sea breeze.

"I'm a farm girl. I've been riding since I was three!"

226

"No mercy, then. Race you back!"

He lost the race. Only when they were approaching the ruined graveyard did she fall back. A clutch of perhaps thirty people, both men and women, were standing among the broken headstones—the small flotilla of gondolas moored near Byron's boat explained how the celebrity chasers had gotten there. When they caught sight of Byron, at last in the lead, they let out a bay of triumph and trotted toward him, English reserve cast to the winds, every voice straining to outshout the other.

"'Childe Harold,' your autograph, please!"

"Autograph! Autograph!"

"Hardstaff, *The Times*! Have you really just sold your ancestral home?"

*"The Morning Chronicle.* Is it true you've just received a letter from Napoleon? What does it say?"

"Crabtree of the *Enquirer*! Are you going to help Napoleon escape from Saint Helena?"

The poet outflanked his tormenters by spurring his horse through the ruined graveyard, hooves be damned, and thundering down the sandy slope to where his gondola waited. He leaped from his horse in a fury, dived into his gondola, and hastily drew the blinds.

Charlotte, who had proceeded through the field of splintered marble at a more sensible pace, found Byron hiding in a dark corner. "Is it like this wherever you go?" she asked.

Overtaken by a fit of gloom, perhaps because of the question, he didn't answer. He didn't say a word until they reached the watery steps of the British consulate. "Tomorrow's the night of the full moon," he said after examining her with huge, haunted eyes. "I shall go for a ride in my carriage. I shall have the letter from Napoleon. Would you care to accompany me?"

It was improper, she knew. Even dangerous. But how could she say no?

Byron, in the exact replica of Napoleon's carriage, top folded down, came for her as the moon soared above the Doge's Palace. The poet, dressed in a huge black cape and wearing a small ornamental dagger, was the only passenger. The black mood was still weighing him down, because he said nothing, not even a word of greeting, patting the seat next to him and calling for the coachman to drive on.

"You were right. It is a full moon," she said to break the awkward silence.

He stared at her, his eyes made mad by the moonlight. "The bats are out. I've set the werewolves free. Witches soar on broomsticks. At midnight I will let you read Napoleon's letter. It will set you free!"

"What does it say? At least give me a hint!"

"Faster!" Byron yelled at the coachman. "Imagine," he said to her, "that we are careering down a narrow road carved out of an immense rocky mountain, ruined castles hanging over precipices, sheer ravines on every side, rivers raging down crevasses wetting us with their spray, everything mad and dangerous. Faster!"

The coachman whipped the horses; the carriage's rumble became a roar, which was fortunate so that the few peasants still afoot had time to scamper out of the way.

"She walks in beauty, like the night," he sang out.

"Of cloudless climes and starry skies,"

Charlotte, who had caught the mad spirit, sang out. "And all that's best of dark and bright—"

"Meet in her aspect and her eyes."

The same poem she had recited with Daniel in another age and on another planet. But now she was reciting it with the poet himself! The rush of emotions

228

swept Daniel away. She saw him disappearing, growing smaller in the rushing torrent of her imagination. A last wave of his hand and he was gone, and she was back with the poet in Napoleon's windy chariot pulled by horses maddened by the whip.

Byron looked skyward, observing the position of the moon, perhaps. "The time has come," he said. He handed her the letter. "Read it aloud, it's bright enough."

"I can't," Charlotte said. "It's in Italian, I think."

"I'll summarize. Napoleon says that Lady Holland has sent him a copy of *Frankenstein*, clearly meant to be Napoleon himself, who creates a superhuman creature, clearly meant to be me, since I have been molded like clay by his ideas. This creature, me, is powerful but hideous, Napoleon says, a reference to my clubfoot and the way it repulses every woman I meet."

"But that's not true!"

Byron ignored her. "Soon, writes Napoleon, the creature begs his creator to make him a mate, which the scientist is unwilling to do, because even one monster is too much for the world. Are you following all this?"

"Yes, but—"

"Napoleon, of course, goes one better than Frankenstein the scientist. He creates a beautiful woman for the monster. Read the last line."

Charlotte struggled with the Italian.

"Do you know what that means? It means, 'Take her, she is my gift to you.'"

Without warning, he threw himself on her like a lightning bolt. She astonished him by responding like its thunder clap. "Lady Holland said you are a virgin," he said, breaking her fierce embrace. "And that you are to remain that way."

"I am more than that. I am a command from Napoleon."

His second kiss was fiercer than his first. "Which I am going to enjoy obeying," he said.

Afterward Byron called to the coachman, who must have heard everything, with the order to drive back to the consulate. "Thank Napoleon for his beautiful gift," he said. "Assure him that I am doing everything I can to promote our cause."

She was so shocked by his sudden coldness that she lapsed into Yamstock. "I wazz tinking," she began before she caught herself. "I was thinking of visiting Venice for a while. The consul has invited me to stay."

At least her lapse aroused mild curiosity. "Is that your Saint Helena dialect coming out of hiding?"

She shot him a teasing grin. "Eirce—that means yes. As in: eirce, you done be one werry famous poet. Everybody done hear about you. Wot you tink about Yamstock?"

Byron sighed with such a deep sadness she felt tears spring to her eyes. "Charlotte, go back. Europe is bad for you. I'm worse. Go back home and tend to Napoleon. Console him in his desolation. I'm sure you are his favorite creature. Be the dove that Noah released. Take the emperor back an olive leaf from me."

"Perhaps I'm the raven that never returned to the ark," she said, fighting to revive her spirits.

"No," he said. "*I* am the raven. I can never return to England."

"Why not?"

"Why do you think Lady Holland had you dress as a boy? Why do you think I enjoyed you as I did? What do I care about virginity? Housemaids, shop assistants, messenger boys, countesses. All whores!"

"Is that all I am to you?"

"How can you even think that? You are a gift from the other great man of the century!"

With a tired creak, Napoleon's carriage drew up outside the consulate. Byron, eyes fixed on the moon, didn't seem to notice.

"Thank you," Charlotte said. He didn't seem to hear. He was motionless. So was the coachman. It was as if a toy had wound down. The show was over. She let herself out.

As the carriage rattled off, he gave a mad laugh. "Forget about me—if you can!"

She couldn't forget about him. She lay awake thinking of passion. It was a monstrous wave that swept everything before it, expectations, good intentions, promises, vows. Every superstructure of orderly life annihilated, leaving a wasteland in its path. But what an exquisite sensation to be caught up in that torrent! To be thrown skyward like the mists chased up the sheer mountains of Saint Helena by the exuberant southeaster! What could be more painful than a love like hers, an undecided love? Yes, she was in love, but she was torn to shreds trying to decide with whom.

It was dawn before she finally fell asleep. When she woke toward the middle of the day, she put on the emerald dress Lady Holland had bought her, touched up her face.

"The Palazzo Mocenigo," she told the consul's gondolier.

The man grinned slyly. "I hear Lord Byron is a popular destination today," he said.

She told him to wait. She had no intention of staying long. She wanted Byron to see her as a woman, even if it was just once.

Two huge, baying black dogs guarded the open door. When they noticed that she wasn't afraid of them, they licked her hand. Somewhere inside two women were screaming at each other in Italian. She went in, followed by the dogs. The place was a zoo. Caged animals were everywhere. A pair of monkeys. A fox and a wolf in the same cage. Ravens chuckled as they examined her with one eye and then another. Guinea fowl, an Egyptian crane, a sad-looking ostrich, a large snake—perhaps a python. The most curious exhibit of all was a blonde child, a girl by her clothes, who sat placidly in a cage sucking her thumb. She looked like one of the exhibits.

The screeching stopped. A black-haired woman hurried in, frowned when she saw Charlotte, opened the cage, took out the toddler, and planted a kiss on her fat cheek. The kiss was rewarded by a piercing shriek.

"She's just sixteen months. We lock her away when we have to do something," the black-haired woman explained in a German accent. "She sticks her hands in the cages. She's been bitten once already by a monkey. But she goes into a tantrum when we take her away. They're her only friends, poor thing. She hates going home to the consulate."

"Who is she?" Charlotte suspected she already knew.

"Allegra. Lord Byron's daughter. I am Elise, her nurse. You're here so see him." It wasn't a question.

"Yes."

"Still in bed. Upstairs. The door's open—he's expecting you," she said with a flat intonation, as if visits from women walking in off the street into his bedroom were an everyday occurrence, which no doubt they were.

Charlotte looked in the direction pointed out by the nanny's jabbing thumb. A massive marble staircase led up to Byron's lair. She should have turned around right then. But she couldn't. The drumming of the six horses pulling Napoleon's blue-black carriage thundered in her temples.

She was climbing the stairs. At some point the cries of the infant below were drowned by the cries of a woman above. Still she went up, step after step, through a lofty billiard room to a heavy wooden door, as wide open as the gates of hell.

When he had seen her she would leave. She stood at the open bedroom door for what seemed long minutes before he noticed her. He stopped his business under the covers. "Ah, it's Napoleon's Rosebud in full regimentals!" he said with a smirk that ended in an ironic pout. "What a beauty you are. No wonder *mon empereur* sent you to me! Please meet Margharita, who is known as the Furnace for good reason." With a quick movement, he pulled aside the covers, which made the Furnace scream with mock modesty. "See, she has legs as long as yours and not an ounce of fat on her belly. What a brace of beauties you make! Come and join us in our labor of love, *caro*. You know you can't resist!"

Charlotte must have grown wings, she fled down the marble staircase so fast. "The consulate, hurry!" she told the gondolier, as if she was being pursued by the devil himself.

She couldn't resist looking up at the balcony that must have led off the bedroom. Byron was there, draped in a flowing silk gown. "Adieu, Rosebud! Give my love to Napoleon because he has just given his love to me!" he called out. He knew she would take the next ship back to England.

The first night out at sea, she went on deck. The moon was still nearly full, lighting the caps of the sleepy waves. Her lips moved:

> So, we'll go no more a-roving
> So late into the night,

233

Though the heart be still as loving,
And the moon be still as bright.

A flood of tears flushed Byron away. He was a
monster as twisted as his foot.

# Chapter 18: The Submarine

A letter was waiting for her on a little silver tray in her bedroom at Holland House. It was from Daniel. She felt too travel stained to touch it.

A junior lady's maid helped her wash off the grime of the journey in a luxurious bath. A senior maid dressed her in a new but very modest gray outfit she said Lady Holland wanted her to wear.

"Why?" asked Charlotte. "It's nicely cut but awfully plain. Not Lady Holland's taste at all, I would have thought. I look like a servant."

The maid let loose a barely audible sniff. "My lady, I'm simply following instructions."

Her hair, still short, was being shaped by a hairdresser, the third servant to attend to her before she was ready to face the world. Charlotte snapped her fingers at the junior maid and pointed at the letter. The junior maid, oozing deference, brought it to her, tray and all, like a sacred offering.

> *Saint Helena*
> *April 18, 1818*
> *My darling Charlotte:*
> *By the time you receive this letter I hope you will be reconciled to the death of your very dear friend Mary. I also hope that you did not find it offensive that I didn't inform you of the tragedy but left that sad duty to Mr. Burchell in the hope that it would be kinder coming from a loving person than from words scratched on paper. Alas, I have more sad news that I must share with you directly because it is a family matter. Following so soon after the tragic death of Mary, I have to tell you that*

*your dear uncle Samuel was at last relieved of his suffering when he passed on to a better world yesterday evening. It is meager consolation, I know, but it is widely held that he died the wealthiest planter on the island, which is in mourning as if we Yamstocks have lost our king.*

Charlotte stopped reading because her eyes were filling with tears. Dear, gentle Uncle Samuel! He had been like a father to her since she had lost hers. It was he who had given her the material and moral support to get where she was now, wherever that was, playing the part of spy or traitor or adventuress, she wasn't sure which.

And Mary! It wasn't that she'd stopped mourning her and hating Gaspard for taking advantage of her. The rush of events had tidied away both of them into the dusty corners of her mind, from which they ventured out like spiders only when she lay awake on her midnight pillow, haunted by the thundering of Napoleon's carriage in the moonlight, the cackle of Byron's mad laughter.

No! No more! She must never think of what happened with Byron!

She went back to Daniel's letter.

*As so often happens, dear Charlotte, this bad news comes yoked to the good. I am now the owner of Virgin Hall! I am pinching myself black and blue to make sure I'm not dreaming. It's unbelievable, but it's true. This morning Napoleon's valet, that cool customer Marchand, called on me with the title deed already in my name. He said the gift was a consideration from the emperor for services both rendered and to be rendered. It appears Napoleon has owned Virgin Hall for some time but is making the transfer now, so it appears*

*that Uncle Samuel gave me the property. Gave us
the property, for you will very soon, I fervently
hope, be sharing it with me as its beautiful mistress.
I suspect that this astonishing stroke of luck is more
about you than about me. Napoleon wants to lure
you back home with a feathered nest, in which hope
he is second only to me!*

*I lie half-awake at night dreaming that we
are sitting at the Friar's feet together, as we have
done so many times since we were children. I dream
we are going on one of those mad Saint Helena
walks where we pass into a new climate every half
an hour, as if we were flying around the world on
the back of a meteor. I still do those walks,
collecting specimens for the Gardens, but miss you
terribly because I have nothing to kiss but the empty
sky. Put me out of my misery, my darling. Come
home to Virgin Hall!*

There was a polite knock at the door. Yet another
lady's maid appeared.

"Lady Holland requests the pleasure of your
company at your earliest convenience in her private
drawing room," she squeaked.

Lady Holland, enthroned in a large comfortable
chair because her arthritis was still playing up, was writing
a letter in her shrine. Charlotte couldn't resist glancing at
Byron's portraits, feeling a guilty shard of pleasure strike at
her as she did so.

She could tell by a quick flicker of emotion on Her
Ladyship's face, by the way she turned her best ear toward
her, that she had noticed. "So do tell me, how did you get
on with our famous poet?" she said in the teasing way of
someone who already knows the answer to her question.

"Very well, Your Ladyship," Charlotte said, although this was both the truth and a lie. "He is an extraordinary man."

"Does he still support our cause?"

"Yes, Your Ladyship. He says Napoleon is the greatest man of the age."

"After Byron, I suppose?"

"He does seem to have a very high opinion of himself. But he says the emperor created him."

"And so he did. Like that scientist Frankenstein created his monster. Byron does think of himself as a monster, doesn't he?" she added as a whimsical afterthought.

"Sometimes I think he does, because of his deformed foot. He claims to be reminded he's a monster every step he takes."

Lady Holland winced as she flexed her swollen right ankle. "Yes, of course. I know exactly what that's like. Well, what else did he have to say? I know you are absolutely brimming with wicked secrets that are dying to be told."

"He did have an awful lot to say, Your Ladyship. He talks all the time. Or else he says nothing at all, just glowers and bites his nails."

Lady Holland flicked her wrist impatiently, as if she were brushing off a fly of a thought. "Your boy. Daniel. You've read his letter?"

"Yes. He is well."

"*Well* be damned, girl!" Lady Holland snapped. "No one cares about his health! Does he send news of Napoleon?"

"Yes, Your Ladyship. He says that Napoleon has given us an estate for a wedding gift. It's called Virgin Hall."

"Ha! *Virgin* Hall. An ironical gift for someone who has just been tumbled by Lord Byron!"

"Lady Holland, I *am* still a virgin!" Charlotte said a lot more hotly than what was polite.

The old woman's hard eyes glittered with amusement. "However, I hear it was a damn near-run thing, as Wellington would have put it. Wouldn't it have been priceless if you lost your virginity in the same carriage that Napoleon lost Waterloo! But fortunately for you, Byron prefers…Oh, enough of him and his little perversions. Let's talk about something big."

"Your Ladyship?" said Charlotte, not at all sure that there wasn't some sort of wicked innuendo in play.

But Lady Holland's thoughts had taken flight. "I have a glorious plan to rescue the emperor from that damned island of yours! A special boat will spirit him off to the Americas so he can reestablish his empire, in Mexico, perhaps. Then he will forge a grand alliance with the United States. Europe will rise up, cast off its chains, and join in. The alliance will rule the world! The end of deference! Liberty, justice, and equality for all! Now isn't that something worth risking your life for?"

Charlotte kept her feet on the ground. "Your Ladyship, there is a small problem. From the lookout post on Diana's Peak, the highest point on Saint Helena, you can see a ship sixty miles away. If your rescue vessel approaches without authorization, it will be blown out of the water."

Lady Holland stared at her, the joy of triumph lighting up her eyes. "Not if it travels *under* the water!"

Charlotte was so astonished by this outlandish idea that she forgot her manners. "That's impossible!"

"Apparently not. It's a newfangled American invention. It's called a submarine. This is where you come in. You must see this machine with your own eyes so you

239

can describe it to the emperor, confirm that it exists. You have survived his interrogations before, I am told. You know what to expect."

"Your Ladyship, I am not mechanical."

"You may not be James Watt, but you are the best we have. Balcombe is banned from the island. General Gaspard Gourgaud won't be allowed to go back, either. It's all up to you. Will you do it?"

Charlotte nodded, dumbfounded.

"Excellent! No time like the present, I always say. An unmarked buggy waits for you outside. In the buggy is a young Cockney girl called Polly. She is one of our operatives. She will take you to the submarine. That is why I have dressed you more as a maid than a lady. So you do not attract unwelcome attention at the docks. However," she went on with a little smile, "I'm afraid I have not succeeded. You look even more eye catching in plain clothes!"

The unmarked one-horse buggy was waiting at a servants' entrance. Polly was pretty in a vulgar way. She looked like a trollop, Charlotte thought.

"Oh, I recognize you!" the girl cooed when Charlotte slid in next to her. "Daniel showed me a picture."

"Really? How well do you know him?" Charlotte couldn't resist asking.

"Dearie, we got on like 'ouses on fire! Good lad, that one, if you know what I mean!"

Charlotte felt her eyes narrow. *Get back to business*, she counseled herself. "What do you know of this submarine thing?"

"It really is somefink from anuvver world. Wouldn't have believed it if I 'adn't seen it for meself. That's why we need to show you, so you can pass it on to you know who."

"We?"

"I work for Lady Holland, like you do, I s'pose."

Charlotte sensed that underneath the overdone cosmetics and garish clothes there was much more to this girl that met the eye. "So you know Lady Holland?"

"Behind the curtain!"

"What?"

Polly rolled her eyes at Charlotte's ignorance of Cockney rhyming slang. "Means 'for certain.'"

"Oh."

"You excited?" said Polly.

"Mystified," said Charlotte. "How does the driver know where to go?"

"He ought to by now. Lady Holland has sent loads of toffs to see it. Well, at least three or four. Rich Frenchies, mostly. Building a submarine ain't cheap."

"You've seen it yourself, you said?"

"You bet. It's called the *Eagle*. In 'onor of the emperor. It's somefink special, it really is."

"Who's building it?"

"A sea captain. Bit of a devil, in and out of bed, if you know what I mean!"

Charlotte felt herself color. "Really?"

"Oh, yes, is the answer. Over six foot and 'andsome as Lucifer, he is. Children, horses, and dogs adore him. But he drives us women crazy. Best tighten your chastity belt!"

"What else do you know about him?"

"That he's England's most famous smuggler an' escape ar'ist. He's been thrown in the clink more times than he's gone to church. Got out every time, one way or anuvver. Even escaped from Napoleon hisself. Who be'er to spring the emperor and smuggle him away than a professional?"

The dock in Blackwall Reach was surrounded by high wooden walls and a tall floating gate on the river side,

241

which could be closed for complete privacy. At the gate was a freshly painted shack, and in the shack, behind a desk, which was covered by a large map, sat Captain Thomas Johnson, the man who had paid for her dress in Bond Street and whom Gaspard had wanted to fight at Holland House.

"Miss Charlotte Knipe," he said with a dangerous twinkle in his startling blue eyes. "We meet again!"

Charlotte fought to regain her composure. "I didn't know…"

"Lady Holland loves her little surprises. Her Ladyship tells me that Napoleon sent you."

"Yes," said Charlotte. "To help secure his release."

"Oh, we'll soon take care of that! I know His Majesty personally, did he mention it?"

"No. It was Lady Holland who sent me to you."

"He asked me to pilot the invasion of England back in '03. I refused, because I knew he simply didn't have enough ships. He thought it was because I favored England over France, flew into one of his famous rages, threw me into prison. I escaped, of course, and made my way to America. That's where I hooked up with Robert Fulton, a very clever American engineer—fearfully inventive, those Yankees. He introduced me to submarines. Submarines! A smuggler's dream come true!"

"Tell her about the *Eagle*, love," said Polly, who sounded quite breathless with excitement.

"Ha!" exclaimed the captain. He tapped the unrolled map on his desk with a powerful hand. "First you've got to find her. Clue: she looks like an overgrown porpoise. Come closer, Miss Charlotte. I don't bite, except very gently. Find the *Eagle*!"

"Yes, find it if you can!" teased Polly, who seemed to have played this game before. "She's big enough!"

242

Charlotte walked round the desk and stood next to Captain Johnson. As tall as she was he towered over her, his large, athletic body exuding the pleasant smell of salt perfumed with tobacco. He relit the clay pipe he'd been smoking and watched her with a quizzical expression as she examined the map.

That's all it was. A large map of the Thames, showing the docks that cluttered the riverbanks all the way to the sea. There were ships and rowing boats sketched in everywhere, but nothing that resembled a porpoise.

Charlotte looked up boldly into the dangerous blue eyes. "I'm not quite sure of the rules of the game," she said, "but this is just an ordinary map. There is no sign of a porpoise."

Captain Johnson made an ironic little bow. "Of course there isn't! That's the genius of it. It's a ship, all right. It's been just about everywhere on that map today, but when it's underwater, it doesn't exist!" He puffed so exuberantly at the pipe that Charlotte choked on the smoke. Captain Johnson, eyes burning like blue fire, didn't seem to notice. "Tell the emperor that I will tow the *Eagle* to Saint Helena and enter the sixty-mile visibility zone at night. Then, well before dawn, I will transfer to the *Eagle* and the tow ship will flee for the horizon. At dawn the *Eagle* will dive and complete its approach to the island underwater."

"How does the submarine move? Not by wagging its tail, surely?" said Charlotte, who couldn't resist the temptation to ruffle this gorgeous man's feathers.

He favored her with a flash of white teeth. "We tried that, in fact, but settled on a propeller. Do you know what that is?"

"Not really."

"Well, it spins around and pushes you through the water."

"A sort of water wheel?"

Captain Johnson, still working on his pipe, answered with a mouthful of smoke. "Sort of."

"But what drives the propeller? The emperor will want to hear every detail."

"A steam engine. It can drive the *Eagle* at five miles an hour underwater—more on the surface."

"I see," said Charlotte, although she didn't. She was overwhelmed by the technology. She was overwhelmed by the madcap adventurer. She was on a wild, moonlit ride. But this time it wasn't with Byron, it was with Captain Johnson. Polly was right—he was irresistible. He could have most of her anytime he wanted. She could see in those sharp eyes of his, in his secretive smile, that he knew.

Captain Johnson blew smoke at the ceiling, watched it rise. "The emperor will understand. He's very technical, you know. He summoned Professor Volta to Paris in '01. Gave him a medal for discovering the electric battery. Now, if only someone would invent the electric *motor*, the *Eagle* could travel around the world underwater!"

Charlotte recovered her wits with an effort. "Tell me more about the escape," she said.

"Quite simple! We will take Napoleon on board that night, transfer him to the tow ship, and then head for America, where he will be welcomed like the hero he is."

"But how do you get the emperor from Longwood to the submarine? He's surrounded by guards, night and day."

Johnson put down his pipe. "Dr. O'Meara helped us work out this part. We will attach a cable to a peak near Longwood house and run it down to the sea. The emperor will disguise himself as a liveried servant, who, as you know, come and go from the house as they please. Once through the perimeter of guards, he will be taken to the cable chair. The chair will have a footboard behind it for the man who controls the rate of descent with a brake. I will be that man."

During the long moment of silence that followed, Charlotte imagined Napoleon, squeezed into green livery, whizzed down a cliff to the sea by a dashing swashbuckler in the dead of night. The idea seemed utterly brilliant and equally preposterous at the same time.

There was a loud knock on the door. It was a longshoreman who touched his cap. "She's back, Captain. We're opening the sea gate to let her in!"

The dock was about fourty yards long and twenty wide. It was closed by a floating wall the man had called a sea gate, which was being cranked open. Captain Johnson led the way down some steps to the concrete edge of the dock. The muddy Thames lapped at their feet.

"She's coming in," said the captain when the gate was fully open. "Can you see anything?"

There wasn't even the slightest ripple on the surface. "No."

"Totally invisible, you see. Now behold the behemoth!"

There was need for the warning. A muffled clanging noise rose out of the water, as if Neptune had thrown open the doors of his undersea dungeon. A moment later the surface of the water split open, as a great black porpoise hissing clouds of steam lunged out of the water.

"Miss Charlotte, I present you with the *Eagle*, 114 tons, eighty-four feet long. It is the eagle that will fly Napoleon to America."

# Chapter 19: Home

Saint Helena!

Charlotte spent most of the day clutching the ship's railings as the island, the tip of a vast undersea volcano, emerged slowly from the sea. The boat, caught in the teeth of the ill-tempered southeaster, tacked to and fro as it fought to make headway.

The thousand-foot walls of Napoleon's prison, and the vast moat of the South Atlantic that surrounded it, glowed like bronze as the day died, but the highlands were lost in a mantle of weeping clouds. It would be cold and foggy on Deadwood Plain. He would be sitting in front of a tiny wood fire, reading, perhaps, or dreaming of the glorious past.

And Daniel? Dear Daniel! An innocent leaf on the vines of intrigue that infested her life. He would probably still be working away in his Botanical Gardens, aware from the boom of the signal cannon that a ship was coming in, unaware of its troublesome cargo.

Perhaps not so innocent, according to Polly. The thought struck at Charlotte like a viper.

"This is our last good-bye," Polly had told her when the carriage dropped the girl off in Cheapside on its way back to Holland House. "Now that you've seen the submarine they're goin' to ship you straight back to Boney, mark my words, wif' no time for farewells. Lucky fing! You struck gold with that Daniel of yours. I've 'ad your French general Go-Go. I've 'ad Lord Byron, because you know 'ow much he likes to slum it with types like me. I've even 'ad that 'andsome Captain Tom Johnson back there with his submarine. Let me tell you somefink, dearie. Daniel's twice the man in bed as any of 'em, if you know what I mean!"

*Not so innocent at all.*

The confusing dream that had woken her in her cabin the previous night leaked back into Charlotte's mind. She was on a wild moonlit ride with Byron, who was screaming exultantly into the wind. Above them, climbing up the cliff face with superhuman speed, was Frankenstein's monster, lit by great flashes of lightning. Standing on the mountain's pinnacle, waiting for the monster, was Napoleon, wearing his threadbare green coat, Legion of Honor medal, and black hat. Byron was no longer clutching the reins. It was Daniel who whipped on the horses, trying to catch up with Napoleon, who was racing down to the sea on the cable chair with her standing behind him on the footboard, fleeing to America with him.

Just a silly dream.


The next morning the ship anchored in James Bay. According to the census, there were 820 white Yamstocks on Saint Helena, 618 Chinese laborers, five hundred free blacks, and 1,540 black slaves. At least half the Yamstocks were at the wharf to see the island's most beautiful girl, one of their own, return from her mysterious mission to Europe. Of course her mother, all elbows, was there, as were her brothers and sisters and aunts and cousins and all their friends and relatives. Half the island.

The only Yamstock who wasn't there was the one she wanted to see most. Daniel.

"He's waiting for you in the Gardens," her brother Henry, who wore his kilt for the occasion, told her when his quick eyes saw her searching the crowd. "He told me to tell you to slip away and meet him there. He's taking you to see someone."

She excused herself from the impromptu gathering on her mother's porch, said Daniel wanted to see her alone.

There were nudges and there were winks, but not even annoying children dared to follow her.

He was waiting at the door of the little shack where he kept the garden tools. A horse stamped and snorted impatiently. Daniel kissed her and for a glorious moment held her close, his heart beating against hers.

"We're late," he said.

"For him?"

"He says you have a message."

"Yes."

"Let's go!"

The horse was a fine looking animal. "Yours?" she asked.

"On loan from Longwood. I've been practicing my riding."

He mounted first, pulled her up behind him. She wrapped her arms tightly around his waist. His stomach was hard and ribbed with muscle, the reward of hard physical work. He gave the horse its head. The wind whipped through her hair. For a moment she was back in Venice, on the sands of the Lido, racing Byron.

*Daniel's twice the man in bed as any of 'em.*

Napoleon's carriage was waiting for them at Hutt's Gate, the portal to Deadwood Plain. A footman took the panting horse. Another opened the carriage door. Napoleon wore his threadbare green coat decorated with his tarnished Legion of Honor medal with its defiant imperial eagle at the center. His deep-set eyes glowed in his gloomy face.

He didn't greet her. "What did you think of London?" he snapped.

"It is unimaginably huge, Your Majesty."

"I was within a stone's throw of visiting it myself a few years ago," he said with an expression of grim humor. "With two hundred thousand men at my back."

"You would have been greeted as a liberator."

"I will be, I'm sure, as soon as I get off this cursed rock. You have news for me." It was a statement.

"An American has designed a boat that sails under the water. I have seen it."

"How big?"

"Over eighty feet long."

"How is it powered?

"Steam, I think. It belched stream when it emerged from the water."

"Whom have you told?"

"No one."

"Not even Daniel?"

She glanced at Daniel for confirmation. "No," she said.

"My jailer will interrogate you first thing tomorrow," Napoleon said. "He is a clever inquisitor with a nose for secrets. But you must keep the news of the craft a secret. Can you do that?"

Charlotte caught the inquiring look Daniel shot at Napoleon. The emperor's face remained impassive. Her eyes flew back to Daniel. Only then, when she couldn't see it, did Napoleon give him a curt nod of assent.

Afterward, when they were back at the Botanical Gardens, Charlotte and Daniel walked together, keeping their voices low as if there were ears in the breadfruit trees. First she described Captain Johnson, to make him jealous, and then gave him a waspish description of Polly, because Polly made her jealous.

Daniel changed the subject. "You missed Dr. O'Meara by just two weeks," he said.

"Pity. I would like to have told him what a hero he is in England."

"That's exactly what Governor Lowe didn't want."

"It doesn't matter what he wants," said Charlotte.
"Dr. O'Meara will be taken straight to Lady Holland. Lowe
knows that. I'm surprised he let him go."
Daniel pulled out a weed, examined its roots.
"Orders. He had no choice. London had no choice.
O'Meara didn't *commit* a crime. He *refused* to commit one.
England is still a free country, you know."
"Not until it frees the emperor."

As Napoleon predicted, His Excellency Sir Hudson
Lowe sent for Charlotte the next morning. He skewered her
with his suspicious sideways look. "You saw Napoleon
yesterday afternoon," he snapped without asking her to sit.
"Yes. We ran into him by chance at Hutt's Gate,"
she lied. "He was taking a drive around his perimeter."
"By chance? I see. Did he ask you about London?"
"Yes."
"What did you tell him?"
"That I stayed with Lady Holland part of the time.
She said you did her the honor of calling on her several
times. She sends you her most cordial regards."
Lowe's laugh was as dry as Jamestown dust.
"Whom did you meet at Holland House?"
"As you know, Sir Hudson, Holland House has
receptions almost every night. I met a great many people."
"Damn Liberals, all of them, baying for Napoleon's
release."
"Yes."
He seemed startled by her candor, but his words
were calm enough. "I've heard you spread O'Meara's lie,
that I ordered him to kill Bonaparte."
"I commented on it, yes, when asked. It was
impossible not to. It was the talk of the town."
"What did you say?"

"That I had known Dr. O'Meara for years but that he had never mentioned it to me or anyone else on Saint Helena."

"A good answer. Lady Holland seems to have grown a cool head on you. A formidable woman that, formidable. Did she ask you to give Napoleon a message of any sort?"

"She asked me to give him a bag of sugared prunes. She said he can't get them here."

"Prunes? Really?" Lowe muttered, distracted. Then he seemed to pull himself together. "Sit, we need to talk."

Charlotte sat on the edge of the chair, back ramrod straight, as she had seen bon ton ladies in London do. "About what, Sir Hudson?"

"About your duty to report acts of treason, especially as related to the security of the prisoner. Treason is a hanging crime. Did you know that?" he said very softly.

Charlotte, eyes large pools of innocence, nodded. What did this man know?

"Is there anything you need to tell me?"

Somehow she found her voice. "No, Your Excellency."

Lowe nodded thoughtfully. Abruptly his tone became more convivial. "I suppose you know that Countess de Montholon, the woman who's been taking General Bonaparte's dictation, has just had a child, a daughter?"

"Yes, sir. Little Napoleone-Josephine."

"Napoleon's child. Just as well it wasn't a son, or we'd have a second prince imperial on our hands! Another stroke of luck: Napoleon hates the smell of breast milk, can you believe that? Milk for his own child? So he's banned the countess from his presence. It's thrown her into the bowels of a depression—often happens to women after childbirth, apparently. She hardly gets out of bed."

251

Charlotte knew all this. "Which means that he needs someone else to take his dictation."

"My, my, you are quick. But are you quick enough to realize that you will need to keep your eyes and your ears open for anything…irregular, which you must immediately report to me?"

"Oh, yes, sir. You can rely on me."

Long after dark that evening, a lone horseman rode unseen out of Jamestown, up the path that wound itself up the precipice of Ladder Hill, onto the winding road that led to Plantation House, where Sir Hudson Lowe, weary with the stress of the day, was already in his dressing gown, ready for bed.

"What is it, man? You said it was urgent," Lowe said as soon as the valet had bowed himself out.

"It is, Sir Hudson. A monstrous plan to snatch Napoleon away from under your nose."

"Nonsense! I have thought through every possibility, every single one! What is this plan?"

"A submarine."

Lowe's eyes widened with a rapidly growing sense of panic. "A submarine? What in the name of the devil is that?"

"It's a new American invention, sir. Instead of sailing on the surface of the sea, it sails underneath it."

In a vision from hell, Lowe saw a craft of as yet undetermined shape sailing right underneath the fleet of frigates that he had circling the island, day and night, spiriting away the man he hated more than Satan himself. "That's impossible!"

"No, sir, it is not," said Daniel. "Charlotte saw it with her own eyes, in the Thames. It was totally invisible until it surfaced so close to her she could almost touch it."

"She told me nothing of this fiendish invention. Nothing! This is treason! I will throw the lying whelp into a dungeon so deep that not even the rats will find her!"

"It is about eighty feet long, Your Excellency. It can hold a crew of twenty men. It has large glass portholes for navigation. She saw men inside waving at her."

"Good God! Can her report be trusted? Of course she can't, she lied to me!"

"But not to me. And not to Napoleon."

"She told him about this...this thing?"

"Yes, Your Excellency."

Governor Lowe beat the arms of his chair. "And she will tell me as well, even if I have to strip her naked and break her legs on the wheel!"

Lowe was so anguished that Daniel felt quite sorry for him, but he stayed in character. "Sir, with respect, I think there's a better way. If you arrest her, the plotters will know that their secret is out. Perhaps they will come up with a plan that is even more devious. Charlotte tells me everything. I pass it all on to you. We have placed a cuckoo in Napoleon's nest. All we have to do is listen when she sings."

Lowe unclenched his fist slowly, as if the secret to what he should do was written on his palm. "How do they plan to get him from Longwood to the sea?"

"Charlotte says a man called Captain Johnson, a smuggler who has made a practice of escaping from prison, will attach a cable to a mountain crag, perhaps on Horse Point, and run Napoleon down in a cable chair."

Lowe's eyes shot from side to side as if they were trying to escape from his roiling brain. His lips moved, silently as a goldfish. "Damn and blast that blackguard!" he spat. "Liberals everywhere will scream blue murder, but this forces me to make Bonaparte's life even more of a misery than it already is. I'll deny him his carriage rides. I will redouble the guards. Post men on all the crags near Longwood, night and day. I will cut his visitors. I will put his staff on starvation rations. I will strike back at him by making absolutely certain no one sneaks him even a single antihemorrhoidal leech!"

Daniel nearly lost his struggle to keep a straight face.

# Chapter 20: Napoleon's Last Conquest

*Never interfere with an enemy who is making a mistake or with a beautiful woman who is falling in love with you.*

The girl was dressed in a page boy costume, the riding attire she'd worn when she went to Venice to deliver herself to Byron. Short blonde hair curled, sitting at his desk behind a forest of quill pens, waiting for him to start his dictation. Delicious.

The conqueror stood motionless, his hands clasped behind his back, silent as a room he had just entered, his full-faced look penetrating, searching, commanding. A look that made princes and kings shake in their shoes.

Not her. Not this island girl he had sent adventuring in Europe, this Charlotte with the unpronounceable last name who was becoming such a large piece on the chessboard of his life, although not the white queen, at least not yet. There was no defiance in the way she returned his gaze. The emerald eyes remained wide, serene, as if they were looking out over a vast tranquil sea. A chess match, an appropriate analogy. He was playing black.

He took some snuff, spilling twice as much as he shoveled into his nose down the front of his threadbare green jacket, nibbled at the licorice he snacked on all day for his digestion, began pacing up and down with his hands clasped behind his back as he talked.

"Everyone wants to know about Josephine," he said. "She was an island girl like you, did you know that? A Creole from Martinique. Talked with a lilting island accent, like you do, rolled like a sailor when she walked—we had to teach her deportment. Pretty, beautiful, even, although she had bad teeth. Had to learn how to smile with her mouth closed. Sweet nature, people adored her. Wonderful memory for names and faces. A valuable ally.

Promiscuous. I like my women on the promiscuous side, makes them more spirited, except of course when I am trying to breed with them. That's why I sent you to Byron in Venice, so he could make you even livelier." His crude, mocking laugh. "I hear that *ended* well!"

"Your Majesty, am I to take all this down?" said Charlotte evenly.

Napoleon didn't break his stride, as he seemed to be considering this request at length and from all angles.

He wasn't. His restless thoughts were flying. "What? Josephine couldn't give me a child, you see, so I had to divorce her, which was a pity, because she had finally come to accept that I needed mistresses when the rutting season came upon me. I was quite candid about them, you see. Told her about their virtues and imperfections. We were together for thirteen years. She was the most intimate witness of my rise to the ultimate power. I lost part of my past when I had to set her aside. But my dynasty must come first, and it turned out she couldn't breed me a dynasty. I am the revolution, you see, and the revolution lives only in my seed."

That's how it began, his *Story of My Love*, as he called it. It was continued Monday through Friday, two hours a day, a roll call of his amorous conquests spiced with explicit details that excited the girl, he could see that. But exciting her wasn't enough. He needed more. He needed her begging to be vanquished. Power was the ultimate aphrodisiac.

"He doesn't ever ask me read back his dictation," Charlotte told Daniel. "He's just very lonely. He doesn't seem to care if I write down what he says or not. He wanders off topic. For example, today he talked about the submarine."

Daniel looked up from the banana tree he was planting. They were at Virgin Hall, taming the jungle that would become a garden. *Their* garden, when Charlotte finally agreed to tie the knot.

"What did he say about the submarine?" asked Daniel.

"That there was a problem, a temporary delay. It couldn't run submerged for long enough. The steam engine's furnace uses up all the fresh air."

"So he's giving up the idea?"

"Oh, no, far from it. He says someone called Volta has developed a device that stores electricity. It's called a voltaic pile. Napoleon says that he's seen it work with his own eyes, back in Paris. That was twenty years ago. He says it's bound to have been improved since then."

"But even a pile of electricity won't drive a ship."

"It will, Napoleon says, if it's connected to an electric motor."

Daniel gave her a lovely, level gaze, which set her heart racing. "There isn't such a thing. The only electric motor we have is a frog's leg that twitches when you run a current through it."

Charlotte said, "Napoleon says an Englishman called Faraday has invented one. He says that Captain Johnson has installed it in his submarine. He could be here any day now!"


The submarine didn't arrive. What did come to the island, in February 1819, was the news that Dr. O'Meara had arrived in England and was shouting to anybody who would listen that Napoleon's jailer had ordered him to murder his famous patient. The War Office ignored him, but a publisher, correctly sniffing sales, didn't.

By coincidence, curious to many, the same ship carried the news that Gaspard had been arrested shortly

257

after O'Meara's arrival. The charge was that he had been writing seditious letters to just about everyone, including Napoleon's wife Empress Marie-Louise and the emperors of Russia and Austria.

"I told Gaspard to write those letters," said Napoleon when Charlotte read him the article in *The Times*, "since he was bound to be found out."

Charlotte failed to grasp his point. "Poor Gaspard! Why would you want him thrown into prison?"

"Only for a night or two, then off he went on a grand tour of the courts of Europe, spreading the gospel!"

A dangerous thought crossed Charlotte's mind. She put it into words anyway. "Did you order Dr. O'Meara to betray Gaspard?"

Napoleon seemed surprised by the question. "Of course! It was a brilliant way for the good doctor to draw attention to his book and our cause. Dear Gaspard will be writing one soon, I am sure. It will be among the first of the thousands destined to be written about me as the centuries unfold."

Henry Porteous, who had been ailing for some time, died in June and was buried in his kilt. Daniel, with Governor Lowe's patronage, took his place as superintendent of the company's gardens. A month later Albine de Montholon left with baby Napoleone. But the rescue balloon someone had promised did not arrive. Nor the double, which would impersonate Napoleon long enough for the emperor to slip away on a racing yacht. Nor the electric submarine.

Charlotte said, "Sooner or later it will come for you, Your Majesty. Nobody who has actually seen it would doubt that."

Napoleon pinched her cheek so hard it hurt. "Yes, I am relying on your underwater boat as a last resort.

However, I'd much prefer to leave this island like a gentleman, wearing my hat and sword, not sliding down a wire in my servants' livery! Something is welling up in England, a wave of unrest. It will sweep Lord Holland and his Liberals into power, and they will sweep me back to France in a grand flotilla. It will happen! I can feel it in my bones. Write that down."

Something *was* brewing. In November 1819 the news arrived in *The Times*.

"Read it to me," Napoleon barked at Charlotte, "the July report first." He had his hat on, for some reason, and was pacing to and fro in front of his miniature desk, hands clasped tightly behind his back, in an obvious state of excitement.

She saw two copies of *The Times* lying open on his desk. The story was dated July 22, 1819. The headline was: "Napoleon's Release Demanded." A raucous crowd of forty thousand had gathered the previous day at Smithfield in London to hear Henry "Orator" Hunt praise Napoleon and demand his release.

"Go on, girl! What did he say? Read it aloud!"

Charlotte's clear voice rose above the howl of the wind. "'All of us at this grand assembly denounce the imprisonment of brave Napoleon upon a desert island,' it says."

"There's more."

"Yes, sire, there is. This Orator Hunt goes on, 'A desert island where the democratic head of Europe is tormented by the brutal insolence of a hired keeper who will go down in the annals of infamy for being as low as his name suggests! Napoleon is a prisoner, like all of us are prisoners of the aristocracy. I have not the least hesitation in pronouncing Napoleon, both in talent and courage, to be unrivaled in the pages of history. Here is a man who is destined to take the lead in setting us free.'"

"That's enough! Now read the other one. Just the headlines."

This edition was dated three weeks later, August 17, 1819. "'Huge march in Manchester!'" Charlotte read. "'Eighty thousand protestors! Banners say, *Equal Representation or Revolution, Liberty or Death*. Government cracks down. Over five hundred killed or wounded.'"

"What do you think?" Napoleon barked at her.

Charlotte couldn't conceal her excitement. "It begins, Your Majesty."

To her surprise he cursed. "*Merde!* It doesn't begin, it ends! Revolutionary mobs will do nothing but panic the English people and strengthen the hold of the government!" He walked to the window and stared over Deadwood Plain, with its neat rows of army tents, the hives of his guards.

"My spies tell me that the agitators are planning something even worse than street riots," he said. "Their leader, that fool Thistlewood, plans to assassinate the entire British cabinet! Can you believe the lunacy? Not even I could think of a better way to strengthen the iron fist of the tyrant. They have damned Lord Holland and his reformers to insignificance. They have damned me!"

Napoleon's mood changed abruptly. He stared at Charlotte until she felt herself drowning in his deep-set eyes, which were sometimes blue and sometimes gray. "My memoirs. I have saved the best for last. The *Story of My Love* is not complete until I have told you about my beautiful sister Pauline. You've heard of her, surely?"

"Yes, Your Majesty. Lady Holland showed me a statue of her, reclining."

"A copy of the one by Canova, no doubt. What did you think?"

"She's very beautiful."

"As beautiful as you are?"

"More beautiful."

"You lie, you witch. Unless there's some imperfection you're hiding from me. Ugly feet, perhaps?"

Charlotte couldn't help being drawn into his teasing banter. "No, sire. I have been complimented on my feet."

A coarse Corsican laugh. "Show them to me!"

Charlotte did, even wriggled her toes, just once, as she had done for Gaspard on the *Winchelsea*, showing off her high arches. As she did so, the thought struck her that here she was, unchaperoned, flirting with a promiscuous womanizer, all-powerful once, used to having his way with any woman he wanted. She scented danger, found it intoxicating. She left her feet bare.

The ship carrying the birdlike man fought its way into the South Atlantic, pitching and rolling as it was tossed like a toy in the ill wind's white-capped teeth. There were two hundred passengers on board, settlers heading for a new life in southern Africa, plus a creature who admitted to himself that he had no soul to lose. After ten weeks at sea, everybody had told their life stories ten times over. But the creature wrapped in black didn't tell his once.

On the evening of June 6, 1820, the ship dropped anchor in James Bay. The next morning the birdlike man went ashore. Napoleon's valet Marchand was waiting for him at the wharf with a bag of gold and written instructions. A single request at the Almond Tree got him directions to where Daniel could be found.

For the first time in months, the creature flashed his yellow fangs in an approximation of a smile. "Daniel, my boy!" he sang out. "A sorry sight, this little patch of weeds, after the wonders of Kew!"

Daniel looked up from the cutting he was planting into the black eyes of George Edwards. "Edwards," he said, "what the devil are you doing here?"

"Emigrating to Cape Town. Opening a little shop. Going back to painting and sculpting. Done with politics and all that. You have heard the good news, haven't you, about Thistlewood?"

"What news?"

"I netted him, finally. Set a trap he walked right into. You don't by any chance have some brandy hidden in the shrubbery, do you?"

"You netted him?"

"Yes, finally. Thistlewood admired the way the French revolutionaries did things, you see. So what I did was persuaded him to stage a coup that would begin with the assassination of the whole of the British cabinet, every last one of them in one fell swoop." He looked over his shoulder quick as a crow, dropped his voice. "You see, what I did was show him an official advertisement, which announced that all His Majesty's ministers would be dining at the Earl of Harrowby's on a particular night—February 23, to be exact. Persuaded him that this was the perfect opportunity to do the glorious deed. Oh, how eagerly the fool flew at the bait!"

"So all this time you were working for the police?"

The little man nodded like a parrot. "Always played both sides, I did. More butter on your bread that way. Come now, lad, you're a man of the world. Did a bit of double-dealing yourself to keep your little Rosebud safe, didn't you? Delivered all those smuggled Rosebud letters to me and Thistlewood. I wager you never told her you knew the government was reading them as well."

Daniel didn't know what to say, so he said nothing.

Edwards cackled with malicious delight. "I was telling you about Thistlewood, I was. See, he arranged for the assassins to meet him in a loft right around the corner on Cato Street. It was eight thirty in the evening. The murderous swine were about to strike when I sent in the police, thirteen brave men. Thistlewood killed one of them, bullet straight through the heart, then escaped out a window. We took him the next day. Had to deny myself the pleasure of seeing him hang, because I was warned that there was suddenly a very liberal price on my head, if you get my meaning, and that I'd better shake the dust of old England off my shoes. Sad, but no matter. In lieu of services rendered, His Majesty's government was kind enough to give me money and a free passage to Cape Town. I was delighted to hear that the ship was stopping at Saint Helena. You and the beautiful Rosebud, together at last." Edwards gave Daniel a nauseating wink. "I couldn't miss out on that, now could I?"

"What do you want?" said Daniel, struggling to rein in his rising temper.

"Oh, just a small contribution to help me set up shop. A farewell present. Say, one hundred guineas. A trifle for the superintendent of the Honorable East India Company's gardens and lord of stately Virgin Hall. A mere pittance in exchange for a guarantee I will not tell your darling Charlotte you are Governor Lowe's spy. That you whisper everything she tells you about Napoleon into the governor's ear."

Daniel glared at him. "You disgusting blackguard! Get out of my sight!"

Edwards strode off whistling in facetious merriment. The written instructions that accompanied the bag of gold he'd been given at the wharf had told him to go directly to Charlotte with the news of Daniel's betrayal. The detour via Daniel was merely an entertaining attempt to double his money.

Edwards found Charlotte busy with the fruit and vegetable display on her mother's porch. Because she was about to ride up to Longwood, she was dressed in one of the white off-the-shoulder dresses with a plunging neckline that Napoleon liked her to wear.

"Good day, Miss Charlotte, or should I call you Rosebud?"

She eyed the little man coolly, looking him full in the face, a habit she picked up from Napoleon.

"Who are you?" she asked.

The creature bowed like a bird pecking at a seed. "George Edwards, at your service."

"How did you know my name, Mr. Edwards?"

"We are fortunate enough to have friends in common. Daniel Hamilton, for example. I have just had a chat with him in his Gardens. Lovely lad, that."

"You're off the boat?"

"Yes. Just passing through on my way to Cape Town." He glanced at her horse tethered to the fence. "Going for a ride?"

"As it happens, yes. I am riding up to Longwood."

"To see the emperor, of course."

"Yes. I take down his dictation."

"That isn't a sidesaddle, surely?"

"No, it's not. I ride astride."

"In a dress? How daring! The lads don't whistle at you when you pass by?"

"This is Saint Helena. We have our own customs. One of the wealthiest local ladies rides an ox and smokes a pipe!"

Edwards laughed his birdlike cackle. "You certainly do seem to be having the time of your life, which is why I so much regret being the bearer of bad tidings."

"From London?"

"No. About someone much closer to home. Daniel."

"What about him?"

"He pretends to love you so he can use you," said Edwards and told her how.

Daniel heard the thundering hooves. He looked up just in time to see Charlotte bearing down on him at a full gallop, her spurred horse white eyed with panic, her skirt hitched up so she could ride astride, showing off her long, sculptured legs.

"You don't love me. You are using me!" she shouted.

"What? Charlotte!" he yelled as she tried to run him down.

"You know! That man Edwards! He told me everything. You are a traitor! You're the one who told the governor about the submarine. Now I see it all. From the very beginning you have been in the government's pay. We're finished, you and I. You have betrayed Napoleon. You have betrayed me!"

"Charlotte, calm down. It's not what it seems."

She spun the horse in a tight turn. She was bearing down on him again. This time her riding crop was raised. "Swear it's a lie, damn you! But it's not a lie. It's the truth, isn't it?"

"Get off that damn animal!" Daniel shouted, his blood up. Purposely he didn't try to defend himself from her whip. He couldn't live with the indignity. The crop cut his cheek. Charlotte didn't wait to see the blood flow.

*Never interfere with a beautiful woman who is falling in love with you.*

Napoleon listened gravely to Charlotte's angry, heartbroken account of Daniel's betrayal, his face expressionless except for eyes that shifted mysteriously between blue and gray.

265

"All these years, he pretended to love me, but he was just using me to spy on you . He is nothing to me anymore. Nothing. I hate him. You are everything! If you want me, take me!"

He did. They made love in the deep shade of a pomegranate tree. His body was perfumed with eau de cologne. The Pyramids…Marengo…Austerlitz. Borodino. The roar of cannon. The cries of soldiers—or were those her cries?—the blare of trumpets, the thundering of a thousand hooves swept her away. Much too soon, Waterloo.

Afterward he flashed her his cupid's smile. "Rosebud, I have a confession to make, and I want you to know it's very rare for a man like me to apologize for anything."

"Your Majesty?"

"To conquer you I have used deception, as I did in all my battles," he said.

Charlotte was sure he was teasing her. "Deception?"

In a swift, practiced maneuver, Napoleon reached out and pinched her flushed cheek so hard it brought tears to her eyes. "Yes. I used you and Daniel to feed my jailer a poisonous diet of fictional escape plans. For a while, thanks to the scroll in your last packet, we had him believing that the whole of Chile's navy was about to tear me out of his clutches!"

A chill of realization closed its frosty fingers around Charlotte's heart. "Lowe opened my packets?"

"I made sure he did."

Her head was spinning. "Daniel knew?"

"We made him aware. He cooperated to protect you."

"What about the submarine?"

"A decoy. A provocation. It couldn't cross the Thames, let alone the Atlantic. But you had to convince

Daniel that it could. So he would convince my jailer. People lie more convincingly when they think they are telling the truth. I fed you lies. You passed them on to Daniel. On my instructions Daniel passed them on to Lowe."

Charlotte's heart leaped. "So that vulture of a man was lying. Daniel isn't a traitor?"

"Edweeds. He was telling his half of the truth. He is our spy as well as England's. He informed us he was passing through, on his way to the Cape. I had the brilliant idea of using him as my flank attack, to drive you into my arms. A man like me, who has carried the world on his shoulders, has the right to indulge himself with light distractions such as the seduction of a beautiful woman."

"So I am a light distraction while Daniel is—"

Napoleon let loose his bark of a laugh. "Is a hero, not a villain! Now that I have exercised my *droit du seigneur* by deflowering you, I order you to marry him immediately!"

Daniel, biting down hard on his anger, was still doggedly at work in the Botanical Gardens when Charlotte arrived in a whirlwind of dust. The nasty cut on his face, oozing blood, did nothing to offset his smile, because he could see that at last she knew.

"Daniel!" she called out from the saddle. "My sweetest darling!" she called out again as she abandoned her foam-flecked horse and threw herself into his arms. "I am so, so very sorry I doubted you. Boney told me everything!"

She kissed him again, breathing fire. Her lips found the wound. "Your sweet blood," she said with a mad laugh she'd learned from Byron. "It's delicious!"

He pushed her away, laughing too, making the sign of the cross. "You're cursed!"

267

She was crying now. "Yes, I am, cursed by love! Use me now, in the garden shed, use me anywhere. I'm a fallen woman."

He looked at her as if he were trying to find the point of a joke. "What do you mean?"

"He tricked me. He's given up all hope of leaving Saint Helena. He said he needed one last conquest."

Daniel was suddenly eerily calm. This was a side of him Charlotte hadn't seen before, not the lonely, dreamy Gypsy child, not the bookish botanist. A side that was made of steel. He was going to have to be made of steel if he was going to weather what she had to tell him next.

"I was blinded by the Furies. I knew Napoleon wanted me. I could tell by the way he's been looking at me, by little things he said. I wanted to hurt you for deceiving me, to take revenge. It was my fault. I threw myself at him. Daniel, I am no longer a virgin! Do you hate me now?" She was crying. "Because I love you!"

Time stopped as they gazed into each other's eyes, his brown as the honest earth, hers green as the deepest water. "We'd better get married immediately," he said with his lovely lopsided grin. "You may be pregnant with a prince!"

They exchanged vows two days later in Saint James Church, across the street from the Castle. All the Knipes were there in their Sunday best. Henry Knipe wore his kilt. Charlotte's mother was in tears. The tiny clutch of Hamiltons filled half of a pew on the other side of the aisle, Daniel's half sisters and his mother, who had read the auspices and found them favorable. Even with the contingent sent by Napoleon—General Bertrand with his wife, Count Montholon without his, the valet Marchand—it was an empty church until the officers in full dress uniform, uninvited, began to file in. Soon the church was packed.

The minister smiled benignly as if this show of military force were all his own doing. "Dearly beloved, we are gathered together—" he began. He was cut short by a hundred well-drilled soldiers jumping to their feet. The Knipes and the Hamiltons gaped. Even the bride and groom abandoned decorum long enough to glance over their shoulders. Sir Hudson Lowe was striding in at a stately pace, a splendid plumed helmet under one arm and Lady Lowe, cheerfully tipsy, clinging to the other. He was smiling benevolently because, for a change, he suspected nothing.

Two weeks later, when she didn't bleed, Charlotte knew she was indeed pregnant, although she wasn't certain who the father was. She had a strong feeling it was Daniel's, because he was a tiger in bed, as Polly had promised. But when she wandered alone along the paths skirting the precipice that fell down to Sandy Bay, the ill wind gusting in off the sea whispered to her, "The Pyramids. Marengo. Austerlitz. Borodino. Other great battles. The Code Napoleon. An emperor who once had Europe in his thrall. *Father of your child.*"

As soon as the baby began to show, she was banned from Longwood. That came as no surprise.

"I can't stand seeing perfection disfigured," Napoleon told her. "Come back when you've had the child. I want to see him, to make sure he's mine."

Although he wrote to her almost every day, quick notes in his own execrable handwriting, a comical mixture of English, French, and Italian, she only saw him once more during her pregnancy, on October 4, 1820, when he called briefly at Virgin Hall on his way back from a carriage visit to Sandy Bay. The visit was stiff and formal.

269

Napoleon looked pale and ill. The cancer eating at his stomach had begun to torment him, the same cancer, he said, that had killed his father at the age of thirty-nine.

The child was born on March 9, 1821. It did have a large head like Napoleon, but in many ways it looked like Daniel, Charlotte thought. Also, it was a girl. They baptized her Mary Ann, which was what the French called Lady Liberty. She was two months old when Napoleon, who wrote that he heard death calling to him in the howling of the ill wind, asked to see the child. He told her to bring Daniel with her.

Death was everywhere in the converted cow barn that had become the parody of an emperor's palace. Faces were downcast. People spoke in whispers. Napoleon, propped up on pillows, was white as his sheets.

"Out, everyone!" he whispered when Charlotte and Daniel were shown in. When they were alone, he kissed the baby on the forehead and then seemed to lose interest in her. He started to speak in a soft, sad voice, very different to the mocking bark Charlotte was used to. She passed the baby, who was gurgling happily, to Daniel and leaned forward to make sure she heard every word.

"It was the evening of my first great victory, over the Austrians at Lodi," Napoleon murmured. "I was only twenty-six at the time, but as became my custom I was surveying the field of the battle I had just won. The scene of carnage, thousands of Austrians lying dead, was lit by a bright crescent moon, sharp as a scimitar. Suddenly the deep, beautiful silence was broken by a dog's anxious barking, as it leaped up from his dead master's body, rushed at us teeth flashing, then slunk back to the body, tail between its legs, whimpering. As we watched, it tried to wake the dead man by licking his face and when that failed flew at us again, repeating the same sequence of actions, over and over. Nothing on any field of battle before or since made such a deep impression on me. This man, I thought, has friends, family to mourn him. But here he lies, all alone, abandoned by everyone except his dog."

Napoleon coughed weakly. There was a long silence. Eventually he continued, "The closer I approach the end, the more I think of that dog. You see, that poor creature is me, doing everything I can to defend my empire, unable to accept that it is dead." He rolled his head weakly so that he was looking straight at Charlotte. "What do you think of my story?"

"It will haunt me, Your Majesty."

"Not as much as what I am going to tell you next. I'm not like other men. The rules of morality do not apply to me. I used the myth of democracy to reach the pinnacle of power. Then I cast it aside to impose a new line of kings on Europe, my family. Crowned my son king of Rome, dauphin of the new dynasty. My brother Joseph king of Spain, my brother Louis king of Holland, Jerome king of Westphalia, sister Elisa duchess of Tuscany, made Lucien a prince, lovely Pauline a princess, Caroline queen of Naples. Out with the Bourbons, in with the Bonapartes! And then came Waterloo, and my empire shrank to this miserable little shack on this unspeakable little island and my last conquest..." He rolled his eyes to Charlotte, smiled faintly when he saw she was weeping. "You, my Rosebud."

They were back home at Virgin Hall when the thunder of the signal cannons eight minutes after sunset told Charlotte and Daniel what they were expecting to hear. They were alone. Daniel said:

Be not afraid; the isle is full of noises,
Sounds and sweet airs, that give delight and hurt not.

Charlotte was staring at a twilight image under a guava tree, a shadowy figure that wore his black hat sideways, a cupid's smile on his lips. For as long as she could she forced herself not to blink because she knew he would disappear when she did.

The southeaster sighed "farewell."

"Yes," she said.

# Acknowledgements

*The Knipe Family of Saint Helena Island* (which at 468 pages must rank as one of South Africa's most exhaustive family histories) introduced me to the Rosebud legend. I would like to thank its author, Glennis Snell, for her most helpful responses to my endless e-mails while absolving her from any responsibility for my flights of novelistic fantasy.
I would also like to thank Albert Benhamou, author of *L'autre Sainte-Hélène* and *Inside Longwood: Barry O'Meara's Clandestine Letters*, for his valuable contributions concerning the micro politics of the island during Napoleon's exile. It was he who discovered Albine de Montholon's description of Rosebud, which establishes that she was the daughter of an invalided lieutenant (my great-great-great-grandfather Richard Knipe) and not his brother Samuel, the comparatively rich planter.
Two other books I found particularly helpful were Brian Unwin's *Terrible Exile* and R. C. Seaton's *Napoleon's Captivity in Relation to Sir Hudson Lowe*, where Napoleon's campaign of deliberately provoking harsh reprisals from Lowe to arouse sympathy in England, Europe, and America is clearly laid out.
For Saint Helena as the inspiration for *The Tempest* see David Jeremiah's new book *Shakespeare's Island*.
The hero of *Napoleon's Rosebud* is an emperor without his clothes. No book I know of shows us this personal, intimate side, with all its idiosyncrasies, vanity, and cunning, better than Christopher Hibbert's *Napoleon: His Wives and Women*.

Charlotte died in 1835, three days after giving birth to her ninth child. If she had lived a few months longer, because of her botanical connections she would almost certainly have met Charles Darwin, who visited the island on the *Beagle* in 1836.

IF YOU ENJOYED THIS BOOK, PLEASE REVIEW IT FOR AMAZON. EVEN A FEW COMMENTS WOULD BE VERY MUCH APPRECIATED!